I0550180

Fire Island

Book 3 of Kazza's Chatterre Trilogy

by Jeanne Foguth

Cataloging-in-Publication Data is on file with the Library of Congress.

ISBN: 978-0-9913339-9-8

Acknowledgments, Etc.

A special thank you to Paul, Kaj Graham, Kensleigh, Marcha Fox and Pauline Nicolai --- I don't know what I would do without your amazing ability to help me catch typos and inconsistencies.

Thank you also to Kiara Graham for her prowess with digital design. Kiara, I love how your designs give a hint at what the story is about and who is a main character.

~o~

Cataloging in Publication Data is on file with the Library of Congress.

Books by Jeanne Foguth

Kazza's Chatterre Trilogy (Sci-Fantasy):

Star Bridge
Thunder Moon
Fire Island

Xander's Sea Purrtector Chronicles (Fantasy):
Latitudes & Catitudes
The Red Claw
Purr-a-noia
The Vi-Purrs (coming in Spring of 2016)

Contemporary Suspense/Romance:
Deadly Rumors
Fatal Attractions
Passion's Fire

Chapter 1

Tem-aki slid over the slippery rock floor, which might have been easy to skate on, but was nearly impossible to navigate wearing a clumsy space suit. Moving deeper into the treacherous tunnel, her attention was torn between staying upright and peering through the helmet visor trying to figure out her tricorder's strange readings.

Until they had reached this narrow area, with its slick surface, the readings had been typical of a salt mine. Now, they went from strange silica measurements to even stranger oxide readings. Frowning, she pressed the tricorder against the side of the passage, but the odd analysis did not change.

Tem-aki closed her eyes and tried to focus on what she knew about silica. When molten silicon dioxide was rapidly cooled, it solidified as a glass, which could explain the slippery surface, but it didn't explain how or why this area of the mine had been altered from that of a normal, abandoned salt mine.

Opening her eyes, she looked around. Noticing an offshoot passageway, she moved into it and almost immediately tripped over debris littering the rough potholed floor.

After she regained her balance, she realized that the

readings in this area were consistent with an airless salt mine. What in the world had caused such drastic changes in the chemistry of the main corridor, yet had left this area untouched?

Salt was a staple of life and if the deposit wasn't mined out, this discovery would be valuable to her superiors. Perhaps valuable enough to merit advancement. That, plus finding her brother, who everyone else had given up as dead, made this a very good day, because either one had the potential for a promotion and increased pay-grade, but if she could achieve both, her success was assured.

Of course, there was the problem of how to contact her superiors. She frowned, as she wished she had thought of this before leaving Nambaba and its antiquated communications. If Larwin was here, as Thunder claimed, why hadn't he notified anyone of his location?

Had she gotten herself into the same trap he was in?

Tem-aki glanced back down the tunnel to where Thunder knelt as he prepared the explosives, which he claimed were necessary to protect his people from a madrox invasion. Aside from the bizarre belief that madrox would venture trillions of light years across space to enter a deserted salt mine, Thunder seemed like a rational person and if she could find Larwin alive and well, as Thunder claimed, she wouldn't even mind being trapped with him. Having her brother back in her life was worth much more than rank and credits.

Just as she was about to step back onto the slick surface of the main tunnel, Raine glided past, graceful as a ballerina, not even paying attention to her footing as she talked to Reed. Tem-aki cautiously put weight on her right foot, but the turquoise-colored space-boot slipped on the shiny surface and she nearly cartwheeled into the main mineshaft. Arms flailing for balance, she managed to avoid falling, but dropped her tricorder. A quick glance assured her that Raine and Reed were so focused on their conversation, that they hadn't noticed her clumsiness.

Cautiously, Tem-aki walked across the slick, slanting floor of the mineshaft. Perspiration burned her eyes and her heart hammered from the stress of moving over the treacherous ground. When she got to her tricorder, bending over to pick it up nearly had her somersaulting down the slippery slope. Somehow, she managed to grab it without falling flat on her face.

Standing upright, she put her hand against the wall, as she caught her breath and watched Raine move over the tricky floor with the ease and grace of a professional ice-dancer. How did she move like that while wearing a clumsy space suit and heavy boots? Raine was small, curvy and dainty — and graceful, even when wearing an outdated, bulky charcoal-colored spacesuit. She was everything a woman should look like – everything Tem-aki knew she was not, even though her own custom-made suit was the most advanced design and an attractive turquoise color.

Just thinking about Raine's dexterity, made Tem-aki's knees shake and her boots slide.

"I can do this," Tem-aki vowed, as she focused her attention on her analyzer. The difference between the rock of the main tunnel and the smaller side tunnels was a geological anomaly she would have loved to examine in depth, but limited air made a thorough investigation impossible.

At least for now.

Perhaps, after she rendezvoused with Larwin, they could recharge the air of both their suits, and continue researching this old mine. For now, she only needed to confirm that there was something worth further study.

Just when she started to feel confident, her feet slipped, again. She pitched sideways into another side-tunnel and fell on top of something with sharp corners. Fearing her spacesuit had been punctured, Tem-aki rolled to her right and checked for damage.

No rips.

No obvious punctures.

She heaved a sigh of relief, then scrambled to her feet and panned her las-light to see what she'd fallen on.

A perfectly preserved Artelbas IV bench sat at the side of the space. She stared in shock. How had such a rare and valuable antique gotten here?

The bench made the prospect of finding her brother alive and well seem possible.

"You all right?" Thunder asked.

Great, he'd seen her make a fool of herself. "I'm fine." Tem-aki gestured toward the bench. "Surprised at what is in here, though."

He gave the perfectly carved stone a disdainful glance. "Refuse." Her shock must have shown through her somewhat foggy face-place because he added, "Things tend to lose value when a person must choose between it and their own life."

Interesting and probably true, but it was still the single most valuable piece of furniture that she'd ever touched.

"You like the thing?" he asked. She nodded.

"It would be impossible to carry down the mountain, but easy to make one like it." After that strange statement, Thunder turned and strolled back down the tunnel.

How much farther did they have to go? It felt like they'd been walking for weeks. She glanced at her analyzer: 27.4 kilometers. She wrinkled her nose at the distance, which would have taken a blink of an eye, if she'd been riding in a shuttle; or a few moments, if she'd been standing on a fast-track. She couldn't recall a time in her entire life when she'd walked such a long way.

Suddenly a roaring sound surrounded her. Her eyes snapped to where the sound had come from and she saw a distant bright gold glow with bright red dots and a brief azure ripple. Tem-aki stood in shock for a moment, almost unable to comprehend that Thunder's fears about the dragons coming down this hostile hole were valid. Then, her survival instinct kicked in and she sprinted down the tunnel, toward Thunder. "Madrox! Run!"

He stared past her, transfixed, then looked down at the maze of switches and wires.

"Go! Now! I'll blow it when I get there."

He turned and ran.

Moments later, Tem-aki got to the cobbled-together maze of wires and hit the switch, then, she turned to run after Thunder. But saw GEA-4's damaged form slumped against the wall. She paused and threw the android's arms around her neck, then, she started to run after the others.

Abruptly, a deafening boom, followed by a shockwave threw her face down.

Tem-aki screamed, throwing her hands out to cushion the fall.

Instead of hitting the floor, she plummeted into solid rock, hurtling downward, through what looked solid, but she never actually hit anything.

She closed her eyes and fought the need to throw up, which could be fatal inside a space suit.

Moments turned into minutes and minutes seemed to turn into hours. Tem-aki didn't know how long she hurtled through solid stone, which shouldn't have been possible. Was she hallucinating?

With a jarring halt, Tem-aki splatted against something hard enough to knock the breath out of her, despite her spacesuit's protection. Strangely, though her momentum seemed to slow, it felt like she was still dropping.

Then, she hit something so hard that her knees buckled, pitching forward landing on her face. Pain shot throughout her body.

Lungs burning, she gasped for oxygen, but it seemed impossible to inhale.

Desperate, she lay there, waiting for the glorious whiteness of eternity to envelope her.

Everything stayed shades of charcoal and black.

Unable to breath, beneath the crushing weight, she succumbed to the enveloping darkness.

~o~

Heart pounding and face bathed in sweat, Nimri's eyes shot open. It took her several minutes of gasping for breath to realize that she had fallen asleep in the hammock under the ginkgo tree and it had only been a nightmare.

But what a realistic one!

She tried to swallow the lump of fear that still choked her, but the suspicion that dreams could actually be real stayed. This nightmare had been different from the one that she had been having every night for the past half year. But she didn't know if it was a good sign that she hadn't dreamed of hordes of ravenous golden dragons spewing from the Star Bridge or not.

Shading her eyes from the bright afternoon sun, she gazed up at Sacred Mountain's peak and looked for an omen. She thought she saw a thin dark cloud rise above the balata grove, but she couldn't be sure. Gooseflesh rippled over her body and her soon-to-be-born-baby kicked.

An affectionate, leathery nose prodded her elbow. Smiling, Nimri turned her attention from the distant peak and stroked Kazza's muscular shoulders, then tickled the smooth, silky fur at the base of his ear until his tail twitched and his six-hundred-pounds of muscle leaned into her.

A distant bird screamed. Together, Nimri and Kazza turned

their attention to Sacred Mountain's summit, where the small black cloud seemed to be dissipating. Was that a good omen or bad?

Did it mean that Thunder had closed the portal and the threat had dissipated?

If so, why hadn't he returned? He should have only been gone more than a week.

In the beginning of her dream, Thunder had been wearing Larwin's strange suit and he had been with four strangers wearing similar attire. Where had they come from? And why hadn't Thunder returned days ago? Worse, poor GEA-4 had been badly damaged.

Had her dream been real or imaginary?

Nimri caressed her bulging abdomen with one hand and Kazza with her other, trying to sooth them, even though she couldn't sooth herself.

If Thunder had not been able to close the Star Bridge, would any of them survive another assault by the aura-devouring beasts.

Chapter 2

"Tem-aki." Nimri gasped as her eyes popped open from the dream that wasn't a dream. She recognized Larwin's sister's name, as it resonated in her dark bedchamber. Lying there, staring at the ceiling, while listening to Larwin's soft, purr-like snoring, she understood that something catastrophic had happened to Tem-aki.

What she couldn't understand was how she knew this or why their thoughts seemed to have linked.

Worse, how could she possibly help Tem-aki, when she didn't know where she was? Particularly now that Thunder had closed the Star Bridge.

Nimri turned her head so she could look out the bedroom window and see Sacred Mountain's harsh silhouette against the inky sky. She had been concerned about the Star Bridge, since seeing the black cloud dissipate above Sacred Peak, so, before retiring, she and Kazza had spirit traveled there. They had assured themselves that the connection to the old world had been completely severed. They had also noted that despite being missing for so long, Thunder appeared to be well. The strange part was that he was only with three strangers, instead of the four she'd seen in her dream and there was no sign of GEA-4.

Once she and Kazza returned to their myst energy to their physical forms, she felt calm enough to relax.

But now, in the middle of the night, as everyone else slept, she lay awake and worried about Thunder and his companions making their way down the treacherous path. Two of them had looked quite old. Would they be able to navigate the squirrel-thin portion of the path down Sacred Mountain?

They should be here later today or possibly tomorrow.

Could she wait that long to know they were safe and find out all the answers to her questions?

The two companions who looked quite elderly bothered her the most. They moved slowly. What if one slipped, when Thunder was helping and they pulled him to his death?

Still her brother was strong, so it would be unlikely for that to happen. Neither of the old ones was a particularly large person. In fact, one was small, like GEA-4. She frowned and wondered why she hadn't seen GEA-4 with the group.

Why had Thunder taken so long, with what should have been a simple task?

Where had he been when he had disappeared and how had he found other beings on the burnt cinder Solterre had become?

Curious as she was, Nimri knew that all her questions would be answered in good time. With that in mind, she tried to relax and go back to sleep, but the name, Tem-aki, kept swirling in her mind, along with dark haze, darker tunnels and ominous white bones.

She bit her lower lip and twisted the long, dark braid that kept her knee-length hair controlled as she turned to look at Larwin's peaceful sleeping face. Should she share her worries with him or wait until she had a better understanding of his sister's problem?

~o~

Late the following morning, Bryta rushed into the garden, to where Nimri was transplanting basil, "You were right! I saw four coming down the trail!" Face red with excitement, she added, "They should be here by dinnertime!"

"And Thunder will probably be starved," Nimri said.

"I'll make a big pot of soup." She turned with surprising speed and agility for such a plump woman, then rushed toward the kitchen door.

"Good idea. Do you need me to harvest anything for you?" Her question lay in empty air, since Bryta had already disappeared through the kitchen door. Knowing Bryta, by dinnertime, there would be fresh-baked bread to go with the soup and, since Thunder had become one of Bryta's favorite people to spoil, probably even dessert.

Larwin and Kazza appeared on the path from their morning swim. Larwin held up his hand. "I heard. Thunder is finally on his way down. Do you need me to dig potatoes or carrots or anything?"

"With four extra mouths to feed, it would probably be a good idea."

"Four?" Larwin laughed. "I know you think Thunder and I eat a lot, but four?"

"He isn't alone." Larwin gave her a condescending look. "And I am not talking about GEA-4."

"You've been myst-traveling." She nodded. He squatted next to her. "I know you've been worried about him being gone so long, but are you sure it's safe for the baby?" He placed a protective hand over her bulging abdomen.

"I think so. I mean, it wasn't as if I was in hand to hand combat with a madrox or anything. And it was just a quick trip to confirm a dream." Actually, it hadn't been the first time she'd looked for her brother, but it was the first time she had found him.

The baby kicked his hand and Larwin smiled. "Wouldn't

want to encourage that, quite yet." His expression became serious. "Do you know who Thunder is with?"

"No, only that the Star Bridge appears to be closed." She sighed. "My glimpse of him gave me more questions than answers. I mean, where was he for all that time? Where did his companions come from? Why isn't GEA-4 with him?" She took a deep breath, then looked him straight in the eye. "And why am I dreaming of your sister, as if I am her?"

Larwin's brows arched. Nimri swallowed, then plunged on, "In my dreams, she is with GEA-4 and she has been hurt."

"How was Tem-aki hurt?"

"Not Tem-aki, GEA-4. And I don't know how. All I know is that there was a lot of damage." She bit her lower lip to keep herself from telling him that his companion no longer seemed to have a face and that she did not seem capable of using her arms or legs.

Larwin's expression darkened. "It would be just like her to look for me, after I disappeared."

"But GEA-4 knows where you are."

"I meant my sister."

Nimri blinked twice, as she wondered how such a simple conversation had gotten so complicated. "But how would she know where to look? You said that your star ship was thrown many 'whatevers' away after your tracking signal quit."

"Whatevers?" Larwin chuckled. "Close enough to a quadrant. It would be impossible to explain the distances involved and it really doesn't matter that you understand the terms because they aren't relevant."

She studied his expression, and remembered the vast distances she had experienced on previous myst-journeys. While it was true that she hadn't understood the words he used, she was well aware of the vast distances they described. Still, this topic was not worth fretting over. When

Thunder returned, it would be time for questions, because they had a chance of getting answers. "So you think Tem-aki is all right?"

He shrugged. "I hope she is, but there isn't anything I can do for her if she needs help." He narrowed his eyes at her. "And neither can you, so if that's what you're thinking, forget it."

"But what about GEA-4?"

"She's an android, not a person and if something damaged her, it had to have been something catastrophic and we certainly don't want to expose our child to that. Do we?" He gave her a stern look, as he caressed her stomach.

She shook her head, no. Still, she couldn't stop thinking about Tem-aki and wondering if she was all right.

~o~

As Thunder told them everything that had happened since he had headed for the Star Bridge, Nimri smiled, gasped and laughed at all the appropriate times. But she soon realized that he hadn't mentioned GEA-4 or Tem-aki once. As the meal continued and the stories of dragon moons and water worlds continued, she had to bite her tongue to keep from asking why he was not mentioning them.

Strangely, even during the relaxed atmosphere of dinner, neither Larwin or Bryta asked about GEA-4, but maybe that was because Thunder's tale of a land-less world and a moon teeming with madrox, which his petite, blond friend, Raine was a shepherd for seemed so impossible to imagine. How could anyone as delicate as Raine possibly control dragons?

While Bryta got their guest rooms ready, Larwin talked about something called eepyllihg and treaties with Raine, Reed and Coral, who Thunder had met on Kalamar. If she could believe what her brother said, Kalamar treated madrox like some sort of farm animal. Of course, Kalamar was a world covered with water, which apparently protected the people, and they actually kept their dangerous herd on the moon, Vilecom. When her brother tried to explain the problems with Vilecom and eepyllihg, which the people of Kalamar apparently sold as a 'fuel additive' for space ships, Nimri asked Thunder to take an evening stroll in the garden. As they quietly got up, Kazza looked torn between following them and listening to Larwin's confusing conversation.

Kazza chose the discussion about eepyllihg, which was apparently a fancy name for something that was essentially 'ghilly pee'. Raine, Reed and Coral all laughed at Larwin's disbelief over that odd fact.

They were well away from her home, which spiraled around the towering sequoia in the middle of her sprawling herb garden, when she finally dared ask, "Why didn't you tell Larwin that GEA-4 was damaged?"

"He didn't ask."

"And you didn't think he had a right to know?" Thunder shrugged. Nimri pressed her advantage, "Why didn't you bring her back here, so that Larwin could try to repair her?"

Thunder didn't look her in the eye, which was very odd. "I couldn't." She raised a brow. "You know how treacherous that path is."

She nodded. "Yes, I do... So are you telling me that you left GEA-4 and Tem-aki alone on the mountain, hoping she could repair her, then come down?"

His jaw dropped. "You've been myst-traveling. I thought you didn't want to do that because you didn't know how it would affect your child."

"He is fine. Now, answer my question."

"He? You know it's a boy?"

"Yes, stop trying to change the subject."

"Have you told Larwin?" Nimri crossed her arms over her bulging stomach and silently glared at her brother.

"We agreed that it was best to say nothing, until we knew what had actually happened."

"We, who?" Nimri demanded.

"Me, Raine, Reed and Coral."

Fireflies twirled through the shadows behind Thunder. "So you think not knowing is better than knowing?"

"Yes." His answer was decisive.

"Explain."

"Well, as I understand it, on Guerreterre, the family relationships are not as close as they are here."

"So? Just because they seem to send their children away to school at an early age doesn't mean they don't care about each other."

"I know that. But it does mean that they aren't used to seeing each other every day."

"True, but Tem-aki is the one he always mentions and I know he loves her."

"Which is why it would be cruel to tell him that she is probably dead."

Pain shot through Nimri's core, and she sank onto a nearby bench. "You think she's dead?"

"What other explanation is there?" Thunder sat down next to her. He broke off a mint leaf, which he twirled between his fingers, as he marshaled his thoughts. "One minute we were both in the Star Bridge and there was a madrox coming toward us. I was waiting for Tem-aki to get past me, so I could trigger the charges that GEA-4 had planted before we got side-tracked to Kalamar."

"What about Raine, Reed and Coral? Where were they?"

"They were already where the balata used to be."

"And GEA-4?"

"She was with me."

"But you didn't take her, when you ran from the madrox?"

"I thought she would be fine, where she was. I mean, it's

not like she's flesh and blood or anything." Thunder grasped her hands and looked deep into her eyes. "The area where I left her was pretty-much the same, after the dust settled." His grip tightened. "The only difference was that GEA-4 was gone and there was no sign of Tem-aki, but she had to have been there because what set off the explosives if she didn't?"

"I don't know." Nimri sighed and her vision began to blur, as she thought about Larwin's loss. "Do you think the madrox got them or was it the detonation?"

"There were no bits and pieces. No sign they had ever been there. Not even a footprint in the dust, so I just don't know." He chewed at his lower lip. "I'm surprised that Larwin hasn't asked about GEA-4."

"That's because he knows what I have been dreaming."

Thunder stiffened. "Do you still dream of madrox?"

"Yes, but I also dream of Larwin's sister. And in my dreams, I am Tem-aki and she is with GEA-4."

Chapter 3

A distant scream woke Cameron O'ryan. He lay in his hammock, ears straining. After an extended silence, he wondered if the cry had been real or part of his dream. Then, he realized that his frigate was laying so motionless on her anchor that he began speculating if all of nature was holding its breath and listening for another summons.

Heart pounding in anticipation, that he had actually received the summons, which he had told Nolan he hoped for, he waited.

After several long minutes, he heard something rustle in the still night. It sounded as if it was above the deck.

Cameron quietly got out of his hammock, tied his dark wavy hair back with a leather strip, slipped his feet into sturdy sandals, and pulled on his dragon-gold robe, which honored Shaka-uma. Then, fearing the creators would be angered by one of his rank simply wearing the rough threads of an initiate, he added his ornate azure hooded cowl, which tradition claimed was the color or Shaka-uma's tongue, and designating his office, high draco, as the one which could speak for her.

High overhead, an unseen bird wailed its approval to the stars.

Cameron straightened to his full six-feet of height, squared his wide shoulders and ascended the ladder to the frigate's deck. "I am ready," he whispered to the unseen watcher in the cloudless night sky. He paused for a moment and looked toward Dragon Ridge, where the others were preparing for the coming celebration, but he couldn't even see the glimmer of a fire. He swallowed and hoped that the creator's herald could not see the bands of fear he felt tightening around his chest.

Ropes rustled, urging him to hurry.

On silent sandals, he moved across the shadowed deck, climbed down the rope ladder to his dory, untied the knot securing it to his frigate, then paddled his small, but sturdy reed-boat toward the path to the protected place, from which generations of dracos had received guidance.

Behind him, there was a loud splash. Cameron smiled, knowing that his beloved companion, Saphera, was following him.

As Cameron neared the shore, the clouds moved aside and vast barren hectares of massive octagon-shaped objects shimmered in the stars' meager light. Ancient tales claimed that a mighty mountain with a lava-lake at its summit had once stood where the harbor now protected his frigate from the ocean's wild waves.

Over a millennium before, Cameron's ancestors had cobbled together their first bamboo craft, then, catching the wind with rags stitched together to form a sail, they followed the great dragon-mother, Shaka-uma and watched with reverence as she laid her eggs in the lava-lake. A millennium later, even though the mighty mountain no longer existed, Shaka-uma's followers still made an annual pilgrimage to the site.

Unfortunately, after generations of no one seeing dragons, few still followed Shaka-uma and even fewer made the annual journey to honor her. But, if he did not follow the traditions, who would? Their beliefs had been respected for centuries, then one-hundred-twenty-three years ago, the volcano had exploded, raining Shaka-uma and her unhatched young onto the surrounding shore and into the ocean. Many of the eggs had cracked, causing the young to die in agony. Cameron looked at the hundreds of huge, geometric rocks, which littered the shore, unable to imagine the force it must have taken to throw them free of the mountain as it disintegrated.

Legend claimed that Shaka-uma herself had been hurled all the way to Dragon Ridge, then buried there, under ash and debris from the eruption. Though he had faith that she had survived the horrible event, she had not flown the skies to bless the lands, since. And while he told doubters that he had faith that she still lived and would return to bless their harvests, in his heart he doubted if she would return to improve a land which had destroyed her offspring.

What the ancient tales did not explain was if the three undamaged shield-shaped boulders held healthy young dragons or if the uncracked geometric rocks were as dead as the rest. Of course, now that he was the high draco, Cameron needed to pretend to have knowledge and understanding that he did not have so he could project a confidence he did not feel.

Being an initiate had been much simpler.

It was easier to live in the solitude on his frigate than in the home assigned to his station. At least for the few days he was anchored here, he didn't need to oversee the ever-decreasing number of faithful or spend his days feeling like a fraud and he didn't even need to project confidence for the initiates, who Nolan had taken to Dragon Ridge to prepare for the ceremony.

He narrowed his gaze on one of the three large octagonal

mounds which his predecessors believed were pods of living baby dragons, and held his breath. Before he was forced to inhale, a thin tendril of smoke rose toward the slender sliver of moon in the night sky. Gooseflesh rippled over his back at the immediacy of this sign. To think that a young dragon would honor him with this proof of life so quickly! Cameron knelt on the bottom of his woven boat, pressed his forehead to the cold, damp reeds as he renewed his vow of allegiance and told himself that he should not have doubts.

When he sat up, a cloud covered the sliver of moon and shadows obscured everything. He shivered and hoped this was not an evil omen. Picking up his paddle, he quickly moved the rest of the way to shore. With every stroke, he tried to convince himself that the creators had chosen him for something special and that all that he hoped to understand would soon be revealed. He also assured himself that the creators would help him guide the ignorant, who believed that their profits and baubles meant that they had value. When, in truth, they were merely weighing themselves down with clutter.

When the water abruptly thinned and his dory's flat bottom scraped the rocks, he stepped out, secured its rope to a nearby stone, and then waded ashore on the only area of the harbor that didn't have a sheer drop into deep water.

Step by step, the water pulled at the hem of his robe. Cameron smiled at the token tests the creators were giving him.

Twice, he stubbed his toes on unseen protrusions, which hid in the shadows and he smiled. Finally, assured of his devotion, the clouds moved aside to reveal the thin foot path, which priests had used for centuries to pay tribute to Shaka-uma for leading them to this bountiful island. At least, it had been bountiful while the dragons flew over it. The trail snaked past craters that had pocked the land since the dragon father, Shaka-dun, died fighting the money-loving infidels, and his mate fled into the volcano's magma to protect her pods and escape persecution.

Saphera leaped onto the battered shoreline and shook the water from her ivory and black coat. In the thin moonlight, her five-hundred-pound body inside the iridescent cocoon of droplets appeared delicate against the harsh beauty of the stark black rocks.

When his steps faltered, another screech from high overhead spurred him onward.

The farther inland Cameron O'ryan walked, the more the ground warmed and the sky lightened. He tiptoed over licorice twists of cooling lava; two steps later an unexpected acrid breath of earthly steam bathed him. He bowed, then blinked in surprise at the sight of a tiny fern that was miraculously growing in a crevice of the hot stone.

He had never heard of anyone being given so many signs! It was almost as if the dragon-creators knew about his doubts and wanted to assure him that he was their chosen representative.

But why him?

Why hadn't they cured Draco Moore when he became ill? Draco Moore was more respected and actually had liked leading the flock, while Cameron had almost fled the priesthood because of his own lack of conviction.

It was easy to doubt. Many generations had passed since anyone had claimed to see the dragon-mother, Shaka-uma. Decade after decade and century after century, it became more difficult to lead the believers when no dragons flew overhead casting their magic on the fields below. Now, people whispered that the stories about dragons living in fiery pits and coming out at night to spread fertility over the fields were silly stories grannies invented to entertain babies.

Worse, since no dragon had been seen in generations, some doubters claimed that the dragons had never made the soil fertile.

Others claimed they had never even existed.

His ancestor, Draco Hale Cameron, had lived to be over a century old and even he had never known anyone who had actually seen a dragon. Now Draco Hale lay in the most sacred graveyard at the heart of the Protected Place and Fire Island's fields continued to produce a bit less each year.

In many ways Cameron could understand why the faction that extolled earthly possessions kept gaining followers. The thoughts of the starving masses were easy to sway when they saw fat pontiffs feasting off the fruits of their schemes, instead of spending their time on honest labor.

What if the accumulators were right?

What if the rain and harvest ceremonies were a sham?

Had Draco Hale really lived so long because Shaka-uma loved him or had his mother told him the story as a means to encourage a small boy who hated sweating in the cinder fields or because she'd known he'd need to hold onto something long after she was gone? Had they sat in the shade of the sacred red blooms of the 'ohi'a trees so he would understand that the words she spoke were truth about his ancestry? Or had they sat there so he could see the blooms as he listened to her voice and believe that if those magnificent flowers were real, that her words were, too?

Again, the unseen night bird urged him to hurry.

~o~

Pressure crushed Tem-aki in the dark unknown. She looked forward, but everything in front of her was black. She turned her gaze to the right, but only saw a menacing haze. She blinked, then looked to the left, where a rock's harsh lines seemed to blur in and out of focus in the dismal, hovering shadows. She squeezed both eyes closed, counted to one-hundred, then squinted to her left; the rock appeared more solid. She managed to draw a burning breath into her starving lungs. The more she became aware, the more suffocating her situation seemed. Tem-aki frowned, as she tried to understand her predicament, but nothing made sense. Tentatively, she took a deeper breath. It felt like she was lying under a ton of rocks, but enough oxygen made it into her aching lungs for survival. After a few more breaths, she levered herself into a sitting position, which caused the haze to thicken to near-opaque, but it also changed the weight that she felt and made it easier to breath.

How odd.

Dazed, she sat still. Gradually, the swirling murk surrounding her settled in a filthy film.

Where were Thunder and Raine?

Using the least movement possible, she keyed her analyzer. Neither of them were within range.

I'm alone.

Lost.

Or maybe in the here-after.

A chill wracked her body.

Or else they're behind me being quiet and the tricorder is malfunctioning, she thought, as she recalled the bizarre way its screen had rolled.

Tem-aki shivered.

Or else this is a really, really bad dream and I needed to wake up, she thought as she recalled all the other improbable events that had led up to the analyzer's malfunction.

"Or else I'm awake, have limited oxygen left and that means I'm in deep kimchee," she muttered.

"You're not in sauerkraut," an odd, thin voice said.

Tem-aki turned to look behind her and dislodged the arms of the android. As its weight fell away, the haze obscured, again. She'd forgotten about the android, which could account for some of the heaviness, but only some. Tem-aki ground her teeth together. Didn't the fool machine, which could supposedly translate over a million languages and dialects, understand the concept of colloquialisms?

"You're in H2O at a depth 43 meters. Your oxygen supply should last 37 hours at the present rate of consumption," GEA-4 said, as if reading her mind. Tem-aki swallowed the lump of fear and told herself to breathe. "You cannot stay here," GEA-4 added.

Where did the stupid droid expect her to go? "Which way are Thunder and Raine?"

"I lost my fix on them when the magnetic properties of the portal shifted."

"I beg your pardon?" Tem-aki willed herself to calm down. "Are you telling me your sensors are dysfunctional?"

"That is a possibility. My systems have suffered significant damage and need repair."

"Fine, then which way did Thunder and Raine go?" she again demanded.

"Unknown."

She knew it'd seemed like a long fall, but that was probably a hallucination. "Are you trying to tell me I'm alone?"

"There is one other 11.7 meters away on bearing 278."

Did the blasted android have a bad sense of humor? "Right. There's someone else down here. Are they running out of air, too?"

"They are at a higher elevation, so theoretically the individual has an adequate oxygen supply available."

"So, if I can get to them, I should have a better chance of surviving."

"Affirmative."

If she didn't need the blessed heap of fried wires to help her find bearing 278, she'd dump the infernal machine here and now.

Tem-aki struggled to stand upright. Why hadn't Thunder warned her they could become separated? If she'd known, she'd have stayed closer to him. It took her seven attempts before she managed to stand up without pressure sending her back down to her knees and creating an ever-increasing particle haze. Eventually, she managed to stand as well as secure the droid so that she could carry it, but now she couldn't even glimpse the rock through the silt. "Okay, which way do I need to go?"

"Toward the school of angels."

"What?" This was the information she needed to save her life?

"In front and to your right. You should be able to see them."

All she could see was something silvery darting in the murk near the edge of her vision. With nothing to lose, she took a step in that direction, then another. After forty paces, she still didn't know why she was trusting directions from a damaged android, which directed her toward mythical beings that supposedly went to something as mundane as a school.

But with no other viable option for survival, GEA-4's 'school of angels' was her best bet.

After what seemed like days, but was less than six hours, according to her chronograph, the rocky, sandy bottom began to sprout vegetation, which gradually got taller and thicker, the blades grasping at her legs.

Suddenly, Tem-aki tripped and fell. She threw her hands forward to break her fall, and landed hard on her knees. Exhausted, she focused on breathing and calming her hammering heart. After several minutes, feeling a bit calmer, she turned to see what had caught her boot.

Something glistened and beckoned against the sandy muck. Pushing GEA-4's arms aside and wriggling back to the thing, Tem-aki dug around it with her hand, excavating what looked like a dark twisted stick with an ornately knotted top. Very peculiar construction, but sturdy and potentially useful as a walking stick. Standing up, she took a tentative swipe at the clinging leaves. As if by magic, their grip on her boots slackened.

The stick was useful.

While it had obviously been manufactured, it could have been made thousands of miles away, so it didn't guarantee there was any land nearby.

Tem-aki sighed. "I thought you said that there was another person 11.7 meters away. Surely I've gone ten times that far."

"Correct."

Her hands clenched in rage. "So this person is now behind me?"

"Negative."

"Well, they are not here."

"Correct."

"Well, they obviously were not 11.7 meters away on bearing 278."

"At present, he or she is 534 meters away on bearing 322."

"Why did you allow me to move so far off course?"

"You were not the only one in motion."

Had she ever had such a frustrating conversation, before? "And this is the first time you thought it appropriate to mentioned this?"

GEA-4 did not respond.

Tem-aki tried to control her breathing to calm her temper. "Is it normal to get separated when going through the wormhole?"

"Cannot calculate probability due to limited data."

"Excuse me?"

"I have only passed through the vortex in question four times. The previous times were stable, which would suggest eighty-percent probability of arriving in the cave atop the peak of Sacred Mountain. We are not there."

Great, first the infernal machine advised her to follow a school of spirits, now it was telling her that she'd hiked deep into an asteroid and should have come out on top of a mountain.

And she'd been dumb enough to follow the advice.

Tem-aki turned her attention to the area around her. Since she'd been still, the silt in the water around her had begun settling and she realized she was sitting in a strange grassy plain, which had a multitude of odd silvery things darting amidst the leaves. Even more interesting, when she looked up, she thought she could see sunlight glistening on the top of the water. "Are we still under 43 meters of water?"

"Negative. 5.93 meters."

"Did the wormhole return us to Kalamar?"

"Impossible to determine."

"Well, what can you determine?"

GEA-4 remained quiet.

If the wormhole had somehow returned them to Kalamar, then no matter how many miles she walked, it was doubtful if she could find the planet's spec of dry land before she ran out of air. Tem-aki looked at the strange waving grass and the odd swimming creatures. Having grown up on Guerreterre, where water was sold by the drop, she had always thought that in nature, it was a scarce commodity, then she'd seen the water-world, Kalamar. Now, she was somewhere unknown and surrounded by the stuff. Tem-aki decided that it was most likely that the Star Bridge had malfunctioned and returned her to Kalamar.

Being surrounded by water made it seem common, but it was also impossible to breathe water, so she had to find a way out.

"Is there any land nearby?"

"Probabilities indicate that the other humanoid is on land."

"And that would be 534 meters away on bearing 322?"

"Correct."

Tem-aki considered leaving the infernal droid behind, then changed her mind and readjusted her burden. "If I do not find another person or land in 534 meters, I am dumping you. Understand?" Twenty paces later, she stood in front of a dark, vertical wall, which seemed to keep climbing higher, even when it soared above the water. "Any suggestion on how I'm expected to get over this?"

"Swim."

The droid was insane to think that anyone on Guerreterre, which had no natural water, knew how to swim, much less could do so carrying a malfunctioning droid. "Other than that?"

"There is a tunnel to your left, but my scanners are not adequate to determine if it would get you to your objective."

"And that is?" Tem-aki asked, to see what GEA-4 would say.

"The humanoid signal, which has not moved for the past three minutes."

"And is on land?"

"At an elevation above water-level."

Vowing this was the droid's last chance, Tem-aki moved along the sheer, high wall to her left, then found the promised tunnel, which wasn't as big as the old salt mine had been, but fortunately was large enough to stand inside. Squaring her shoulders, Tem-aki stepped into the unknown.

~o~

Cameron O'ryan knelt in front of the fire pit, which was in the ancient lava tube at the heart of what his faction called their Protected Place. He hummed the song of creating, as he carefully placed dried bits of moss in a cone shape, then added shreds of kindling. As the pyramid grew, he added larger sticks until it resembled the volcano at Fire Island's heart. Finally, he began intoning the proper incantation.

As the first rays of dawn shone through the cracked rock into the area, Cameron lit the fire.

The flame coughed and sputtered before it took hold.

As the strengthening light caressed the designs which had been carved into the walls of the ancient lava tube, he sprinkled sage on the blaze as an offering of respect to the creators.

When the flames reached high enough to meet the rays of morning light coming through the entrance to the Protected Place, he altered the ritual incantation. Now, instead of habitual praises, he murmured petitions for his tribe's health and safety as well as specific pleas for individuals who had been desperate enough to pay for his intervention. Cameron tried to sound sincere in his requests, even when the farmers' pleas for good rains for the crops clashed with petitions for good weather during the Tribe's spring-time equinox festival.

Cameron hoped the creators were wise enough to sort out what was important and ignore frivolous requests.

When the morning rays glinted off the rising smoke, he dropped to his knees, and offered the petitions close friends and family had entrusted to him.

~o~

Tem-aki cautiously walked into the black tunnel, using the twisted stick to verify the solidity of the ground prior to taking each step. After several paces, the gritty sandy bottom began to thin and there was an occasional slick spot, which slowed her even more. Thankfully, after an hour of snail-slow going, the passage began to get lighter.

Unfortunately, the water also began to look foggy, so even though it was lighter, it wasn't really easier to see. She vaguely recalled hearing about water's foggy layer phenomena. Unfortunately, she hadn't paid enough attention to something that she doubted she would ever encounter, so couldn't recall if it was supposed to be a good sign or bad.

What was good was that despite getting slicker and harder to walk on, the passage was moving upward at a steady pace, which meant she was probably getting close to air, and the sooner she got to that, the better.

She took a break to analyze the chemical properties of the cave, which remained consistent with the readings she had taken before entering it. Tem-aki took that as a good omen.

When she looked upward, an odd, flickering light seemed to flash off a layer of water. She reached up to touch it and circular ripples of light fled from her flight glove. She blinked in surprise.

With no other option, she refocused her attention on walking up the slick incline without falling on her face. Twenty paces later, her helmet began to break through the water. With her objective in sight, her pace quickened, so every step brought her another inch out of the water and toward the strange, flickering light.

Every footstep also made her burden heavier.

Worse, every step closer to the strange shoreline made it easier to see that someone had carved long rectangular depressions into the stone walls, above the high water mark and placed odd groups of rounded and long whitish things in them. Between the condensation inside her helmet and the gloom, it was difficult to get a good look at the jumbled items, but many of them looked suspiciously like bones.

And the closer she got, the more convinced she was that she was approaching some sort of burial ground. Tem-aki gulped, then asked GEA-4, "Where is the human, now?"

"One-hundred feet directly ahead."

Tem-aki frowned at the blazing fire, which was where the android said the human should be. Still, a living person must have built the fire, right? "Are they alive?"

"Affirmative."

"Near death?"

"I am unable to determine that."

Tem-aki sighed and wished she had had time to repair GEA-4's fried circuits.

Moving to the side of the black tunnel, she used her tricorder to analyze the material; the properties were nearly identical to the ones she had gotten before entering the tube. She blinked perspiration out of her eyes and wondered if the temperature was actually hotter or if it was just her imagination.

Hotter?

The fire was not large enough to account for the increasing temperature.

She bit her lip. Her tricorder indicated the presence of carbonization, on a large scale, that usually meant the rock was volcanic. Add heat to that fact and this probably was not a good place to be. Being under water with limited air was bad enough. Being under water that might have a volcanic explosion was a nightmare.

She had to get out of this place.

Backward was not an option and forward had no guarantees, but it was her best choice.

Fighting her fear of entrapment, she moved toward the higher heat readings as quickly as she could, without falling. By the time she was halfway out of the water, and the water no longer moderated her burden, GEA-4's weight was unbearable. Tem-aki wished she had taken the time to repair GEA-4's ability to walk, because despite the fact that the android was over a foot shorter and much thinner, GEA-4 outweighed her.

Unable to keep moving once her boots were past the tide line, Tem-aki sank to her knees and unhooked the harness. "Is this air breathable?"

"Yes. It is very similar to the air at the market."

Though that sounded confusing, it also sounded promising. Tem-aki took off her helmet and cautiously sniffed the air. Ew, rotten fish. Fortunately, there was also the scent of wood smoke and something oddly herbal.

Unfortunately, without the haze from the condensation, she confirmed that the white things were in fact humanoid skeletons. She didn't know what to think about expending all her energy to get to a cemetery, but assured herself that the good news was that if there were dead humanoids laid out in hand-hewn crevices, others should still be alive and hopefully they could help her find Thunder and Raine, or maybe just direct her straight to Larwin.

Chapter 4

Cameron knelt on a rough, woven reed mat in front of the fire and tried to focus on the proper tones and phrases for petitioning the creators, but odd sounds, from deep within the tunnels' black unknown depths kept distracting him. At first he thought he heard splashes, so he moved to the side, so he could see around the fire, but he still could not see into the darkness.

So, he knelt on his mat again and spent several minutes listening, but the only noise was from the gases in the burning wood popping and spitting. Certain that his imagination was playing with him, he began the chants, again.

As his muscles relaxed, a high-pitched voice said something garbled in the depths.

Cameron jumped up, looking for whoever had dared to enter this sacred space. In the gloom, he saw something pale near the water's edge. Squinting, he realized that Saphera was crouched near the waterline. With a sigh, he knelt and began the ritual, again.

Just as his forehead touched the reeds, he felt a rush of air and felt thuds on the ground, as Saphera ran past him, then threw herself onto the dusty ground behind him, as if she was trying to hide her five-hundred-pound bulk behind his one-hundred-eighty-pound form. Dear companion that she was, Saphera had always shown excessive caution, which was why he often joked that 'fear' was the middle of her name. In fact, many snickered and called her a 'frady cat', but this was ridiculous.

She was merely cautious.

A moment later, from the other side of the blaze, he heard what sounded like snippets of conversation. At least it sounded like two voices uttering consonants and vowels, but there had not been one intelligible word.

Were the creators testing him because they sensed his doubts?

Testing poor Saphera, because of her timid ways?

Squaring his shoulders, Cameron focused on his duty as mediator between the creators and the faithful and began to pray, only to hear a high-pitched voice rasp, "Yes. It is very similar to the air at the market." Chills ran down his spine at the high, thin clarity of the voice.

Were the creators speaking to him?

Why couldn't he understand what they were saying?

Unable to focus on his devotions, Cameron sat up, and saw a brief glimpse of something azure, where Saphera had been looking prior to her latest panic attack. Azure was the most sacred color. Why would she run from that? He stared without blinking, the fire's heat making his eyes water, then, he saw the apparition again. Closer this time, and fully out of the water, it knelt in front of the bones of most ancient dracos, as if paying homage.

Heart slamming against his ribs, mouth dry, Cameron forgot to breathe as he watched the miracle.

After the deity set aside its offering to the dead, it almost looked human. Then it made some odd movements and seemed to be taking off its round, crystalline crown.

The flames leaped, blocking his view.

With a gasp, he remembered to breath and then, he cautiously moved to his right, so he could see around the fire. The vision in azure was still there, and with the round hat-thing off, it had the face of a beautiful woman. Deity, really, judging by the golden halo. But it also seemed to have a second face; at least he thought the mangled mess was a face, beneath a mess of horrid, strange dark hair.

Was it part angel? Had it emerged from the underworld because it was a demon?

As he watched, the azure figure separated into two beings, the one tall, with lovely cheekbones and divine golden-reddish curls remained the sacred color, but the smaller one, which appeared to be all shades of lights and darks was pathetically homely and probably injured, since the attractive one needed to assist it to lie down properly.

He silently watched, while the azure one laid the injured one down, then knelt beside it, holding an odd black box, which it slowly moved over the sick one's head. After punching the box a few times, the golden-haired being moved it from the sick one's head, to its torso and lower. As Cameron's gaze followed the movements, he tried to understand what was being done.

If the angel was trying to help the other one, the strange one probably wasn't a demon.

Was it?

And it was female, wasn't it?

Would an angel help a being from the underworld? He blinked at the memory that they both had come from there.

Confused by his conflicting thoughts and emotions, he studied the strange pair. As his gaze traveled over the injured one, he noticed that something long and dark was lying next to her. He squinted, trying to see the details, then swallowed hard, when he realized that it looked remarkably like the sketches of the staff of power, which Draco Shakura, his sect's founder, had used to harness the dragon-mother's power and convince Shaka-uma to lead them to this island sanctuary.

The sketch of the staff of power was in the ancient journal, right next to the entry explaining that it had been lost during a violent storm at sea, even though the sacred volcano was in sight.

It was momentous that the deity had chosen to materialize, but why did it have the staff of power?

How bad were things going to get?

~o~

As a geologist, Tem-aki Atano thought she had encountered every type of anomaly associated with geology, but discovering that someone or some unknown group had carved the walls inside a lava-tube and was using the recesses as a tomb was something she had never imagined finding. She frowned as she studied the way the bones were laid, with all heads to the North and feet to the South. Was that fact significant or had the corpses been laid that direction because the tube itself had flown molten rock that direction?

Were compass readings important, here?

Was a culture that buried bodies like this advanced enough to consider compass bearings or have a way to determine the direction, when they could not see the stars?

She shook her head and decided such random thoughts could wait. The crucial thing, for now, was to see if she could repair GEA-4 enough so that the android could walk; because, without the water to moderate the load, there was no way she could continue carrying her.

Tem-aki trained her tricorder on the android and confirmed that, despite the strange fall and submersion, there was no additional damage.

That was the good news.

Unfortunately, the bad news was still the same. Tem-aki was great at a lot of things, but electronic repair was not one of them. When she fixed the shorted out wires for GEA-4's speech circuit, she had accomplished more than she imagined possible. She chewed her lower lip. "Okay, where is the system to control your limbs?"

"The part connected to my visual, auditory and gyroscopic sensors, is in my neck. Circuitry to move arms is at the base of my skull and the main circuitry to move my legs is where you humans have a belly button."

Rats, the android's face and belly had suffered the majority of the damage. But the back of its head didn't look too bad; at least she could tell one wire from another, instead of it looking like a half-melted slag-heap. "Um, if I can repair the damaged wiring in your neck, do you think your arms might work well enough for you to help?"

"Possibly."

"Okay, then we have a plan." Tem-aki began cleaning the exposed circuit board, then scanned it with her tricorder and showed GEA-4 the readings. Following the robot's directions, she carefully began repairs, but the harder she worked, the more difficult it was to see.

Glancing up, she realized that the once-bright fire had burned down to embers, but what was even more surprising was that a human and a big furry creature were sitting behind it, staring at her. "How long have you been there?"

When the silhouette didn't respond, GEA-4 said, "He was here first."

Hmm, maybe the robot's information wasn't so suspect after all. Tem-aki sat back on her heels and studied the alien as intently as he was examining her. At least she hoped GEA-4 was correct about it being male. It was impossible for her to tell because the flowing yellow robe and ornate blue cowl camouflaged gender, height, weight, and just about everything except long dark hair, strong cheekbones and steady gaze, which seemed very male. Since GEA-4 had said 'he', Tem-aki decided to think of the stranger as male, until she found a valid reason not to.

Whoever and whatever this person was, she needed his help finding food, shelter, tools and parts to repair GEA-4. Most importantly, she needed to find Larwin, but, if the silent man's attire was any clue, he came from a very backward culture.

Tem-aki smiled at him and introduced herself. He didn't bat an eyelash or introduce himself. "GEA-4, can he speak?"

"Unknown."

Great! Alien cultures had never been her strong suit, but she recalled that in some cultures, it was prohibited for females and males to interact unless they were either mated or part of the same family unit. "What should I do?"

"Fuse the relay."

That was not the answer she wanted, but probably the best advice, at least for the moment. Tem-aki pulled her las-cutter from the tool pouch, which was designed into her spacesuit, calibrated it to emit a soldering beam and did her best to refasten the delicate wire to the circuit board.

~o~

Cameron watched in fascination as the golden-haired woman – at least he thought the apparition was a woman – bent over the smaller, damaged one. Was it her child? The posture of the one in the strange, turquoise outfit looked like she was trying to heal, but he didn't know how she could do that, when she was fiddling with a barely visible hair. And why was a tiny silvery hair, which appeared not bigger than an eyelash the focus of her attention? Furthermore, why was it sticking out of a cut at the base of the injured one's skull?

Surely the other injuries were much more severe than the tiny hair. With that thought, the back of his own neck began to tickle. He moved a hand to scratch it and encountered whiskers. A backward glance confirmed that Saphera was as fascinated by the two unknowns as he was.

Reaching behind, without taking his attention from the unexpected pair, he patted Saphera's neck. A soft, tentative purr came from deep within her chest. Crawling forward, she leaned against his side and together they watched the odd pair.

Once, when it looked like the taller one was having difficulty trying to move the smaller one, Cameron considered offering his assistance.

But he realized that if she/they wanted his help, they have would asked, so he stayed on his mat, without seeing anything more earth-shattering than the pair emerging from the underworld.

Then, as the sun climbed high in the sky and the embers began to die, the smaller one suddenly sat up and clasped the taller one's face between her damaged hands. Saphera shivered so hard, as she leaned against his side, that Cameron nearly fell over.

The pair remained motionless for so long that he began to worry that he should do something. But what? Chant? Without being sure if they were sent by the sky creators or from the underworld demons, he couldn't decide what they were doing here.

How could he know what to pray or which chant would be appropriate, when he couldn't even decide if they were friend or foe?

His entire body began to feel stiff and cold, but he stayed still, watching.

Abruptly, the small one let go of the other's face, then with a swift, fluid movement stood upright, raised her hand in friendship and said, "Greetings."

Assuming it was her word for salutation; Cameron bowed with the respect due an injured child and responded in kind.

Unexpectedly, the taller one stood, then bowed deeply to him. She pointed to her chest. "I am Captain Tem-aki Atano," then she pointed to the small one, "and this is GEA-4." She gestured to the shorter one. "I am looking for my brother, Colonel Larwin Atano, can you direct me to him?"

Cameron blinked in confusion and looked from the possible demon to the possible angel, wondering what to do and what had been said, after what was obviously an introduction.

Saphera nudged him.

Belatedly, he remembered his manners and introduced himself and Saphera, then, deciding it was wise to give them the benefit of the doubt, with a great deal of pantomiming, he invited them to his frigate to share a meal.

When he was halfway back to his dory, it occurred to him that ones who healed by fiddling with nearly invisible hairs at the skull might not survive on the same things he did. But, by then, it was too late to back out on his offer, so Cameron continued forward.

Captaintemakiatano lagged behind when their path went by an octagonal-shaped rock, which his faction believed to be the birthing pod for a young dragon. He paused and watched her move the black box over it, as she had over the smaller one. Was she checking the dragon's health?

Had she come because a dragon was ready to return to their needy island?

If so, that would explain why she had brought the staff of power.

Hope bloomed in his soul.

Chapter 5

Tem-aki's fingernails dug into the craft's golden sides, as she held on for dear life. With each stroke, the tiny craft moved forward, the front point dipped down, so water sloshed over GEA-4's bedraggled form, as she perched in the small bow. Tem-aki looked over her shoulder at Cameron, whose back was toward their destination and wondered if she should bring his attention to the problem.

But how could she ask him if it was safe to have GEA-4 sit there?

Would GEA-4's weight sink them before they got to the big boat?

Seated on the bottom, in the middle, and getting damper with each stroke, Tem-aki's stomach cramped against the flimsy little boat's unsteady motion, and her fingers dug deeper into the fragile reed sides. She shut her eyes tight so she didn't need to look at all the water surrounding her.

What had she been thinking, when she allowed a man wearing a long, flowing dress to talk her into getting into this unstable thing?

And, had she understood him properly, when he pointed to the other boat and explained that was where there was food?

How would she possibly be able to eat anything if the other vessel also felt like it would flip over at any moment?

Cameron knelt in the stern and hummed a cheerful-sounding tune as he propelled the unsteady thing backward.

Hearing a big splash, Tem-aki risked a peek, to make sure that GEA-4 had not fallen in, but the 'droid was fine and to her surprise, the big furry animal was swimming next to their craft. For some reason, she had thought it would stay on the safe solidity of the rocks.

Obviously, she had been incorrect.

She glanced forward and was surprised to see that their destination was much larger than she had expected. In fact, it looked like it was at least two stories tall. She frowned and wondered why anyone would float a building. Then she remembered all the odd roundish things on Kalamar, which she had determined were homes and shops, so perhaps if a world had water, having buildings float was common.

The good news – or perhaps it was the bad news – was that their destination did not resemble anything she had observed on Kalamar. So wherever she was probably was not in that quadrant. Now that she thought about it, she realized she had not catalogued any volcanic activity, old or new, on Kalamar, and she certainly hadn't observed anything with the bizarre readings like the big, rocky, octagonal-shaped things on the land.

Her tricorder had given similar readings to the octagons as she had gotten from the walls of the old salt mine, but the truly strange part was that there was also a reading that indicated life signs.

Where was she?

What happened to Thunder and Raine?

Would she ever see Larwin or their parents, again? Not that she'd ever seen much of them to begin with; Guerreterre culture evaluated children on their third birthday and then sent them to the appropriate training facility. She had only been a year old when Larwin had left the security of home for military school, and did not have memories of him living at home. But she cherished her memories of the four-week-long breaks they had shared each solar revolution, when they went home to their parents.

A thump brought Tem-aki back to the present and the reality that she was surrounded by water. Fortunately, they had arrived at the sleek golden side of the big boat. Unfortunately, Cameron was gesturing for them to precede him up a weak-looking rope ladder. Tem-aki swallowed, but the lump of fear remained. "GEA-4, can you climb that?" she managed to ask.

"Affirmative." The droid surged to her feet, which sent the boat wildly rocking. Tem-aki screeched and dug her broken nails into the small boat's sides. GEA-4 grasped the woven fiber and bamboo ladder and hoisted her weight out of the boat. The tipsy craft bucked like an unbalanced mordike and she was sure she would be pitched into the deep, dark water.

Instead, the motion calmed. She opened one eye, then both and looked around, only to see Cameron's hazel eyes looking at her as if she was the oddest thing he had ever seen. Would he find her reaction as strange if it was his first time in a boat, which moved in unpredictable ways, all threatening to pitch him into unbreathable water?

At least he wasn't laughing.

Tem-aki took a deep breath and told herself that if the flimsy ladder had held GEA-4's weight, it would hold her. And if the droid could climb it, even though she was still severely damaged, so could she. She took another deep breath, then loosened her grip on the small craft with the hand closest to the ladder and grasped it. In reaction, the small boat moved. Quickly, she half stood and grabbed the ladder with her other hand, then, before she had a chance to let her fears overwhelm her, she climbed as fast as possible, while wearing a space suit and chunky boots. Which meant that she slipped with every movement, until the ladder miraculously moved away from the golden side of the big boat, so that she could get a secure foothold.

Glancing down, she realized Cameron was holding it out, and anchoring it. Smiling her thanks, she turned her attention to the climb. Once she got to the top, flat deck, she threw herself aboard, kissed the smooth golden surface and vowed that if this boat was as stable as it seemed, she would never leave it.

With that plan in mind, she began removing her space boots and suit.

~o~

Cameron took his time securing his dory to Sirocco's side and wondering why the deity had left Draco Shakura's staff of power in the dory. And now that he saw it in the light of day, he was positive it was Draco Shakura's lost staff. Reverently, he leaned forward to touch the magical wood. Immediately, power raced up his arm.

Why would she leave something so important behind?

He pondered that mystery so long that Saphera heaved herself onto the dory, gave herself a good shake, which soaked him to the skin. Then, she stood on her hind legs, braced her front paws on Sirocco's deck and vaulted aboard.

From above, there was a scream.

Catching the ladder, as the dory shot backward, he scrambled to the deck to see what the problem was.

Saphera's sudden appearance was probably what had startled Captaintemakiatano, but he couldn't be sure.

Once Cameron could see above the deck, he stopped

transfixed by the sight of the strange turquoise skin hanging from her body as she stared at the open doorway to his cabin.

Saphera was nowhere in sight, which meant that she was probably hiding under the table in his galley.

Now he could see that the turquoise layer was some strange form of clothing. And, since it was half-torn away, he was positive that Captaintemakiatano was a female. Thankfully, he could also see that she appeared uninjured, so he assumed her scream had been a response to Saphera leaping aboard.

Captaintemakiatano's scream had apparently terrified his dear companion, and she had probably done what she always did in such a situation. Hide.

Taking her attention from the galley door, Captaintemakiatano calmly began pulling at the strange azure layer. There was no blood and her expression didn't appear pained.

Obviously, the stuff was removable.

Clothing?

Judging by the methodical way she was moving, he was inclined to think it was the most likely possibility.

The shedding of the turquoise layer revealed a glimmering silver layer, which was very similar to the ill one's attire, which made him wonder about their relationship. Were they from the same group, or was the silver layer coincidence?

As he silently watched, Cameron was reminded of a butterfly emerging from its cocoon, except for the fact that she didn't appear wet or have wings. At least none that he could see from his vantage point.

Knowing that she was all right, he quickly stepped back down, grabbed the staff of power, then climbed aboard, nodded to Captaintemakiatano, as if seeing a creator's emissary disrobing on Sirocco's deck was normal, and hurried to the galley to check on Saphera and prepare their mid-day meal.

Chapter 6

Thankfully, the larger boat was steadier than the small one had been, so Tem-aki was able to eat the food the strange man offered. As she chewed the dark bread and chunky whitish thing, which he called 'sandwich', she studied Cameron. If he put on normal clothing and got his shaggy hair cut to a normal length, he would probably be quite handsome. For certain, his food tasted wonderful. Perhaps long hair was typical here. Thunder's hair had been worn long too, but Cameron didn't have any tiny braids with beads and feathers, so the style was different. Perhaps the braids weren't as important as the hair's length and it fashionable, on this planet, for males to have long hair.

And if so, she might actually be on Thunder's world, but that didn't explain why GEA-4's language program hadn't worked.

Again, she thought of Thunder's dark hair, which was well past his shoulders with four small braids, two near each ear, which blended in with the rest of his thick hair, except for the beads and feathers decorating them. She studied Cameron's hair, which was a similar dark brown/black color, but there was no sign of any tiny braids. Aside from the color, there didn't seem to be any similarities, so she might be wrong about being on Thunder's world.

And their clothing was decidedly different.

Which might mean that she would never see her brother, friends, or her parents, again.

Tears blurred her vision and the sandwich threatened to come back up. She clenched her jaws, closed her eyes and tried to focus on calming thoughts. Several minutes later, when she finally felt like she might be back in control of her emotions, she sighed and opened her eyes.

Cameron was staring at her with a worried look.

"I'm fine," she said, as much for her own sake as his.

His expression didn't change, so either he still couldn't understand her or he didn't believe her. He chewed his lower lip and glanced from the food left on her plate to her. Did he think he'd made her ill? If so, would he stop providing food and shelter?

Tem-aki tried to smile assuringly and took another bite of the too-sweet red gel-food.

Cameron's concerned look calmed somewhat, but not entirely. How could she assure him that her roiling stomach had nothing to do with his strange food and everything to do with her uncertainty over her future?

Whoever Cameron was, he obviously lived wherever here was and knew how to survive in this water-infested environment. She needed that knowledge.

After she figured out how to survive here, she could figure out if she could find a way to either find Larwin or a way to get back to Guerreterre.

If anyone had ever told her that she would be sitting at a table that was on a boat, which was surrounded by an unimaginable quantity of water, she would never have believed them. Yet, now that this impossible-to-predict situation had happened, all she could think of was how to get back to her waterless home-world.

While a cup of water was wonderful, when there was enough to drown in, it was evident that even marvelous things had a point where they became a liability. Until this moment, if anyone had told her she would ever think such a thing, she would have laughed at them.

Tem-aki gave Cameron another smile and thanked him for the food. Just because he had found her, had not obligated him to help her, much less feed her. At least he hadn't tried to clothe her. She glanced at his shapeless saffron-gold toe-length dress. If the males of this world dressed like that, what did the females wear?

The feline took that moment to crawl out from under the far end of the long table. Huge as the black and white creature was, it seemed timid, which was as reassuring as it was curious.

Why would something that had teeth bigger than her pinky and claws that looked capable of shredding the flesh from a madrox fear her?

Tem-aki looked down. The feline, which he had called a Saphera, was studying her with intelligent blue eyes.

Gooseflesh rippled over her.

~o~

Cameron didn't know what to think about his unexpected guest. At first, he had thought she and her companion had materialized in response to his prayers.

Now, he wasn't so sure.

His attention moved from the one with matted golden hair, who was poking at her berry sorbet, but not really eating it, out the open door to the damaged one, who stared at the sun, with sightless, silver eyes. Uneasiness rippled through him.

Perhaps he made Captaintemakiatano uncomfortable. If so, Cameron didn't know if he should sit down and eat with her, or leave her alone. Since his stomach was clinching with stress, it wasn't wise to try and eat. With a gesture to Saphera to follow, he went onto the deck to meditate or at least try to figure out why the smaller one was so obsessed with sunlight.

He sat on the deck, his back to the mast and Saphera plopped down next to him, as they studied the ill one. The more he watched her — at least the curves made him believe it was a her — the more he realized this one was even stranger than the tall one. While there were traces of soot from burning and several slashes in her skin, there was no sign of blood. Furthermore, if he or anyone he knew had been hurt that badly, their bones would have been laid to rest.

Could this one, and perhaps the other, be demons instead of the creator's emissaries?

His mouth went dry at the thought, but it made a horrible sort of sense. The damaged one didn't seem to understand, or fear, the burning power of the sun. Which probably meant that she had never seen one previously. That probably meant they had come from the underworld.

A sudden chill made him shiver.

Saphera put her massive paw on his lap and began to purr.

~o~

Now that the cat and man were no longer staring at her, Tem-aki could eat with her fingers instead of the strange, slick slicks, which had been provided, so she made quick work of the too-sweet food. Then, with nothing else to do, she watched the odd pair stare at GEA-4 and noticed that while they did not speak, they seemed to be communicating. The feline hadn't spoken to her, either, but she had not considered that strange.

Now that she thought about it, though, it was odd that the only time she had heard Draco Cameron O'ryan speak was when he had given her his name and that of Saphera. All their other communications, assuming you could call gestures and facial expressions communication, had been silent.

For the first time in her life, Tem-aki wished she had taken more of the social studies classes, which explained why individuals behaved the way they did. Instead, nearly her entire curriculum had targeted earth-sciences and eventually centered on rocks and minerals. While her education had prepared her well for doing the geological survey she had been in the middle of when she initially spotted the rogue madrox, it certainly had not prepared her for wherever she currently was. And it didn't help her understand why Draco Cameron had moved close to GEA-4 or why he seemed to be inspecting the repair she had done on the circuit at the back of the android's neck.

She watched with interest as he fingered GEA-4's shredded uniform. Primitive as the cloth his own robe was made of, she wondered what he thought of the high-tech fabric and if he understood how catastrophic the event had to have been to rip and burn the protective fabric.

As he fingered the material, Cameron got a strange expression on his face. Suddenly, he grabbed GEA-4's face in both of his hands and seemed to stare into her face. Tem-aki jerked out of her chair and shouted, "Don't do that to a droid!" But, GEA-4 had already grabbed Cameron and flung him away.

Within a blink, he disappeared over the side of the boat. Tem-aki sprinted to the rail, but Saphera beat her, and dove into the horrible water.

Oh Keus, now she needed to help them both!

But how?

She stared at the ripples expanding over the water. Her education hadn't prepared her for anything like this, either.

Tem-aki whirled to confront GEA-4, who had resumed solar-recharging. "Did you need to throw him overboard? He is the only one here who knows how to exist wherever here is! I needed him. But you didn't think about that, did you? Of course not, all you need to exist is to stand in sunlight." Tem-aki glared at GEA-4. "Well, do you have anything to say for yourself? Can you show me where to find food or other humans?"

"There is no need; Draco Cameron O'ryan knows how to swim as do most on this planet."

"I beg your pardon? Are you suggesting that you know where we are?"

"We are on the planet we were headed to."

"Larwin is here?"

"On this world."

"And you can take me to him?"

"Negative."

"Then how do you know where we are?" Tem-aki slapped her forehead, at her stupidity. Now that the 'droid was able to recharge, of course, she had taken the opportunity to do a celestial survey to determine location. "Never mind. Dumb question."

Hearing the sound of splashes, she rushed back to the railing, where she was grateful to see Cameron dragging himself onto the little boat. He had lost the bulky, blue collar and the robe's gold fabric now clung to his well-toned physique. If he was that fit, why had he hidden his body under the ridiculous tent of a garment?

Cameron sat down in the small boat and appeared to either catch his breath or be deep in thought.

A moment later, Saphera rocketed out of the water, landing lightly beside Cameron, then gave her huge body such a shake that she resembled a fountain. As more water dripped off Cameron, she casually hopped onto the deck next to Tem-aki, then sprawled in the biggest pool of sunlight, put her chin on her crossed paws and stared at GEA-4.

Now that she knew that neither had drowned, Tem-aki moved away from the railing and looked around the big boat, as she wondered what to do.

Chapter 7

After GEA-4 finished recharging, she and Tem-aki began repairs to the android's damaged face. "It almost looks like you were in an explosion."

"I was."

Tem-aki blinked in surprise and waited for GEA-4 to continue, instead, the android silently continued bonding her damaged tissue. With a sigh, Tem-aki asked, "Do you think you will be able to find Larwin's coordinates, once your sensors are repaired?"

"Time will tell what is repairable." The android's hands paused and she raised her silvery gaze to meet Tem-aki's in an oddly human way. "However, even if I can determine that, the crucial question is if we will be able to get to him."

"What do you mean?"

"Probables indicate that the rocky landmass we discovered is an island. It is the only landmass within sensor range. Assuming my calculations are correct, while we are on the same planet as Colonel Atano, the land mass that he is on, is on the opposite side of this planet. Your suit does not have adequate air to walk that distance."

The tiny flame of hope, which she had been nurturing, died and tears of despair blurred her vision. "Cameron has the big boat. Couldn't he take us?"

"Unknown." GEA-4's hands paused, then she added. "I do not know of any world map for this world, so do not know if the water all interconnects."

That was a problem. Tem-aki chewed her lower lip. "Then what are we going to do?"

"That is the true question, isn't it?" GEA-4 went back to working on repairs.

"I always thought that the material covering you was pigment infused during manufacture, but your covering is stark white on the back and tan on the top."

"Nimri helped me look more human, so I would fit in better."

"Nimri?"

"The healer and protector of the Chosen."

"The Chosen?"

"Nimri's Tribe."

Again, Tem-aki waited for the android to continue speaking, but, again, she remained silent. "You have no intention of telling me about her, do you?"

"At the moment, Nimri is not relevant."

"Oh, really?" Tem-aki's fingernails dug into her palms, as she fought the urge to smack the infernal machine. "What is relevant?"

"Survival. Second: repairs. Third: assessing our situation. Fourth: once we know exactly what our situation is, what resources we have available and where Colonel Atano is located, then we can make a plan to reunite with him. Until then, planning anything is a waste of time and energy." GEA-4 bonded the largest torn piece of dermal-layer covering her cheek back into place.

"That makes sense." And it did, even though she hated to admit it and the only thing she really wanted to find was Larwin, immediately. "Since we have survived, and are now on step two, how do you propose that we assess our situation? Other than the fact that we are in the middle of water and have no way to go anywhere?"

GEA-4's hands, which were fitting bits of plastoid to repair her ear, stilled and, again, she turned her silver stare on Tem-aki in an oddly human way. "We listen and watch."

"Listen to what? Words we can't understand?" Tem-aki ran her hand through her hair. "Watch what? How he slices bread and makes something he calls a sandwich? Or maybe how to use a board to move a little boat through the water?" She exhaled, but the pressure inside remained. "Just what valuable information am I supposed to learn from that sissified dress-wearing guy?" The words exploded with a violence she couldn't hide.

"Draco O'ryan obviously lives here and if we watch him and his feline-companion, we can learn much."

"How do you figure that?"

"Do you not remember that he was waiting for us and he had lit a signal fire?"

"You think he expected us and went there to meet us?"

"On this world, that would be my best explanation."

"Why did you phrase it that way? Does this world operate that much differently from Guerreterre?"

"Nimri's tribe values natural resources and does not squander them, as Guerreterre does. She, Thunder and Kazza all have the ability to use myst power."

"Mist what?"

"The books you had as a child would have called it magic."

"You can't be serious!" The android ignored her and continued repairing the damaged tissue. Already, there was a marked improvement on the left side of her face. "Who is Kazza?"

"A feline, very similar to Saphera, though he has much more gold in his fur. He is approximately twenty percent larger and his eyes are amber instead of blue."

"And this so-called-feline works magic?" Her tone squeaked with surprise.

"Correct. I therefore postulate that Saphera could have the capability for magic, as well, and if so, there is a possibility that she could let Kazza know our location."

"You cannot be serious!"

"If you knew Kazza, you would not say that."

"Whatever." Since the android was now spouting crazy speculation, Tem-aki turned away. Walking to the railing, she studied the shore, and focused on the strange octagonal rocks, which had fascinated her. From this vantage point, she could see hundreds littered the shore. Calibrating her tricorder, she checked each for life signs. Only two other than the one she had taken readings from, while going to where Cameron had tied his small boat, showed life signs. Strange.

Very strange.

No matter how hard she thought about it, there was nothing in her geology books that mentioned anything similar, much less had the silica-based readings that also could indicate life.

Could GEA-4 be correct about magic being a factor in this world? As a chill rushed over her, Tem-aki rubbed her palms on her arms and wished she had ended up somewhere understandable.

Somewhere, where she didn't need to worry about drowning.

Somewhere, where men dressed like men.

Somewhere, where rocks were rocks, not some form of living thing.

~o~

Cameron watched the tender way Captaintemakiatano touched GEA-4, and, again, wondered if they were related. And if they were not related in some way, why did GEA-4 allow Captaintemakiatano to touch her? Again, he studied the smaller one's extensive injuries.

Had she been attacked by a man?

That could explain why she had reacted to his touch the way she had.

However, he could not imagine how anyone had gotten close enough to hurt someone that strong.

Yet, when he had first seen her, she had been so badly wounded that she couldn't walk. Could that be done from a distance? It didn't seem likely, but then neither did the rapid way her torn flesh healed.

Cameron had no idea how any person could cause another such extensive harm, but was also aware that humans were capable of bad things. As a draco, he had watched far too many families suffer because one member became unbalanced by either mental or physical illness. And too often, their illness spread to those closest to them. Since he could not figure out how or why bad thoughts and deeds could move from person to person, he still accepted his mother's lesson that it was like having one bad apple in a basket, which tended to taint the rest of the apples, if it wasn't removed and the bad parts cut out.

And that made him think of Varlet, whose attitudes and laziness were already starting to affect Dirk and Malin. It was bad enough that their beliefs were attacked from outside, nearly unbearable that he had to tolerate Varlet's negativity from within their group. Yet tolerate it, he must. At least until Varlet gave him solid reason to dismiss him.

Cameron clenched his teeth until his jaws ached. Then, he forced himself to focus on GEA-4 and the way she and Captaintemakiatano were apparently healing her torn flesh, instead of think about the thorn named Varlet, which had been his problem for over a year. Shaka-uma willing, he would find a solution for Varlet. But right now, he needed to understand why she had sent him these two strange females.

Cameron wished he knew what to do to heal the injured one. Keeping his distance from the strangers, he noticed that Captaintemakiatano was not actually healing GEA-4, but somehow seemed to be supporting her while she healed herself.

Was that the secret?

Did the ill need to heal themselves instead of seek help elsewhere?

He chewed his lower lip as he contemplated the idea, which was the exact opposite of everything he had been taught.

Yet, the more he watched them, the more certain he became that they were some sort of supernatural beings. Even though, the only other way he might be able to describe their arrival from the underworld was speculating that they were demons, he had never heard of demons healing anything or anyone. And when he had first seen her, Captaintemakiatano wore the color of Shaka-uma's tongue. Though it was strange and troubling that he could not understand most of her words.

Regardless, a demon would not have come bearing the staff of power.

So, that doubt was settled. Whatever they were, they were not demons.

After over an hour of watching them and nothing dramatic happening, Cameron went outside and looked at the desolate coastline. Draco Shakura, his sect's founder, had controlled the dragon-mother, Shaka-uma with the staff of power, then lost it in a violent storm, which nearly cost him his life.

Now, it had been returned.

Why? There had not been a dragon sighted in generations. Why had the supernatural beings returned it, now, unless it was needed?

Cameron's gaze traveled around the peaceful bay. Were the legends true?

Had this bay once been a tall cone-shaped mountain filled with fire?

Had Shaka-uma lived here?

Had Shaka-uma been killed when the mountain exploded in the cataclysmic disaster which formed this harbor, as the profit-makers claimed?

Was his faction merely following an elaborate myth?

Or was Shaka-uma sleeping under Dragon Ridge as she waited for her eggs to hatch?

He remembered the thin tendril of smoke, which had risen toward the slender sliver of moon. Again, gooseflesh rippled over his back, along with the certainty that the eggs would soon hatch, Shaka-uma would soon wake and he would need to figure out how to control them with the staff of power.

Cameron's grip tightened on the railing, as his gaze traveled to the distant formation named Dragon Ridge. Soon, it would be time for the annual pilgrimage to its summit, where, for centuries, dracos had built bonfires on what they claimed to be the top of Shaka-uma's head. It would be the first time he officiated at this most sacred ceremony.

Legend said that fire built this island.

Fire protects and feeds the faithful.

Fire burns out poisons.

And supposedly fire called for Shaka-uma to return.

Would she come for him?

Or, had his strange guests brought the staff to use themselves?

A pinging sound from GEA-4 caught his attention. He turned in time to see a spark leap from her fingertip. Had the sound she made been the same tone dracos had used in their healing ritual for the past thousand years? He couldn't be positive, because it was so short, but he thought it was the same frequency he used to move a sick follower from a place of imbalance to a place of balance.

He cocked his head to one side and concluded that this could be another clue about his guests' divine origin.

Like fire, sounds helped facilitate shifts in thoughts. By using rhythm and frequency, it became possible to change thoughts from normal waking consciousness to sleep, where healing could happen.

Sound therapy could be both passive and participatory, but he had never known anyone to practice it on themselves. For one thing, the passive aspect was achieved by lying down and slowing your breath. Cameron squinted at GEA-4's chest and marveled at her control. Never, in all his years of training, had he known anyone who could slow their breathing so much that no inhalation was detectable.

Had sound helped GEA-4 create the pathway to perfect stillness of meditation?

After she finished healing herself, would she teach him how to transcend the need for air?

And would Captaintemakiatano teach him how to use the staff of power?

Chapter 8

As the sun neared the horizon, Cameron hung up two hammocks in the salon for his guests, then, he went topside to bring them down. Oddly, neither of them seemed to know how to get into a hammock, so he hung his, then demonstrated.

Captaintemakiatano gamely gave it a try and nearly flipped over before she collapsed, white-knuckled, into the wildly swinging bed. GEA-4 tentatively tested the fabric's strength with her palm, and apparently decided it was not strong enough, because, without uttering a sound, GEA-4 turned, walked back to the ladder and went back above-deck.

After his startling dunking, he was unwilling to urge her to give the comfortable hammock a try.

Watching her leave, Cameron noticed that the last rays of sun were shining through the eyes of the huge feline crystal skull, as it sat in front of the porthole. The skull had been given to him when he earned the rank of high draco. But, for the first time since he had seen it, it looked like something was moving inside the skull. He took a step closer, to get a better look and squinted at the tiny moving figures inside. It looked like Saphera, who appeared to be the size of an ant and some even smaller people were inside the skull and either dancing or fighting with some fiery, golden dragons, which appeared as large as dragonflies. Having never seen such a bizarre phenomenon, previously he bent forward until his nose pressed against the skull.

Now that he was closer, he thought that he recognized himself and was even more certain that one of the two cats was Saphera, but he did not recognize the other humans or understand why they seemed to be fighting three dragons. He was also surprised that by comparison, one of the dragons looked larger than Sirocco's hull.

He blinked as he stood upright and wondered why he would fight something as revered as a dragon.

Suddenly, the crystal skull filled with a blaze of blinding light, then a few moments later, it was back to normal; the vacant eyes staring out the porthole to the last rays of the setting sun.

Heart hammering against his enclosing ribs, Cameron continued to stare at the skull. He nearly forgot to breathe, as he tried to understand not only what he had just seen, but why he had seen it.

The only explanation was that this had something to do with the tendril of smoke and the two strangers, who had arrived with the lost staff of power.

The vision couldn't be an omen, could it?

No draco in the entire history of his faction had ever considered harming one of the magnificent, life-bringing creatures.

Yet he had seen himself and others fighting the dragons in the skull, hadn't he? Had he actually recognized himself or had it been his imagination?

Before the light totally faded to shadows, he climbed into his hammock and tried to relax enough to rest, but all he could think about was the tiny figures, and the more he thought about it, the more certain he was that they had looked like they were locked in mortal combat.

Saphera padded into the salon, curled up on her pile of cushions and began to purr. Cameron couldn't recall the last time he had felt so agitated that she had purred him to sleep, but he soon felt his muscles relaxing and his breathing return to normal.

Then lapsing into sleep, he dreamed he was high in the night sky, soaring, like a bird and looking down at Sirocco's deck. He woke in the middle of the night thinking his dream had almost been as disorienting as the vision inside the skull.

~o~

Tem-aki woke from a dream where she had been heavy with child. By the time she had blinked away the remnants of the strange dream, she realized she was staring at the big translucent plastoid, alien skull, which, if she understood what she had witnessed yesterday, was apparently some holographic display, but judging by the way Cameron had reacted, he didn't understand it any better than she did.

'Skull of doom, skull of death' flickered through her thoughts, making her shiver. She continued to stare at the unusual artwork. At least she thought it looked like some sort of artistic creation, even though it might be some sort of entertainment system or maybe even a communication device.

What if it had supernatural powers?

The small hairs on her arms stood on end. She quickly glanced around to see if Cameron was watching her, but his hanging bed was empty.

Darn, she'd hoped she could watch how he got out of this unstable thing, again. Yesterday, when he had demonstrated getting in, it had looked simpler than putting on socks. Then, she had tried to do it. Tem-aki swallowed at the memory and was still amazed that she had gotten in without landing face-first on the floor.

But now, she was stuck in the darn thing.

The cat was gone, too, so there was nothing to grab onto, except a saffron robe, which was useless.

At least, there was no one around to watch her make a fool of herself.

Tem-aki carefully sat up. The flimsy fabric jiggled. Quickly, she put one leg over each side to balance it, then sat up the rest of the way. She began to move her left leg to the other side, but that sent the hammock rocking so violently, that she quickly grabbed on with both hands and put her left leg back. Sitting there, felt surprisingly stable, as long as she didn't move.

Was this odd bed some form of prison?

She shook her head, quickly discounting the idea. The man had slept in one, too, and she could see where several ropes had previously been secured to hold over a dozen of the things; it was most likely that this was a normal thing for their culture.

She sensed a gentle movement through her feet. Picking them up, the hammock began rocking, again, so she put them back down. She realized that before her feet had touched the floor, the boat had seemed stable as a normal building. So maybe whoever had come up with this bed's design had been clever. Except this was one of the most treacherous things she had ever tried to get on or off of.

Well, this and that slick tunnel floor.

After several failed attempts, Tem-aki grabbed the hammock's sides with both hands, folded her legs around the crazy bed and flipped the thing over. Once she was suspended under it, she released her grip with her legs, then lowered herself the short distance to the floor, and then she released her hands. She quickly got up, dusted herself off, flipped the crazy bed back and draped the saffron robe over it.

Now free, she went to the skull and took out her tricorder.

To her surprise, instead of plastoid, it had a 4 on the hardness scale. Further analysis revealed that it was made of a single piece of quartz crystal. She blinked in surprise, having assumed a culture where men wore tent-like dresses and moved their little boats by muscle power, was too backward to use, much less build, technology. And now, she learned that Cameron had the technology to shape a giant quartz crystal into a complex 13.0 by 15.1 inch sculpture, which not only had a mirror-like finish, but was capable of some sort of visual depiction.

Amazing.

Had the holographic aspect been a trick of the light?

Was this thing capable of verbal communication, or did this culture use ESP or something else equally bizarre?

For certain, Cameron was not much of a talker.

The only other things her tricorder was able to verify about the skull was that the jaw was articulated and that there was no electromagnetic current. In short, the oddly beautiful piece seemed to be nothing more than an inanimate sculpture.

A lump of artistic quartz with a moveable mouth. Yet no sound had come from it.

Yet, she was sure it was much more.

As she contemplated that riddle, she smelled something delicious. Mouth watering, she headed up the ladder to the eating area.

~o~

Cameron used two bamboo cooking sticks to turn the strips of bacon in the deep skillet and wasn't surprised when Captaintemakiatano followed the aroma into the galley. In fact, the only thing that surprised him was that she had not put on the robe he'd left for her. The rest of the group should soon return from their pilgrimage to Dragon Ridge, where they had begun preparing things for the Summer Solstice Ceremony.

While he could appreciate how comfortable it was to walk around in one's under-garments, many of the others would not. In fact, some, like Varlet, who seemed to think that everyone should be perfect clones, would be outright hostile about anyone being in public half-clothed. Particularly a female.

What a boring, repressed world it would be, if Varlet and his pals had their way.

Pain in his hand brought Cameron's attention back to the cooking. As he moved out of range of the bacon's spitting grease, he had to admit that perhaps Varlet had a point about how distracting a half-naked woman could be. Moving the pan to the side, he hurried below, grabbed the robe he had laid out for her, brought it up and handed it to her.

Her confused expression was comical. It almost looked like no one had ever given her clothing, before. It also looked like she didn't have a clue that he meant for her to put it on.

Before he thought about the possible ramifications, he grabbed the robe out of her hands, shook it out than flipped it over her head.

There, she could not mistake his meaning, now.

Recalling what had happened, when he'd touched GEA-4, Cameron quickly stepped out of range, before Captaintemakiatano got her arms through the sleeves, and went back to tending their breakfast.

"You expect me to wear this tent?" She flapped around in the robe, as if she was a fish caught in a net. "Are you serious?" she demanded.

He plucked the cooked strips of bacon out of the pan and placed them on parchment to drain off the grease, then, he poured the excess fat into the canister and placed the egg-soaked day-old bread in the hot pan.

"Are you going to tell me why you put this thing on me?"

Cameron flipped over the fried bread.

"You aren't going to talk to me, are you?" Captaintemakiatano stormed out of the galley. "GEA-4 where are you?"

Her companion, who had made no complaint about putting on a similar robe, answered from the bow. "What?"

"He made you wear one of these ugly things, too?" After that, there were more unintelligible words, but softer.

Cameron grasped the fully cooked slices of fried bread and put them on three plates, then added two eating sticks and a few slices of bacon to each dish. Even as he placed the dishes on the table, he couldn't understand why Captaintemakiatano was unhappy over wearing the robes of an allocate. Putting on his first robe had been a high point of his life.

With a sigh, he rang the bell, then sat down to eat.

~o~

Nimri opened her eyes to find both Larwin and Kazza staring at her, concern in their expressions. "What's wrong?"

"You were having a nightmare."

She struggled to sit up, the bulk of her pregnancy, plus linens damp with perspiration, making this simple task difficult. "Did I kick you out of bed, again?"

Both Kazza and Larwin nodded.

Wow, it took a lot to move Larwin and even more to budge Kazza; she was in better shape than she'd thought. The baby kicked her ribs, making her wonder if her unborn baby had helped clear the bed. Nimri winced. "Sorry about that."

"Do you feel alright?"

Larwin's expression was so serious, that doubts began to nag her thoughts. "Yes." He arched a brow, letting her know that he knew she was not telling all. "Well, aside from being hungry, that is."

He didn't move. Neither did Kazza. Worse, now both of Larwin's brows were arched in question. This was not good. "Did I do or say something – aside from kicking you out of bed, that is?"

"You were kicking, scratching and screaming that someone stole your cone."

Memories of the tiny pinecone she had magically received made her clutch the amulet bag at her throat. "Did I hurt either of you?"

While Kazza snorted in disdain, Larwin shook his head, and asked, "Is our child all right?"

Now that she understood what he was so concerned about, Nimri smiled, took his large, callused hand in both of hers and placed it on her abdomen. Almost immediately, their son began kick-boxing his hand. Larwin smiled with relief.

"In my nightmare, there were four madrox. Three smaller ones plus one huge one." She swallowed. "It was difficult because they moved fast and confusing because the small ones looked alike."

Larwin's smile vanished. "They attacked us, here?"

"No, that's another thing that was strange. They seemed to be cooler and were able to dive in and out of water without problems." She frowned as she tried to remember the details of her bizarre dream. "There was a lot of water. Not like our river... when I stood on the shore and turned my back to the land, there was water as far as I could see and it looked like it was rolling." She shivered.

'Was it rolling because the dragons were diving into it?"

"I don't think so."

"So the water was rolling for no reason?" She nodded. "And there was no sight of land." She nodded, again. Larwin frowned. "Do you think you dreamed that because Thunder and Raine told us about Kalamar?" he asked.

She chewed her lower lip and considered that possibility, but the certainty increased that wherever all that water was, it was not on Raine's home-world. "No, not really." Nimri wondered if she should tell him that wherever it was, his sister was there and she'd held the staff of power, as if she knew how to use it. And a man, who was garbed in the same saffron-gold as Tem-aki, was trying to direct them how to deal with the madrox without harming them, which didn't make sense. There was also a white feline, who acted more lady-like than Kazza, and oddly enough there had been three crystal skulls. In many ways that was the strangest thing about the dream, because it was well known that she and Thunder were caretakers of the only two skulls in existence.

Her gaze went to the translucent skull, which was sitting on top of the table in front of the window. Its vacant eyes seemed to be staring at Sacred Mountain's peak. Was the skull as magical as her great-grandfather had claimed or was it just a mysterious creation, which repelled dust?

After the dream she'd just had, Nimri was inclined to believe that, for once, her great-grandfather had told her the truth. She wished that made her feel better, but keeping others ignorant of how to do things was Rolf's main form of power-play, because it kept others dependent on him.

Kazza's whiskers brushed her arm; she turned her attention to him and caressed his silky fur. His serious eyes proclaimed that he knew what she had dreamed and that he was as worried as she was. For the millionth time, she wished they could communicate better.

"In many ways, communication with Kazza is more straightforward and honest than with most humans," Larwin said. Kazza's whiskers twirled in agreement.

Heat spread from her neck to her cheeks, as Nimri realized

that she must have articulated the thought. "What do you mean by that?" she asked.

"Simple, most humans tell you what they think you want to hear, which may or may not be true. Or they tell you what they think should be said to get the sale or the support or whatever it is they want."

"You always were cynical."

"True, but that doesn't mean that the average person is honest."

"You want honest?" He nodded. "Fine!" Nimri took a deep breath, and wondered where to start and what to say. "I am scared." There, she had admitted it.

"We all are."

"What if my dreams are true?"

"There is no if. Your dreams usually are accurate premonitions."

"Are they?"

"You know they are." Remembering the horrible dreams, which she had had prior to the madrox invading the Star Bridge, Nimri was forced to nod in agreement. Larwin pressed his point, "Without your dreams, we would not have known to prepare."

"As is, we barely survived," Nimri said.

Larwin took her knotted fists in his large comforting hands and began to caress her wrists. "But we did survive, and we will survive whatever is haunting your sleep this time, too." His words along with his touch soothed, her but she still feared that a confrontation was looming.

"Are you sure?"

He nodded, then kissed her forehead.

"How can you be?" Shaking off his grip, she got out of bed and went to the window. "How can we fight something when we don't even know where it is? With my past dreams, we knew it was coming from the Star Bridge." She gestured to the window. "Now, I dream of water as far as the eye can see. Where is that? All I can see from here is trees and the river." She turned to face him. "Even when we were at the peak of Sacred Mountain and could see forever, we didn't see that much water."

"We will find it."

"How?"

He shrugged. "Don't know, but I do know that we are meant to, so we will."

"I wish I had your confidence."

Larwin wrapped his arms around her in a comforting hug. "I have confidence in you, Kazza, and Thunder."

"While that makes me feel good, it also scares me. What if I can't figure out where the danger is? What if we can't fight four madrox?" She pushed away from him. "Did I mention that they could dive in and out of water?"

"Perhaps it only looked like water."

She blinked at his words and a kernel of hope for their survival began to bloom.

Chapter 9

Tem-aki watched Cameron as he puttered around the boat, frequently looking toward shore. Shortly after mid-day, she spotted tiny dots of saffron slowly moving across the distant landscape. Was that what he was looking for?

She consulted GEA-4, who confirmed her suspicion and added that the group had come from the distant ridge, which Cameron had referred to as Dragon Ridge, adding, "That is where the Summer Solstice Ceremony will begin on the next moon cycle."

Tem-aki digested that information. "You can communicate with him?"

"Verbally?" Tem-aki nodded. "No," GEA-4 said, "not yet, but I am working out the language based on the writing."

"What writing?"

GEA-4 gestured to the odd scraps of rustic paper, which had strange squiggles of charcoal, or at least something that looked like charcoal on them. "Draco Cameron is apparently some form of leader who rules based on celestial cycles."

"I could tell by his attire that he didn't have access to much technology."

"Technology isn't the answer to everything."

Tem-aki blinked and stared at GEA-4, who was a product of said technology. "I can't believe you said that."

"Fact is fact."

Just before sunset, Cameron went over the side and rowed his small boat to the shore, a few moments later, a group of golden-robed individuals arrived on the shore. There were hugs and back-slapping, as ripples of conversation and laughter were carried across the water.

"Now there should be enough for me to hear their spoken language and start breaking it down for you," GEA-4 said.

"Excellent, once I can communicate with them, I can begin getting answers and find out where Larwin is."

Things were looking up. Then all of them turned, as one, and stared at her.

A chill ran down her spine.

"Why are they looking at us, as if they've never seen a female before?"

"Perhaps they have not seen one," GEA-4 said. "All are males."

"Well, they all look humanoid too, so they had to have a mother. I mean they don't seem advanced enough to have been grown in a lab or anything."

"This is true." GEA-4 studied the group on the shore, as they climbed into the small boat. "None appear hostile."

"I'm glad to know that."

"However, three have elevated blood pressure, which suggests high emotion."

"Which can be bad." Tem-aki sighed. "Until we know that they are not hostile, please stay by my side."

"Understood."

~o~

Varlet glared at the strangers on Sirocco's deck, then spun to face Cameron so fast that the small boat rocked dangerously. "Those are females!" Varlet's face turned an unhealthy shade of red as he spat out the words.

"Yes, they are fe-"

"How dare you allow them to defile the order's vessel!"

"I told you, they came to me in the Protected Place."

Varlet's eyes bulged, as he tried to find words to continue his tirade. "You allowed them there, too? You do not deserve to be high draco."

"What would you have done, if they walked out of the water?"

"Thrown them back," Varlet said.

"Walked out of the water?" Emmet asked. "I thought you said they came to you in the Protected Place."

"Exactly," Cameron said, as he calmly looked at the thirteen priests and initiates. "You have noticed that there is water within the Protected Place, haven't you?"

Emmet's eyes widened until they were brown dots surrounded by white. "But that's impossible."

"If I had not seen them arrive, I would agree," Cameron admitted. He nodded toward Sirocco's deck. "I also advise you not to touch either of them. They are far stronger than the normal female." Cameron turned his attention to Varlet, who was not only the tallest and thinnest, but also the most obnoxious. In fact, Varlet was so obnoxious that he was one of the top five obnoxious people Cameron had ever met. "If you have any thoughts of throwing them overboard, feel free to try, but I expect that you will be the one swimming."

"Is that a threat?" Varlet snarled.

"Just a warning," Cameron said. "Yesterday, I merely touched the smaller one, and the next thing I knew, I was flying through the air, over the rail and into the water."

"It doesn't take much strength to offset another's balance, if you get them close enough to the rail."

"True, but I was mid-deck."

Everyone began to murmur, as they gazed at the strangers.

"How are we supposed to achieve Ba-Tal with females aboard," Varlet asked.

"Ignore them," Cameron said. "They will turn in at sunset, and as soon as we have enough moonlight and a good offshore wind, we will pull up the anchor and sail home. If you are worried that two females can ruin your joy, peace and harmony in such a short of time, perhaps you should consider a future other than the priesthood."

Varlet's hands fisted and his jaw clenched. "I was not worried for myself." He gave the younger novices a significant look.

"We will all be too busy to notice their presence." At least he hoped they would be. "For now, we need to get on board, have a meal, then get some rest before the winds change. Tristan, can you secure the lines to tow the dory?" Tristan looked pleased to be chosen, and eagerly nodded. "Excellent. Benji and Emmet, head to the galley and begin serving cold cuts."

"Yes, Sir!" Emmet said.

Benji paused a moment to ask, "Will our guests be dining with us?" Cameron nodded. "Okay." He scurried up the ladder.

Nolan put his hand on Cameron's arm, silently asking him to linger. "They seriously came to you in the Protected Place?" Cameron nodded. Nolan sucked in his breath. "What kind of message did they bring?"

"I wish I knew," Cameron said. "After we are through the passage and the younger ones turn in, you and I need to talk."

"You didn't tell everything." It was a statement, not a question.

Cameron shook his head, then leaned close and lowered his voice, "Our guests brought the staff of power with them."

"The staff of power? As in the staff Draco Shakura lost?"

Cameron nodded. Nolan's legs gave out and he sat with a thud.

Cameron sat next to him. "And that isn't all. Things have been unusual, while you and the others prepared for Shaka-uma's Festival." He glanced upward to make sure no one was near the rail. "I don't have time to tell you all now, but I need your advice and insight. But I promise that once we are under way, I will tell you everything."

"It will be just like when you were an initiate," Nolan said.

"Thanks." Cameron clasped his mentor's shoulder. "It is always much easier to see things clearly when I share them with you."

"It is the same for me."

"Do you regret it?"

"What? Not accepting the cowl?" Cameron nodded. Nolan shook his head. "Never. At my age, I do not need the stress of dealing with everyone and their dramas." With that, Nolan stood back up, then began to climb the ladder and Cameron bent over to secure the paddles for an ocean passage and wondered for the thousandth time, if he should have passed on the offer, too.

But, again, he had to admit that if he had passed, Varlet would have become draco and he could never allow that to happen.

~o~

Tem-aki woke with a start. Eyes wide, she wondered what had woken her. She looked to her right, then left, but the only other entity in the room was GEA-4, who was standing by the crystal skull. As her ears and eyes strained, she heard footsteps above and voices talking. Abruptly, there was a loud thump, which sent Tem-aki half leaping and half falling out of the treacherous hammock.

"What's happening?" Tem-aki asked.

"I believe they are preparing to set sail," GEA-4 said.

"Set what?" The floor beneath her feet tilted slightly. "Is this thing moving?"

"Affirmative."

Slowly, the view from the porthole changed. It didn't take a physicist to know the boat was now pointed away from land. This could not be good.

"We have to stop them!" Tem-aki said as she grabbed GEA-4's arm and tried to haul her toward the ladder.

"Why?" the obstinate, unmoving android asked.

"What do you mean, why? The boat is moving; it needs to be stopped."

"You do realize that boats are a primitive form of transportation and are meant to move, correct?"

"Well, yes, but-"

"Then why would you want this group to cease what they are obviously doing on purpose?"

Tem-aki opened her mouth to respond, but couldn't think of anything she could say without revealing her fears. "Then what do you suggest we do."

"Exactly what we were doing. I will stay on watch and you will sleep." GEA-4 turned from the window and touched Tem-aki's arm. "If there is any danger, I will protect you."

"And wake me?"

"Affirmative."

"Fine." Tem-aki climbed back into the unstable bed and tried to block out the voices speaking gibberish above. Her only consolation was that the voices sounded cheerful. Unfortunately, she had no idea what they were saying. For all she knew, they were headed toward the deep, mysterious sea to throw her and GEA-4 overboard.

Tem-aki lay in her hammock, staring at the planking overhead and realized that she needed to find a way to make herself important to this group, so she could assure her survival, and eventually their cooperation in helping her find her brother.

Chapter 10

Pain slashed across Nimri's back, like the claws of a madrox. Tears streaming and gasping for breathe, she sank to the kitchen floor. Bryta screamed and dropped the menthe leaves she had been cleaning. Kazza howled so loud the rafters shook. A moment later Larwin, burst into the kitchen, panic in his expression. Seeing her on the floor, he dashed to her, "What happened?" he asked Bryta.

"I d-d-don't know."

"I'm fine," Nimri said. With each syllable it was a bit easier to breath. Seeing Larwin's white face, she found the strength to sit up and take his trembling hand. Looking into his eyes, she could tell he didn't believe her. "Really." He gathered her into his arms and sat on a chair.

"If you are fine, why did you collapse?" Bryta asked, distracting her from Larwin's uncharacteristic panic.

"There was a deep, slashing pain in my back."

"Lower back?" Bryta asked in a calm, collected tone, which helped Nimri regain her own composure.

"Yes."

Bryta nodded knowingly. "That is how your mother experienced labor, too."

"That was labor?"

"Probably."

"That's not how the others experience it."

"The others aren't Tramontains. You are."

Bryta did have a point there and while it helped her relax, poor Larwin looked ready to faint. And she doubted if colonels in the Star Dust Fleet ever fainted, so this was probably a first for him.

Larwin gently squeezed her hand, "I can carry you up to bed, unless you'd be more comfortable elsewhere."

She nearly laughed because, at the moment, he didn't look capable of carrying his own weight to the stairway. Instead, she squeezed his hand. "It takes hours, sometimes even days for a baby to come. Lying in bed will only prolong the time."

Larwin's complexion went from pale to white. "Seriously?"

Nimri nodded. "Think about it. If you have some physical thing you want to do, do you prepare for it by taking a nap?"

"Sometimes that is the best strategy."

Nimri laughed. "Be serious."

"I am."

She shook her head. "I'm fine, but I could use a hand standing up." Larwin did just that. It would be good when Mica was born and her body was her own, again, particularly if her nightmares were omens and somewhere in her future she needed to fight four of the deadly creatures. The good news was that in her most recent vision or nightmare, or omen, or whatever she was experiencing – she had not been pregnant. The bad news was that she had no assurance that they could handle four of the horrid beasts, when they had barely managed to handle a lone one.

Of course, Larwin had been a big help, as had Thunder. Perhaps Tem-aki and the gold-clad man would be a big help, too.

Kazza purred and gently rubbed her arm.

Yes, and Kazza had been a major help, so perhaps the pretty white feline would be, too. And hadn't Raine claimed that her job was herding the horrible creatures? That should make it six humans and two felines against four madrox. When Nimri thought of it that way, she realized that she might live long enough to raise Mica.

~o~

When Tem-aki got back into the hammock, she could no longer feel the odd movements of the boat. That was a good thing. When she shut her eyes, she could no longer see how the view beyond the porthole was changing.

That was good, too.

But, even though they were muffled by the floor, she couldn't shut out the boisterous voices of the men, or forget the evil looks a few of them had given her and GEA-4.

How did she know they weren't taking her somewhere to get rid of her?

Even as she had the thought, she recalled how the others, even the nasty ones, had looked at Cameron for leadership. She was sure he didn't want to hurt her. Make her wear the ridiculous robe? Yes. But that wasn't exactly hurting her, at least not if she moved slowly and cautiously, so the cloth couldn't wrap around her ankles and trip her.

She lay in the hammock, mind racing to understand her situation and alert for any hint of treachery, but nothing happened, unless she counted a shift in the breeze and that she could no longer see land out the window.

Though Tem-aki assumed she was too stressed to sleep, she did sleep and dreamed she was giving birth to a child. The unexpectedness of the dream fascinated her. The best part was that Larwin was there. He looked different, because he wasn't wearing his uniform, his skin was darker and his hair was longer, but somehow, despite the differences, he was still her brother.

The strangest thing was that he looked at her differently. She'd always known that she could count on her big brother's unconditional love, which was the main reason why she was so determined to find him. But now, as she gave birth, she could see warm, loving emotions shimmering in his eyes.

When the birth was finally over, a cheerful, chubby woman handed the baby to Larwin, who began to hum and sway. Tem-aki had never seen her brother look so happy and content. Was this because she was seeing the man he might have been, if he had not been selected for the military at age three? She had only been a year old, when he had left for the academy, and had no memory of him for her first three years, when she had been sent to the geological institute. Leaving home should have been that for any memory she had of her biological family. However, her mother not only was one of the governors, she and her father had made a lifetime bond, which was unheard of in their culture. But the most extraordinary thing was that they both thought that the family unit was important. Due to her mother's position, her parents had been able to arrange that all four of them shared the same leave time every year. So, for a month of each year, they were a family. And that felt great.

It also meant she was different.

The chubby, graying woman massaged her back and urged her to relax. Tem-aki closed her eyes and her thoughts drifted to how much she had resented her parents and Larwin when she was twelve. What right did they have to demand she spend her month of unrestricted time with family, instead of take a trip to see the rings of Torin or the moons of Ido with her friends?

How she had envied her classmates' freedom from family

obligations!

By the time she was fourteen, she had met a dozen others who spent their free month with their parents too, but none of them had a brother, at least not a brother who shared both parents and she had begun to realize how special their relationship was.

By the time she was fifteen and had been accepted to the specialized field of geology, she had met three others whose parents still maintained a committed relationship.

That had been new proof that her parents were strange and possibly even backward, so she had fought even harder to have her month of freedom.

Now, Tem-aki was glad she had never won that fight.

And now, she worried what her parents must be thinking – feeling – about having both children listed as missing. How soon would she be registered as 'presumed dead', like Larwin?

Would her parents look for her?

She doubted it, since they had not demanded a special search for Larwin. Regardless, she wished there was some way to contact them to let them know she was fine and would return, if possible... after she found Larwin, of course. But how could she do that, when she not only didn't know where here was, but where Guerreterre was.

How could anyone not know where they were?

A wail brought Tem-aki's attention back to Larwin and the red-cheeked baby. Again, she marveled how happy her brother looked and how settled. Strange, she would never have used those words to describe him, before. Smart, definitely. Driven, absolutely. Lethal yes. But happy and settled?

Never.

And she certainly could never have imagined him tenderly holding a newborn and humming to it while it beat its tiny fists in the air and screamed.

Though Tem-aki knew she was having a dream, and could objectively evaluate it, one part of her also had the feeling that this glimpse of Larwin was fact and she had somehow found her brother, if only in her dreams.

~o~

Cameron adjusted the sails as he rounded the far point and the breeze shifted. A glance at the horizon assured him that there were no storms coming, so they should be in place by the time the sun rose to create the morning's onshore wind, which would blow them into safe harbor.

They would be home by mid-morning bell, but what would their reception be, when the followers discovered that they had returned with two strange females?

Cameron sighed because he already knew there would be problems explaining why he had broken a tradition that dated back more than a millennium. The question was how to minimize the peoples' shock. And the other question was how to make the announcement before Varlet told everyone a distorted version of the story.

He didn't realize he was muttering his thoughts aloud until Nolan said, "Forget about minimizing their shock. Maximize it."

"What do you mean?"

"Tell me what you thought when you first saw them."

"I thought they were a vision." Nolan nodded and motioned for him to continue. "At first, I wasn't sure if they were even human." Cameron frowned. "I'm still not, if you want the truth, GEA-4 never eats and seems capable of healing herself by laying her hands on herself."

"You told me that as soon they came from the Deep, they knelt at the bones of those who have passed on." Cameron nodded. "Which is why you decided they were supernatural beings, not demons."

"That plus the fact that when Captaintemakiatano took off the strange hood that I showed you, her hair -"
"What there is of it," Nolan said.
"True." Cameron sighed. "You've seen that it's the color of sunlight and golden dragons, and her strange outfit is the color of a cloudless sky on a beautiful day."
"Aren't you forgetting something?" Nolan asked. Cameron arched his brows. "The staff," Nolan said.
"Exactly!" Cameron nodded emphatically. "All signs point to them coming to aid us. The only thing I can't understand is why I can't understand their speech."
"Perhaps you don't need to."
"Why do you say that?"
Nolan shrugged. "It is my experience that when the time is right, so is everything else."
"So you believe they are waiting for something before they reveal why they came."
"Do you have a better explanation?" Cameron shook his head. "Then, I suggest that before we disembark, you do two things." Nolan leaned close to Cameron, so no one could hear him counsel the addition of deep hoods to help conceal their faces and have one of them carry the staff of power, then as he stood at the top of the gangway, to introduce them to everyone within earshot.
"Then, finish with a plea not to disturb them. It's the only way to beat Varlet," Nolan concluded.
It wasn't a perfect plan, but with no other alternative, Cameron started trying to figure out how to convince them not only to wear the robes, which they seemed to dislike, but hoods, too.

Chapter 11

Nimri tucked Mica into his carry-basket, then went outside. The garden still glistened with morning dew as she settled down on the long chair that Larwin had designed and built. He called it a lounger and she had spent many hours during the past couple months putting her feet up on her lounger, instead of weeding the garden and planting seeds. Fortunately, the weeds hadn't used her difficulty in bending to take over.

Nimri sighed with contentment and breathed in the garden's healing fragrance as she watched the honey bees and butterflies flit from flower to flower.

If only every day could be peaceful and beautiful like today.

Kazza strolled into the garden, looked around, then ambled over to her and sprawled in a sun-puddle on top of the mother-of-thyme carpeting the ground. Soon, his breathing indicated he was asleep.

With both Kazza and Mica sleeping, Nimri's eyes soon closed, too.

Fat noisy birds soared in the sky, and more of them perched on top of huge rocks, which stuck out of the lapping water.

Nimri frowned, wondering where she was and why she had

never noticed a flock or big white flying birds or these rocks in the river, before.

And why couldn't she see the other side of the river?

A gentle breeze brought a spicy aroma, which made her mouth water and her stomach growl. Turning away from the rocks and water, she followed footsteps in the sand along a sheer rock wall. They led her to steep stair steps, which had been carved into a gaping crack in the imposing rock.

She climbed up, until she came to a flat rock shelf, which overlooked the rocks and water. Nimri paused to look down and estimated that this shelf was about the same height as her bedroom, which Larwin described as being about a hundred feet above the ground. Since he had to climb it so often, he often joked that it was part of his physical fitness program. Whatever that was. But what surprised her the most, was that even from this height, looking toward the horizon, she still could not see land on the other side of the water.

Shaking her head in confusion, Nimri resumed following her nose past huge urns holding fruit trees and trailing plants toward the mouth-watering aroma, which seemed to be coming from a window, which appeared to be carved in the sheer rock wall, much as the doors and windows in Thunder's home were made.

As she approached the window, she was surprised to see her crystal cat skull sitting on top of a table just inside the room. For some reason, she sensed it was watching her approach.

How had her skull gotten into this dream, when everything else was like nothing she had ever seen?

And why was she wearing a toe-length saffron-gold robe? Nimri ran her hands over her body and was surprised to notice that her figure had returned, as well as her muscle tone.

Nimri rubbed the back of her neck in confusion and discovered that her braid was gone. In fact, most of her hair seemed to be missing. She grasped a hair and pulled it. Ignoring the momentary pain, she stared at the wheat-colored strand of hair, which was no longer than her pinkie. Larwin's hair was this color, and though it was now below his shoulders, it had been shorter than this when she'd met him.

She ran her hands over her body, again, and confirmed that it was female.

As Nimri mulled over this confusing situation, she spotted the friendly dark-haired man, she had previously seen in her dreams. This time he waved, then motioned for her to come inside. Instead, she stopped and studied him. He was wearing an identical robe, but instead of the golden hood, he had a huge blue cowl, which looked like it could also be worn as an over-large hood. As encouragement, he, again, motioned her forward with one hand and held up a plate of food with the other.

Were they dressed alike for some reason?

Was this man her mate?

Why else would he cook for her?

Nimri smiled at him to cover her confusion, then, as she stepped back to look for the door, Mica's cry woke her.

~o~

The cry of a bird soaring overhead snapped Tem-aki back into herself. She realized that was a strange way to think about it, but for the past hour or so, she had felt like she was somehow locked out of her body, yet at the same time, she was seeing and feeling everything around her.

Tem-aki stared at the strand of hair she held in a white-knuckled grip and wondered what had possessed her to pull it out. And why, after she'd pulled it out, had she stared at it so long?

It was just a hair.

Holding her hand up to the breeze, she let it fly away, and hoped that the residual strange feelings would go with it.

They didn't.

Taking a deep breath, she headed toward the heavily carved door, which depicted two madrox soaring through clouds, talons ready to slash the other to kindling. Tem-aki pushed down on the rustic handle, then pushed the door inward. While she would never admit it to Cameron, it had taken her far too long to figure out the door's simple latching system and she had initially suspected there was a heavily encrypted security code.

Only to have GEA-4 casually walk up, push down on the wooden lever, then pull the door open for her to go out. Tem-aki's cheeks heated at the embarrassing memory and she fervently hoped that no one else had noticed her ignorance.

Until she could find out where Larwin was, she needed these people for food and shelter, but she certainly didn't need them to be in a position of power over her. And history taught that strangers, particularly alien males, were known to take every available opportunity to maximize any perceived weaknesses. Though she had not sensed any intent to dominate and overpower in Cameron, she certainly had in the shifty-eyed one called Varlet.

Tem-aki carefully closed the door and went to the eating area, where Cameron and the friendly gray-haired man called Nolan had already begun eating.

Her mouth started watering even before she was seated. Grabbing the two pointed sticks, she carefully arranged them, as Cameron had taught her, and focused on getting the food from her plate to her mouth without dropping anything. This was always easier planned than executed, but meal by meal, she was getting better. In fact, she hadn't needed GEA-4 to distract Cameron's attention, so she could eat with her fingers, since the humiliating first day.

She frowned and looked around for the android, sighting her by the window of the cooking space, next to the crystal skull. It was strange how often she seemed to be near that strangely beautiful, yet somewhat sinister-looking thing. The first time Tem-aki had noticed GEA-4 there, she had assumed she had chosen the location because it was at the window. Now she wasn't certain it was that simple.

The morning, after the boat had been tied to the floating dock, GEA-4 had followed the freckled boy with red highlights in his dark hair, who carried the skull. In fact, she had followed him so closely that it would have been considered an invasion of personal space on Guerreterre.

And now, GEA-4 was standing over the skull, like a protector.

The eating sticks paused halfway to Tem-aki's mouth as she wondered if the android had suffered permanent damage and if its judgement could be trusted.

Cameron said something to Nolan, and she abruptly realized they were both staring at her. Before she dropped the morsel of fish, she popped it into her mouth and smiled at them.

They turned their attention back to eating, but she couldn't get past her misgivings about GEA-4's reliability and kept wondering if she could be considered an ally or not.

Worse, in light of the way she had felt since she was on the beach, she wasn't even sure that she could rely on herself.

It was a terribly vulnerable feeling – one that she needed to camouflage with an air of confidence.

~o~

Cameron tried to focus his attention on Nolan's report about the preparations for the up-coming ceremony, he had supervised at Dragon Ridge, but instead of focusing on the papers, his attention kept returning to Captaintemakiatano, who seemed preoccupied and kept distracting him by muttering unintelligible things under her breath. He wished she would communicate with him instead of using the celestial language with GEA-4, but apparently, her reason for coming to him did not require verbal communication.

At least, not yet.

Her lack of verbal communication lured him to give her more attention than he had ever given any woman. Even including his mother and Annosha, the non-stop-talking high priestess, who he frequently needed to coordinate plans with. The thought of Annosha made the fish taste off, so Cameron took a sip of lemonade. Since coming upon Annosha one day at the shore, and hearing her talking to nothing but the water, he had wondered if she talked in her sleep or if females saw the world in a different way.

And now, he'd met her opposite, a woman who barely spoke and usually didn't even respond, when spoken to.

"Has she told you why she's here, yet?" Nolan asked softly, as he tilted his head toward Captaintemakiatano. Cameron shook his head. "Have you asked?" Again, he shook his head. Nolan raised a brow and silently urged him to speak.

Cameron laid down his eating sticks, took a deep breath, then turned toward her. "Captaintemakiatano?" It seemed to take her a moment to realize that he had spoken directly to her, but she swallowed and gave him her full attention. "What is your purpose here?"

Her expression indicated that either she didn't know why he was asking or didn't know how to answer. Then, she smiled, pointed to the food and nodded as she licked her lips.

Well, that hadn't gotten him anywhere. He cleared his throat and began, again. "Captaintemakiatano -"

"Tem-aki."

He bowed his head in acknowledgement of the privilege

she gave him to address her by an intimate name. "Tem-aki, thank you." He gestured to include Nolan. "We are honored by your presence, and wonder if you will tell us why you came."

"Isn't it obvious?" Nolan asked. "It is the end of the thirteenth cycle and the beginning of the new era."

"I am certain that is part of it," Cameron said. "But I wondered if there were more."

Tem-aki watched their interchange, but showed no sign of answering. Perhaps she considered his question shallow. After all, in the 1066 years since Draco Shakura, his sect's founder, had followed the Goldens through the portal, for the most part, the 82-year-cycles had continued calmly into the future. After their faction had established their settlement and farms, the only real blips in their peace had been when dragon-father, Shaka-dun, died in the storm; then centuries later, when fire mountain exploded and the rumors began that dragon-mother, Shaka-uma, was dead as well as all her young had passed.

The problem was that the rumors seemed to gain more power and the faction lost more followers each year.

Worse, he could not prove that they lived, any more than his predecessors over the past century could. Still worse, his prayers for good crops certainly were not being answered with abundance.

Since this was the end of the thirteenth cycle and with it another eighty-two year life-span, it was particularly important that the year's Solstice Ceremony be special. Cameron had hoped that Tem-aki and GEA-4 had come to assure that, but day by day, his doubts grew.

How could he lead, when he, also, felt uncertain?

His gaze narrowed on Tem-aki and he wondered if the other tests had been small because she had come to test his faith.

~o~

After the meal, Tem-aki approached GEA-4. "Are you making progress on the language decryption?"

"Affirmative, but it is incomplete."

"Do you have any idea when you will finish it?"

"Negative. However, it is proceeding more quickly now that others are present and I have the opportunity to listen to conversations."

"Yet during dinnertime, you stayed in here."

"I am capable of multi-tasking."

Some of Tem-aki's frustration at being so isolated evaporated. But only some. "What is your fascination with that thing?" She pointed to the carved crystal-quartz. "I mean, I can see how pretty it can be when the sun hits it just right and rainbows of light dance around the room, but I didn't think androids were attracted to art. Is it the sunlight angle?"

"Nimri and Thunder have skulls very similar to this one."

That statement surprised her, since she had assumed this was a unique piece. "I had no idea this culture was capable of mass production."

"They aren't. This was handmade. Possibly myst-made."

Tem-aki wondered what manufacturing style the latter was, but wasn't interested enough to ask. "Why would anyone make three of these things? I mean, I know they are interesting and well crafted, but they're sort of gruesome." The first thing she had noticed about this culture was the bones lying on that hand-carved shelf in a lava tube. This skull was obviously based on a natural bone skull, so apparently they considered the skeleton important. "The strangest mystery is why they chose to carve a feline's skull instead of a human one."

"That assumes that a human was the artisan."

"What other type of artisan could have executed it?"

"If it was myst-made, perhaps Kazza or another of his kind could have made it."

"The feline?" Tem-aki asked in disbelief.

"Affirmative."

Now, she knew for certain that the android's logic circuits were damaged. "And just how could a feline, which does not have opposable thumbs to hold tools, create something this intricate?"

"Myst-energy."GEA-4 turned away from the skull and leveled her silvery stare on her. "You saw Kazza's magical abilities when you were fleeing Kalamar and he rescued Nambaba from attack. Do you doubt he could build something with magic?"

"What I doubt is that any feline would spend the hours, days, weeks or even years that it must have taken to carve and finish something this perfect and intricate. I mean what would be the point?"

"I believe this could be some form of communication device."

"Are you serious?"

"Affirmative."

"And that is why you've been staring at it?"

"Affirmative."

"Oh." Tem-aki squinted at the polished crystal-quartz and wondered if GEA-4's assessment was another anomaly of a faulty logic program or if she could be onto something.

But who would design a communication device to look like a skull? And why? Surely, if someone wanted to create something functional out of quartz, they could have found a simpler design to carve. Probably even a more aesthetically attractive, yet simple design. She frowned. "Do you know how it works?"

"Negative."

"But you are trying to figure that out."

"Affirmative."
"Well, good luck, then."

Chapter 12

Nimri was startled awake, but didn't know what had woken her. She lay in bed, listening to Larwin and Mica breathing. Nothing wrong there. A night-bird's lonely hoot echoed in the distance, letting her know that she was not the only one awake. The rhythmic drum of the waterfall sounded constant.

She hadn't been having a nightmare, so what had startled her?

Opening her eyes, she looked around her bedchamber. Moonlight flickered as clouds flitted through it, but that wasn't uncommon. A moth fluttered past the window. Nimri rolled onto her side, so she could see Sacred Mountain's peak, but there was no omen to be seen there.

So, what had woken her?

Her gaze dropped to the crystal skull that looked out the window. The way the moonlight was caressing it looked as if a magical light was coming from inside it. This was not the first time she'd noticed the skull appear as if it was filled with light, but it was the first time she'd noticed what looked like another face staring out the back of the skull. Nimri narrowed her eyes, certain that they were playing tricks on her, but she still saw a face with shining silver eyes.

GEA-4!

Quietly, she shook Larwin's shoulder. "What?"

"Shhhh," she whispered, "you'll wake Mica. Look toward the window. Do you see anything strange?"

"Other than the skull being filled with light?"

"That's mainly it." She swallowed before she added, "Do you see anything in the light?"

"A face, but that can't be. How'd you get GEA-4's likeness in there?"

"I didn't do this and don't know how or why it's there."

"It's your skull." Larwin got out of bed and went to the window. "There isn't a candle in it, does it use moonlight?"

"I have no idea."

"Why not?" Larwin asked.

"It was great-grandfather's." Nimri sighed. "You know how little he told me." The skull and staff of power had been his most prized possessions. She'd witnessed him using the staff, and knew how powerful it was, but until now, she had assumed that the skull was some sort of strange artwork. Now, she realized that it must possess some sort of power that she did not understand.

"Does Thunder know?"

"I don't know. I mean, I know he has one, but I always assumed that... I don't know what I assumed."

"Too bad Rolf was so afraid someone would be more powerful than him."

"You believe that's why he acted the way he did?" Nimri asked in surprise.

"Makes sense to me," Larwin said. He returned to the bed and sat next to her. "When I was in school, there was a teacher, whose reputation at planning a campaign was top-notch, so I was excited to learn strategy from him. The only thing was that he was the worst teacher in the world. He seemed to bury us in trivia and be extremely critical of anyone who came up with a new idea. After a few months, some of us realized that he was taking our innovative ideas – the ones he'd ridiculed – and claimed they were his own to the War College."

"How did you find that out?"

"Battle strategy would be reported after the conflict. It didn't take a lot to figure out."

"What did you do?"

"Not a lot we could do other than boycott his class."

"Did that work?"

"Not really."

Somehow, Nimri wasn't surprised to hear that. If Larwin's teacher had been like her great-grandfather, no matter what anyone else did, they would look incompetent or worse, while he would appear skilled. She took his hand. "I'm sorry."

"For what?" he asked in surprise.

"For that man taking your good ideas and making you feel inferior."

"He did it to everyone, not just me." Larwin turned his attention on her. "It wasn't like what you had to deal with. Rolf made sure you were isolated and dependent on him for everything. Plus, you really didn't have anyone to talk to other than him or people he had control over." He caressed her cheek. "I had a barracks full of classmates to talk to and conspire with. Trust me, you had it a lot worse than me."

While she wasn't so sure about that, it wasn't worth arguing about. Besides, it was nice being held in the dark while looking at the skull and listening to the sounds of night.

"Tomorrow, if you like, I'll head over to Thunder's and ask him what he knows about the skull," Larwin said.

Nimri kissed his chin. "Thank you."

"That is what you wanted, right?"

Nimri nodded. "I believe GEA-4 is trying to tell us where she

is, but I don't understand what she is trying to tell me."
"And you hope Thunder does." She nodded in agreement.

~o~

To Nimri's surprise, Thunder arrived at her kitchen door shortly after morning meal. While Bryta bustled around, happily making him something to eat, Nimri knew that he hadn't come for Bryta's biscuits, no matter how mouth-watering they were.

And when he zeroed in on her, instead of Larwin, she knew he hadn't come to discuss a new construction project.

Transferring Mica to his carry-basket, she motioned for Thunder to follow her outside. Once they were out of earshot of Bryta, who not only tended to overreact, but also was one of the tribe's worst gossips, Nimri asked, "Did you see something in your skull?"

"How did you know?" He quickly held up a calloused hand. "That was a dumb question. For a moment, I forgot you had one, too." He pulled her into the shade of a stately pine tree and faced her. "Did you see them, too?"

"Them?"

He nodded so vigorously that the tiny feathers, which were woven into his hair looked like they were attempting to fly. "Of course, them. GEA-4 and Tem-aki."

"You saw Tem-aki, too?"

"You didn't?"

"No."

He frowned. "What do you think that means?"

She chewed her lower lip, before she admitted, "I don't know. I woke in the middle of the night and noticed the skull was glowing, but at first thought it was the moonlight." Thunder nodded in agreement. "Then, I realized that two shiny eyes were looking out the back of the skull, and initially thought it was an odd trick."

"But it wasn't."

"I woke Larwin and he studied it, too."

"But only saw GEA-4?" Nimri nodded. "What do you think caused it?"

"Don't know." Nimri continued chewing her lip, as she looked past Thunder to her sleeping son. "I thought that maybe she was trying to tell me she was alive."

"And now?"

"If you saw Tem-aki, too, then I'm not sure what it might mean." She rubbed her temples. "I always associated that thing with death — it is a skull, after all, and an image can't get much deader than that."

Thunder plucked a pine-bud off the tree and rolled it between his fingers. The strong, clean scent of crushed pine began to surround them. "Dad once told me it was used to communicate with those who were gone."

"Did he mean dead?"

Thunder shrugged. "That's what I thought he meant at the time, but since last night, I wonder."

"Why? Are you afraid that if you now have proof that Tem-aki is dead, we should rethink telling Larwin?" Nimri rubbed the back of her neck, bent down, repositioned Mica's basket and sat down next to it. She lightly wrapped her arms around her legs and put her chin on her knees. "What good would telling him serve? He can never return to his world, so he will never be able to see any of his family or friends, again. In fact, they are already gone."

"True." Thunder leaned back against the tree's rough bark. "But what if she isn't dead?"

"What do you mean?"

"Exactly that: what if she isn't dead and is trying to contact us to help her?"

"How did you arrive at that conclusion?"

"GEA-4."

Nimri blinked, not following his logic.

Thunder pushed away from the trunk and began to pace. "Think about it. GEA-4 is something called technology. If she died, which is something I'm not sure is possible, would she be at the same place as a person?"

That was an excellent question and one she didn't have an answer for. "Would Larwin know?"

"I don't know, but if anyone does, it would be him." Thunder frowned, "But to tell him and explain all this, we need to tell him about his sister." Thunder sat down on the dried pine needles and faced her. "Do you think that would be wise?"

"I don't know, but if there is a possibility that she is alive and we can rescue her, then yes, I think so."

"You don't sound confident."

"I'm not." Nimri's fist clenched in frustration. "Despite what you apparently think, I can't read minds and while I know Tem-aki is special to him, I don't know how he'd react."

"React to what?" Larwin asked as he emerged from behind the pine tree's trunk.

The feathers in Thunder's hair stood out straight and he gulped. Nimri's fingernails dug into her palms and Mica woke with a scream. Nimri picked up Mica and soothed him, leaving Thunder to explain why he had not mentioned Tem-aki to Larwin, when he had initially returned from securing the Star Bridge.

Larwin glared down at them. "Well?" Fisted hands, on hips, his glower urged them to speak. "Which one of you is going to tell me why you felt it was necessary to have a chat about my sister way out here?"

"We didn't come out here to talk about her," Thunder said.

Larwin's fist smacked the palm of his other hand, as he silently urged her brother to defend his statement.

Thunder cleared his throat. "Did you see the skull when it was glowing, last night?" A brief look of confusion crossed Larwin's face and his stiff posture relaxed, as he nodded.

"Well, my skull glowed, too," Thunder said, "and that is what I came here to discuss with Nimri. We came out here to talk in private because I don't think either of us knows what to think about this and we didn't want to alarm anyone." Thunder looked at her for confirmation.

Nimri nodded as she settled a now calmer Mica into her lap. "You know how Bryta gossips. If she knew that the skull had glowed and we had seen GEA-4, she'd be running down the mountain, right now instead of making biscuits."

Larwin looked from one to the other, his expression unreadable. "And she would get the facts mixed up, and get everyone upset." His eyes narrowed. "Is her gossiping your only reason for coming out here to talk?"

Nimri felt heat climbing up her neck. "You saw GEA-4 in the skull, too."

Larwin gave a short nod. "You know I did."

Nimri swallowed. "Thunder saw her in his, too."

"Fine, so what does that have to do with my sister?"

"I sat up looking at the skull for most of the night," Thunder got to his feet, then added, "and for a brief time, your sister was shown in there with her."

Both Larwin's hands clenched into fists. "And how would you know the person you were seeing was my sister?"

Thunder tensed, then straightened his shoulders and looked Larwin straight in the eye. "Because I met her during my return from Kalamar."

"And it took you this long to mention that to me?"

"I apologize."

Larwin turned to Nimri. "And you knew about this." She nodded. "But you didn't say anything, either." She shook her head. "Explain."

Nimri looked at Thunder, willing him to talk, instead his lips flattened, which meant he was not about to speak. "It was complicated."

"Of course it was, but if he could figure out the words to explain it to you, then why not me? She is MY sister, after all."

"Exactly!" Nimri stood up to face him. "You have an emotional attachment, I don't."

Larwin put his fists on his hips. "So she is hurt?" Nimri chewed her lower lip, uncertain what to say. Larwin's eyes widened. "DEAD?"

"We don't know!" Thunder said. "And that is our problem. We didn't want to burden you before we knew facts."

Though Larwin grabbed Thunder's arms in a bruising grip, her brother didn't attempt to fight. "You," Larwin said, "will tell me everything from the beginning and this time, do not skip any details." When Thunder nodded, he relaxed his grip, but did not step back.

"I don't know where to begin."

"How about the beginning?"

Thunder frowned. "I'm not sure when that is, because where it began for Tem-aki differs – a lot – from where it began for me."

A small muscle in Larwin's jaw twitched. "And how would you know when it began for her?"

"She told me," Thunder said.

Larwin stiffened. "You spoke to her?"

"After she came aboard Nambaba, yes."

"And that was – is Raine's ship," Larwin said. Thunder nodded. "And you have not mentioned this until now." Thunder nodded, again. The small muscle in Larwin's jaw twitched several times. "Might I ask why not?"

"The unknown," Thunder said, as if the simplicity of his reason was obvious.

Larwin closed his eyes and Nimri could hear him counting in his native language. "Unless you want a lesson in hand to hand combat, you'd better explain your remark."

"The fact is that we lost her and don't know how, where or why." Thunder cleared his throat. "I assure you that as soon as we discovered something concrete about her location, we – I – would have told you."

"Why should I believe you?"

"Have I ever lied to you?"

"By omission, yes." Thunder's eyes widened. Larwin's eyes narrowed. "And I'm now wondering just how many times you didn't bother to mention things that you didn't understand or have all the facts about because you didn't want to bother me with something you consider to be obscure."

"Start with what Tem-aki told you," Nimri suggested.

Thunder reminded Larwin of what he'd already told him about his journey through the Star Bridge to the surface of the old world and how he and GEA-4 had been attacked and taken aboard Nambaba.

"Yes, you told me all that, already, what does it have to do with my sister?"

"Apparently she was doing something called a geological survey on the asteroids near Solterre and something about your magic suit made her think I was you."

"So she boarded Nambaba."

"Not right then."

Nimri watched her mate control his frustration and wondered if she could have done as well if their situations were swapped.

Eventually, Larwin let go of Thunder and listened intently to the explanation, sometimes even nodding in agreement, when Thunder said something about Tem-aki, like the fact that she seemed to lag behind and be more interested in her lumpy black box, than keep up with the others.

Larwin sighed, "So her obsession with rocks and science killed her."

"Maybe."

"What do you mean, 'maybe'?"

"We don't know for a fact that she is dead."

"You just said that she was still in the Star Bridge when the explosives went off." Thunder nodded. "But you're not sure she was killed." Thunder shook his head. "Explain."

"No body."

"Probably buried under the rubble."

"Except that there was no rubble. The Star Bridge reformed into what appears to be a solid rock wall."

"How did that happen?"

"That is one of the unknowns that I am trying to figure out."

"Any others?"

"If GEA-4 died, would she go to the spirit realm?"

Larwin blinked rapidly. "Excuse me? Are you asking if she would go to heaven?"

Thunder nodded as he chewed his lower lip.

"What makes you ask that?"

"Last night, did you see her in the skull?"

"Her image, yes. What does that have to do with my sister?"

"GEA-4 vanished the same time Tem-aki did."

"That almost makes sense."

"And Thunder didn't just see GEA-4 in his skull, he saw Tem-aki, too."

"How?"

"We don't know," Nimri said.

"So that means she's alive," Larwin said.

"No. It's another unknown," Thunder said. "That's why I asked if GEA-4 had a soul and could enter the spirit realm."

"Our parents gave us the impression that if the skulls showed messages, they were from beyond the barrier of life," Nimri said. "But we never knew for certain."

"And we've never seen them give omens, before," Thunder

added.

"Well," Larwin said, "to the best of my knowledge, GEA-4 is a machine. A very smart machine, but still a machine, so I doubt that she has a soul, but I really don't know for certain, because I don't exactly know what a soul is or if it could be replicated by science." Larwin frowned. "How do those skulls work?"

Nimri and Thunder shrugged and Mica sucked his fingers.

Just then, the kitchen door opened and Bryta called them in to eat breakfast.

"This is not over," Larwin warned. "And furthermore, I intend to examine that skull."

Chapter 13

Tem-aki sat with her back to the endless expanse of water and watched Cameron direct the others to do various activities. A gentle breeze kept bugs away from the flagstone-covered patio, which was good, since many tables and chairs had been added and all thirteen – fourteen, if she counted Cameron – were industriously working on various projects, none of which made any sense. Tem-aki wondered why they were making dragons by folding paper and a huge dragon head made of soggy paper over woven reeds. While she could see there was a theme, she didn't see how it related to grinding minerals to dust in a mortar or carefully molding candles with bee's wax, much less why they acted like their projects were important.

Beyond them, she could see GEA-4 studying the creepy skull – again. Tem-aki's hands clenched and she glared at the scene in the window. What was it with the droid and that thing? Could robots be fascinated by dead things or so-called-art? How many times did she need to instruct the infernal machine to decipher the language, so they could communicate?

Getting up from the bench, which was next to the protective

railing overlooking the beach, that was at least one-hundred feet below the sheer cliff, Tem-aki headed for GEA-4. Once inside, she demanded, "Why aren't you compiling a language program. We have to figure out a way to communicate with these people."

"I am," GEA-4 said.

Tem-aki's jaw clenched. "It looks more like you are obsessing over that hunk of carved quartz."

"I am capable of multi-tasking."

Tem-aki closed her eyes, counted to ten and reminded herself that a moment of patience during a moment of anger often saved her a hundred moments of regret. After the count of ten, she still wanted to throttle GEA-4, so she counted to twenty before she asked, "How soon will you have a verbal program done?"

"Unknown."

Patience. "And why is this unknown?"

"The conversations I have been able to overhear are limited in topic and verbiage."

"And this makes you unable to compile a program, because?"

"It would not be complete."

"Yet you previously told me that you were able to create a language program for my brother and presumably, you only had limited conversation to base that on. Why is this situation different?"

"That program was not built solely on the spoken word. Nimri had a collection of ancient books, which the initial language lesson was built on, then I was able to add to this by listening to conversations."

"So you are saying that you are currently trying to do this in reverse."

"Negative. I am searching for books, which will give me a better idea of the proper language."

Tem-aki blinked, and reminded herself to be patient. "Does that mean that you don't believe verbal language is proper language?"

"Affirmative." The sweet boy with freckles began painting the huge paper and glue dragon head sulphur yellow.

Tem-aki looked at the ceiling. "Why?"

"Written language, when used in non-fiction, utilizes proper grammar and words. Spoken language utilizes slang and is often spoken using improper grammar."

Tem-aki hated to admit it, but the droid had a valid point. "I appreciate that, but I would really like to be able to begin communicating with them, even if it is with improper grammar. Perhaps we could ask them if there is a library here or something."

GEA-4's attention remained on the skull, which was starting to glow. Tem-aki closed her eyes and reminded herself to be patient. "Do you think you can do that instead of stare at that thing?" When she opened her eyes, the skull was dark.

"I am trying to decipher its frequency, to determine if this is some form of data storage device." Outside, a strong gust of wind created a flurry of activity, as the yellow-robed people grabbed supplies and paper projects.

"Why would you believe that?"

"Bubble technology."

"What is that?"

"Bubble memory is a type of computer memory that uses magnetized areas, known as bubbles for storing data."

Now that GEA-4 mentioned it, she had heard about some cultures mining quartz crystals to use for some sort of data storage, so perhaps the droid was onto something. "And you think it might be possible for you to access this data, assuming this is some form of storage device?" She eyed the sinister looking thing and wondered what sort of person would keep information on such a thing. "How certain are you that it could have books?"

"Fifty-fifty."

"Have you had any luck accessing anything like data?"

"Possibly, by transmitting this frequency," GEA-4 paused and though Tem-aki couldn't hear anything, the skull began to glow. "There is a resonate reaction."

"And this indicates that your theory is correct about it being a storage device?"

"Negative, but it does corroborate that the material is compatible with use of wave-technology."

Outside, shouts of laughter broke out. Tem-aki looked and saw that someone had put the huge dragon head over their own and was running around the patio like a demented, sightless bird.

She shook her head at the antics and wondered if there was data on the skull, and how useful it could be.

Tem-aki took a deep breath and told herself that if there was information there, it would be valuable as long as GEA-4 could use it as a base for a language program.

~o~

As Nimri carried Mica into her bedroom, she noticed the skull was beginning to glow. She quickly tucked Mica into his sleeping basket for his nap, and went to study the fading light.

Why had it done that?

Did the light mean something? And if so, what?

Had the skull always done this? It was impossible to know, since her great-grandfather had always kept it in his room – an area that children were forbidden to enter. By the time she was able to talk, she knew better than to invade Rolf's personal space.

Now, Rolf was dead and she had the responsibility to protect The Chosen, as Tramontains had for over a millennium. Unfortunately, her grandfather had made this very difficult, because he had only allowed her to learn the healing powers of plants. Since his death, she had made a lot of progress, learning to manage myst-energy and using that to both heal and protect her tribe, but still, she had not learned a fraction of the knowledge Rolf had known and she still did not feel completely worthy of being her tribe's Keeper of the Peace.

She stared at the back of the skull, as it sat on its special table and its sightless eye sockets starring at Sacred Mountain's peak. Why had this been one of her great-grandfather's special things? Why hadn't he explained what it was used for? All she knew about it was that one day, her great-grandfather had been angry at Bryta for moving it from its place looking out the window.

With many apologies and tears, Bryta had promised never to touch it, again.

Nimri had been afraid to touch it, too, yet now, she might need to.

The skull might be a key to solving Tem-aki's disappearance, so she needed to figure out how it worked. She wondered if it could reveal where GEA-4 and Tem-aki were, and if they were alive and well. Nimri frowned and wondered if those terms were even valid for something like GEA-4.

Mica murmured in his sleep. Nimri went to him, knelt by his basket and stared at the beautiful miracle that was her son.

Larwin entered the chamber and briefly stood behind her, sharing the wonder of Mica, then he went to the window and took his lumpy black box out of his tunic's pocket. Soon, the skull began to glow.

Nimri scrambled to her feet and went to stand beside Larwin. "How did you do that?"

"I haven't done anything, yet."

"Then how?"

Larwin shrugged, as he punched some of the black box's lumps and pointed the thing at the skull. The light was different than it had been when she woke to see it; this time, instead of a bright light, as if someone had lit a small candle inside or perhaps like pulses of sunlight on a hazy day. Some white symbols flashed across the smooth black part of the box.

"What does that mean?" Nimri asked.

"I don't know. At least not yet," Larwin said. "It would be a lot easier to figure this thing out if GEA-4 was here to help analyze it."

"If she's alive, maybe she is somehow trying to send a message to us."

"Perhaps." Larwin tapped some more buttons, but Nimri doubted that he had actually heard her. Still, it would be nice if GEA-4 was attempting to contact them. Nimri sighed and told herself not to get her hopes up. After assuring herself that Mica was sleeping soundly, she went down to weed the garden.

~o~

GEA-4's hands clamped on either side of Tem-aki's head and the rudimentary language program began. It was quickly over.

As GEA-4's hands dropped back to her sides, Tem-aki said, "Keep compiling this program and plan for daily updates. We need to begin communicating with these people as soon as possible."

"Understood."

Tem-aki sighed, knowing that the android was simply following some cultural protocol for polite verbal discourse and could never understand how frustrating it was to need to find a loved one and not be able to ask where they were.

Now that the language transfer had been made, GEA-4 returned her attention to the skull.

What was that thing's attraction? If Tem-aki didn't know that 'droids were incapable of obsessing over things, she would think that was exactly what she was seeing. So what if GEA-4 knew of other cultures that used bubble technologies to store information? She was supposed to be a logical machine, so couldn't she look around and see that this culture was so primitive that they used feathers and berry juice to write on primitive leaf-pulp paper?

Tem-aki blew out a breath and then went outside to listen to the conversation surrounding the work tables on the patio and see if she could understand anything they were saying.

As she casually moved around the tables, she understood random words like, candle, dragon and eat, but the majority was still gibberish.

And she was still lost.

Jaws clenched and eyes watering, she went to the sea-side railing and looked out over the magnificent view. "Harbor," someone said, and she knew he was talking about the water she was looking at. The blues of the water and sky seemed infinite as they receded into the distance. In fact, it was difficult to see where the water ended and the sky began.

Closer in, arms of land jutted into the water and of course, there were some large rocks in the smooth water near shore. The ship, which they had arrived on, was tied to the long, thin wooden platform, which jutted into the large, roundish water, and while it was the largest boat, it wasn't the only one. Hundreds of the tiny type of boats could be seen around what the locals called the harbor, while many of them were pulled onto the beach, others were moving across the water, as if on some unidentifiable and random mission. Farther out, four more big ships sat alone in the water, almost as this one had seemed, when she first saw it.

Tem-aki had never seen a more alien landscape or one quite so beautiful.

"But she is a woman!" an angry voice said. Tem-aki blinked in surprise at knowing a complete sentence. Unfortunately, she didn't understand the rest of the speaker's angry rant and she resisted the urge to look behind.

Cameron's soothing voice began speaking and while Tem-aki couldn't translate what he had to say, she had the distinct impression that he was talking about her to someone – probably Varlet.

Varlet was a tall, wide-shouldered man who might have been attractive, except he had shifty eyes and thin, angry lips. While she had not felt welcomed by several of the group, Varlet was the only one who had seemed outright hostile, at least toward her. Even though he seemed perfectly nice to the younger boys, and constantly seemed to smile at them, pat them on the butt or put his hand on their shoulders as he helped them with their projects. She did not like or trust the man and suspected the feeling was mutual.

Tem-aki kept her attention on the horizon, but thought of the group behind her and frowned. She had not seen a single woman since her arrival on this planet. The men, at least she thought they were all men, didn't all seem to know how to act toward her. Some, like Cameron, treated her very well, but others like Varlet made her wish she had eyes in the back of her head. Perhaps they were some unisex race. It was difficult to be sure, with the tent-like clothing they wore, but if they were unisex, that could explain a lot of the strange looks and most of the stares she and GEA-4 kept getting.

Had they ever seen a woman before?

Recalling the angry voice saying 'But she is a woman!' Tem-aki concluded that they must have or have had females.

Why else would they have a word for her gender?

Unfortunately, that did not explain why so many stared at her or why Varlet and a couple of others, who always seemed to be near him, acted like they hated her.

She wasn't going to figure out where she was or find her brother by gazing at the magnificent horizon. Tem-aki straightened up and went to see if she could find any new information.

Chapter 14

Larwin plopped down at the dinner table, his posture so slumped, that Nimri's stomach clenched in sympathy at his glum expression. She silently passed him the ceramic bowl of mixed vegetables. Larwin plunked a spoonful on his plate, then speared a piece of chicken and started cutting it into bite-size pieces with a determined vengeance Nimri hadn't seen since the madrox had broken through the Star Bridge and invaded their world.

Bryta chewed her food thoughtfully. "No luck?"

"No!" Larwin said.

"Not surprising," Bryta said, even though Nimri signaled her to be quiet.

"No!" he said, again.

"Bryta, how is Tansy?" Nimri asked.

"Fine."

"So, she's over her head-cold?"

"I would have said, if she wasn't." Bryta's eyes snapped with irritation and Nimri knew she wanted to continue pestering Larwin about his sister. Why did the woman poke at sore spots?

"Well then, I imagine you will want to go visit her, soon."

"What, me visit her on the other side?" Bryta half-stood at the idea of crossing the river to visit her granddaughter, who now lived on what had previously been called the side of the Lost.

"Isn't it about time?" Nimri asked, keeping her tone mild. "You are one of the few who still holds to the old hostilities."

"I do not!"

Nimri raised a brow. "Really? Then why do you only see Tansy when she comes to Market Day?"

"I am too busy here to leave more than one day per week."

"With what?" Nimri held up her hand. "Don't tell me cooking and cleaning because, while you do a wonderful job, you need to take time for yourself, too."

"Are you going to sweep and polish?"

"If that is what it takes," Nimri said, even though she privately thought that polishing the furniture once in every eight-day-week was enough and that Bryta's constant waxing was a waste of time and energy. Not that the scent of bee's wax didn't smell good, but it was a wonder that a colony of bees hadn't moved in, due to the mistaken belief that her home was a long lost hive.

"Maybe I'll think about it."

"Do more than that. Pack a bag and go for a nice long visit."

"And where would I stay?"

"Thunder has a lovely guest room."

Bryta's eyes widened at that thought and a great deal of the starch seemed to go out of her. "You said the climb up to his home was difficult."

Nimri nodded. "Particularly in the dark, but not really worse than the one to get here and you do that once a week."

"Have those bartons of his come back?

"Not that I know of."

"He doesn't have anyone to take care of him. I imagine his home is a disaster." Bryta's eyes began to gleam with a light

Nimri hadn't seen since her great-grandfather died.

Nimri put down her fork and studied Bryta. Had her surrogate mother been suffering from depression for the past year and a half? If her present look of animation was any indication, it was likely. Self-doubt gnawed at Nimri as she wondered how many other obvious ailments and problems she was oblivious to. How could she have lived with someone for months and not noticed their unhappiness? Didn't Bryta realize that her brother and Raine could take care of themselves? Or did she need to believe she was needed by a Tramontain?

What kind of a keeper of the peace was she, when she didn't see a problem right under her own nose?

Nimri's attention turned to Larwin. While she saw her mate's pain, what was she doing to help him? Aside from trying to distract Bryta, nothing. Was that what a keeper of the peace should do?

Probably not.

Still, she didn't think it was her responsibility to try and make everyone happy. So, where was the balance?

A large, warm hand covered hers, and gave it a quick, tender squeeze. She looked into Larwin's warm brown eyes. "I love you," he said. Another soft squeeze and he resumed eating, fortunately, with much less bottled frustration.

Nimri smiled. "I love you, too."

"Well!" Bryta snapped, as she got up, took her plate and left. "I can see when I'm not wanted." Head high she went toward the kitchen.

"Bryta, that's not what I meant."

The plump shoulders stiffened and she disappeared through the door. Nimri started to rise, but Larwin held her back. "Let her go and don't worry about her feelings."

But-"

He put a gentle finger on her lips. "Some people need to exhibit anger in order to do something new."

Nimri blinked. Was Bryta that sort of person? Probably. She sighed. "Most of the time, I think you see things much better than I."

Larwin shook his head. "I just have a different perspective."

"How long have you realized she was depressed?"

"About five seconds less than you."

"Honestly?" He nodded. "Did you find out anything about the skull?"

"I think it responds to thoughts."

"Something like myst power?"

"Rolf's other things work on myst, so it's logical." If it worked on myst, she might be able to figure out how it worked and help him find his sister.

~o~

As she had done each morning since arriving, Tem-aki went down the steep steps from the cliffside house to the beach. Sitting on the next to the last step, she took off the leather and rope sandals Cameron had given her, and put them on the stairs, then walked toward the lapping waves, until they caressed her toes and she needed to raise her robe to keep it dry.

She had never imagined anything like this secluded beach, or the way that each receding wave took grains of sand from under her feet, so little by little she was buried up to her ankles.

The first time this had happened, she had been terrified, fearing that she was being sucked into the earth and could not break free. But now, she was merely amused to feel hydro-power in action. Of course, she had also learned not to test the power of the water over her ankles.

Pulling her feet from the sucking sand, she ventured down the shore to a boulder, which was bigger than the cubical she called her home. Carefully, she climbed the rough granite until she could sit on top of it. Lying back, she watched fluffy white clouds drift by. Some reminded her of the tasty grains Cameron had popped the night before. Others almost seemed like they were some sort of placid animal floating past. Thankfully, none of them looked like the terrifying images she had seen battling to the death in the crystal-quartz skull, which GEA-4 was preoccupied with. Until she had witnessed the android's fixation with the strange object, she would never have thought an android could act so obsessive, unless they were following a direct order.

Was GEA-4 correct in her theory about the skull being some form of informational archive? She hoped so, but even if it was and she figured out how to access it, would it do them any good?

Gradually, Tem-aki realized that in addition to soothing sounds of the water and the cries of the birds, she heard human voices, which were gradually getting louder. Closing her eyes, she concentrated on the rhythm of the words.

"I thought you said the golden-haired one came down here."

"She did."

"Well, then, where is she?"

"She has to be here, somewhere."

"Doesn't look like it."

"Keep looking. There isn't another way up from this beach."

"Only if you want to keep dry."

"What's that supposed to mean?"

"Don't you remember Draco O'ryan saying that the golden-hair had walked out of the water?"

"So you think she comes down here every day to return to the water or something?"

"I don't know, but have you watched her? Noticed how often

she stares at the water? Never helps with preparations for the festival – just stares at the sea." The voices sounded like they were getting farther away.

"Now that you mention it, yes, I've noticed. Why do you think she came from beyond if not to participate in the Dragon Ceremony?"

"I've been trying to figure that out for days. Summer Solstice is in twenty-two days, yet she doesn't help prepare in any way. Not with the costumes; not with the decorations; she doesn't even practice chants or her dance steps."

Overhead, a bird seemed to shriek in agreement and Tem-aki wondered what they had been talking about and why she was so sure that they were talking about her, even though the only word that she had understood had been 'dragon'.

She lay on the rock until her face began to burn, then retraced her steps to the stairs, put her sandals on and began to climb toward the terrace, where she could hear raised male voices. Fortunately, none of them sounded hostile.

Tem-aki quietly approached the top of the stairs and was rewarded when she heard someone say, "Do you know when Annosha will be here?"

"Draco O'ryan invited her for the mid-day meal."

"And Annosha accepted?" There was an odd sound that Tem-aki interpreted as agreement. "Imagine, the high priestess here! It is unprecedented!"

"Is it?"

"What do you mean?"

"The two females have been staying here for days and before that, they were on The Sirocco. Seems to me the old tradition of a division between the sexes in their ways of dealing with the masses has been broken."

"Cracked, maybe, but not broken." A snort of disdain, which

did not require any translation, followed that comment. Tem-aki wished she understood what was being said, but the only word she had understood had been females. At least she thought she'd understood that, but the fast way they talked and slurred the words together made their language particularly difficult to decipher. Perhaps their language was a gesture-based one and not completely verbal. If that were so, it wasn't surprising that she and GEA-4 were having so much difficulty.

The worst language she had ever heard of was Calpurn, because on Calpurnia, everyone spoke in metaphors and one needed to know the event and people involved in order to understand the idea. Tem-aki shivered and hoped that this language wasn't similar.

She studied the people, who reminded her of a chattering flock of saffron-gold birds, as their robes fluttered with their movements and they chattered, while doing whatever it was that they were doing. Though there were still at least a half-dozen separate projects going on, she had the impression that they were all working on small parts of one bigger thing. Unfortunately, watching and listening for days had not given her a clue about what that might be.

Abruptly, everyone became silent and hands stilled. Tem-aki looked to see what had caused such a reaction. A small figure had appeared. Aside from the new individual barely being larger than GEA-4, it was dressed in a layers of a thin, green fabric from the top of its head to the curled up points of its shoes.

Someone whispered, "Annosha." Tem-aki assumed it was the individual's name, but was no closer to figuring out the reason for the sudden quiet, which reminded her of the silence preceding an attack.

"Annosha, welcome," Cameron said, as he strolled to greet her, hands outstretched in welcome. "You honor us with your visit."

"Do I?" The voice was high-pitched and seemed to talk without taking a breath. Was the new person either a child or a female? Tem-aki squinted at the fluttering green figure, but could not get any clues from the body shape, nor could she see the person's face, which was half-hidden by a layer of fabric.

She glanced at the window, to assure herself that GEA-4 was paying attention to this talkative person, but, for once, she was not hovering over the hunk of quartz. Tem-aki wished she knew where GEA-4 was, so she could find out what a scan indicated, but the robot was nowhere in sight. Which was as strange as it was unexpected. In the past few days, any time she wanted to find GEA-4, all she had needed to do was go to the skull, but today, it sat in the window, its vacant eye sockets staring silently at the unprecedentedly peaceful patio. In fact, except for the chatty green figure, who seemed to pat Cameron's arm with every word, it was so quiet that she could hear waves land on the beach below. Glancing at the yellow-clad figures, she realized that many seemed to be holding their breaths.

Why such a dramatic reaction?

"Permit me to present you to our guests," Cameron said, as he ushered the stranger directly toward her.

Tem-aki gulped, but stood her ground and the next thing she knew Cameron seemed to be introducing them.

Up close, the heavily-lashed eyes, with the equally heavy makeup appeared female, which could explain what the topic of conversation had been about, but the eerie thing was that the irises of her eyes were orange.

Tem-aki gulped, then squared her shoulders, tried not to shiver and pasted a smile on her lips, as Cameron said, "Annosha, Captaintemakiatano. Captaintemakiatano, Annosha."

Tem-aki nodded at the eerie eyes, then directed her, attention on Cameron. "Tem-aki." She was tempted to say, 'just Tem-aki', but feared that with their communication issues he would begin calling her 'Justtemaki'.

"Tem-aki," he repeated. She smiled and nodded. His answering smile warmed her enough to look back at the freaky orange eyes and smile.

Annosha's look was cool and calculating, but instead of looking her in the eye, she seemed obsessed with something just beyond her shoulder. Abruptly Annosha's arms emerged from the thin, fluttery layers of emerald fabric and her ring-laden fingers grasped her hair and gave it a pull. With a yelp, Tem-aki jumped backward. Pain screamed through her mind, as several strands of hair ripped from her scalp. She put her palm to her injured head and glared at Annosha. "What the heck is wrong with you?" Of course, the obnoxious person totally ignored her question, since she probably didn't understand her any better than Tem-aki could understand their speech. What baffled her most was that both Annosha and Cameron appeared to be fascinated by the blond hairs she had pulled out.

What was wrong with these people?

And why were they staring at her hair as if they had never realized it could be pulled out?

Did they not realize it hurt? Tem-aki clenched her hands, to stop herself from giving them that lesson. When Annosha opened her palm to display the seven golden hairs, and began another round of chattering, more of the saffron-robed ones crowded around to see. There were many hushed comments about pale roots and divine origins, whatever those things were.

Tem-aki slowly backed away from the cluster and went inside to find GEA-4.

~o~

Nimri sat down on the nearest rug to the skull and folded her legs into the hatha position, then she relaxed her neck and shoulders, placed her hands palm-up on her knees and began to tone the Ooooommmm Mantra to clear her mind.

"What are you doing?" Larwin asked, distracting her.

What a dumb question! He had been the one to teach her this mantra. "What does it look like I'm doing?"

"Meditating?"

She nodded. "So why ask?"

"I've never seen you do that indoors."

Understanding dawned. "When I am outside, it is easier to link my energy with the energy of nature."

"Are both types the myst-energy you and Thunder talk about?" She nodded. "And do I have it, too?"

"You must, otherwise I don't see how you could control the staff of power."

"But I don't," Larwin protested.

"Perhaps not consciously, but I believe you did," Nimri said.

"What makes you think so?"

She tilted her head toward the twisted black staff, which was leaning in the corner of the room. "Pick it up."

With two strides, Larwin crossed to the corner and grabbed the Staff of Power, then turned toward her. "Now what?"

She shrugged. "Just hold it."

Larwin looked at her as if she'd lost her mind, then shrugged and held the staff for a minute. Then, he apparently got bored, because he began twirling it round and round, like the blades of a wind-mill. Nimri, who knew that he was able to carry it, when she could barely keep a grip on the slippery thing, watched his control with amazement. "How long do I need to keep holding this?"

"You can stop whenever you wish. You've made my point."

The stubby bottom of the staff plunked to the floor. "What do you mean by that?"

"Don't you realize that you and Thunder are the only two who can carry that for very long?"

"I know that the tribe has all sorts of legend attached to it, so that people think it is extremely important and thus, they respect it."

"That's true, but it's not what I meant." She worked a kink out of her neck. Seeing the strain that looking up was causing her, Larwin settled down on the floor, and casually laid the staff across his lap. She pointed to it. "You take holding that for granted, and it is easy for you, probably because your myst compliments its energy, but for me, trying to hold it is like trying to hold buttered peas without pinching them."

Larwin laughed. "You aren't going to let me live that down, are you?" He laughed harder, as they both recalled one of their first meals, when the peas he was trying to eat seemed to fly everywhere except into his mouth.

"Perhaps, but my main intention was for you to understand how clumsy I am with that staff."

"You're serious," he said. She nodded. "Does that mean that I need to practice learning how to use this?"

"It wouldn't hurt, but I can't tell you how, because great-grandfather never taught me."

"Figures." Larwin snorted. "But that could be a good thing."

"How so?"

"Well, it seems to me that half of what he taught you was complete nonsense, so we don't need to expect stupid stuff to work before we figure out the right way."

"I'd never thought of it that way, but you have a good point."

"Think Thunder knows?"

"I doubt it, but you could ask."

"Do you have any idea how I should begin?"

Nimri blinked in surprise. "Seriously? You are asking me, when you can twirl that staff like a pinwheel?" He nodded.

She studied him for a moment, then said, "If I were you, I would probably begin the way you taught me at Thunder's." Both of Larwin's eyebrows briefly rose before he folded his long, muscular legs into the hatha position, visibly relaxed his wide shoulders, and placed his hands palm up on his knees. Nimri did likewise.

"Do you think this staff can help find my sister?"

"I don't know. I mean, I know it is powerful and great-grandfather used it to control the weather, but I have no idea what it is capable of. But it can't hurt to try one more way, can it?"

He shook his head then closed his eyes and began the Ooooommmmm Mantra.

A moment before Nimri closed her own eyes to begin the mantra too, she saw the skull begin to glow.

Chapter 15

Tem-aki found GEA-4 holding a candle at the back of the skull, in such a way that the light came out of the eerie, vacant eyes. She shivered so hard that gooseflesh popped out on her arms, but tried to sound calm as she asked, "Is that doing anything?"

"Unknown."

"Did you see Annosha?"

GEA-4 swiveled to face her. "What is an Annosha?"

"Not what. Who." Tem-aki pointed out the window to the far left, where the group of gold-clad men clustered in a tight group. "I can't see her from here, but she is the first woman I've seen here and she is wearing bright green from the top of her head to the tips of her toes. Half her face is even covered with semitransparent green cloth."

"Interesting. Were you able to determine her purpose?"

"Aside from pulling out a few strands of my hair, no."

"So you don't know if she is mother, sister, friend or foe."

"No."

"Pity. Knowing that could provide insight into their social dynamics."

"Then perhaps you should go observe her, instead of this skull."

"I need to complete this analysis."

"We don't know how long Annosha will be here, but if the past pattern holds, this skull will be wherever the gold robes are and since we are with them..." Tem-aki flicked the sleeve of her own robe and let her meaning sink into the stubborn robot.

As if a switch had been flicked, GEA-4 pivoted and strolled toward the door. Tem-aki watched her approach the group. Looking down, she realized the droid had left the lit candle. With a sigh, she blew it out, but then was surprised to notice what looked like two wispy forms sitting in the hatha position, inside the skull.

She blinked and leaned closer.

Was GEA-4 onto something with her theory that this thing was some sort of communication device?

She bent so close, that her nose touched the back of the skull. Gradually, the forms congealed enough for her to see that one was male and the other was female. She also had vague glimpses of a more distant face, or perhaps the third form wasn't as easy to recognize as human. In fact, she had the distinct impression it was not human, or at least the bold dark slashes were designed to camouflage its humanity.

Tem-aki was so intent on trying to understand what she was seeing, that she didn't notice that GEA-4 was just outside the window until she said, "The readings are unusual." Tem-aki's head jerked upright.

"Yes, they are. It almost looks like there are holograms of two or three individuals in it."

"Which could match the readings I have."

Out on the patio, the group of men began to speak louder. A glance confirmed that their attention still centered on Annosha, and they were now leading her from table to table, as they showed her the odd craft projects, which they had been working on. Perhaps the woman was their superior.

Tem-aki smiled at the idea of a society where women dominated.

While she didn't mind Guerreterre, where women could hold high rank, men still seemed to hold the highest-power positions and she had always wondered if their society might become calmer, like the ones on Tronos and Yarnera where women had an equal voice, if the leaders of Guerreterre adopted an equal rights policy.

"I can't be positive, but I believe these people's language might be an adaption of U-Tsang."

"U-Tsang? I've never heard of it. Can you translate that and build a language program?"

"I believe so. It is an ancient language, which has somewhat backwards grammar rules, but if my theory is correct, I hope to be able to compile a basic communication program within the next fifty hours."

"Excellent!" Having a solution in sight, Tem-aki turned her attention back to the skull, where the two human forms had gained definition, but the other vague face in the background remained unchanged. Now that there were some details in the haze, she could tell that the one she had thought was male had blonde hair to the middle of his back. He wore some sort of unfitted tunic and pants and his toes jutted out the front of hick-looking sandals. From what she could see of his body, he had a good, strong build, so she didn't know why he covered up a good body with unflattering garments. She glanced at the gold robes and focused on Cameron. The man in the skull wasn't the only one who she suspected had an excellent body, which he camouflaged with unfitted clothing.

"I wonder why Larwin, Nimri and Kazza's images are in the skull," GEA-4 said.

What? Tem-aki leaned close to the skull. The male's body structure might be similar to her brother's, but the skin-tone was much darker and the hair was much lighter as well as over twenty times longer than she had ever seen him wear it. Since Larwin entered the academy at age three, he always wore his hair short. The one time, when she had seen it cover his ears was the month they had backpacked in Uyrla's mountains.

No way would he have it halfway down his back!

Still, the vague image could be Kazza. She studied the dark-haired woman, who had strong cheekbones and the longest braid she had ever seen. "Is that what Nimri looks like?"

GEA-4 gave a short nod.

Tem-aki studied the female, whose loose-fitting tunic and pants hinted at a nice figure, but her attention kept returning to her long, dark braid. She had never seen anyone with hair that long and suspected that if the woman stood up, her braid could reach down to her knees. Why did she choose to have it so long? Was this the style of wherever they were? If so, it looked quite primitive.

Maybe even as primitive as where she was.

"Why is the skull showing Larwin?" Tem-aki asked.

"Unknown," GEA-4 said.

"Do you have any theory?"

"It is possible that the information operates on thought waves of some form. You have been thinking of him."

That made sense, but it still didn't really answer any of her questions about how to actually find him.

~o~

Cameron noticed that the two strangers were back with the skull. Again. While it was gratifying to know that they, too, held the skull in high esteem, he couldn't understand why the short one always seemed to be hovering over it. And now, as he watched them through the window, the tall beauty was studying it so closely that her nose was pressed against the back.

The skull seemed to give a faint pulse of light. He squinted and noticed what looked like faint shadowy figures inside the skull. What had that pair done to the sacred object?

How dare they touch the Summoning Skull!

Without conscious thought, Cameron began moving toward the open window. As he got farther from the group, he realized Tem-aki and GEA-4 were speaking to each other.

So they talked to each other! He'd suspected as much.

Listening more closely, he realized he couldn't understand what they were saying. Why were they communicating in some unknown language?

Did they want to exclude him for some reason?

Could this be their normal language?

But why would their language differ from his?

Cameron got close enough to see that a feline similar to Saphera plus two humans, one male, one female were depicted inside the skull. He stopped and stared at their strange attire.

What was the meaning of this?

As he watched and listened, Cameron began to suspect that Tem-aki and GEA-4 were as surprised by the Summoning Skull's strange message as he was. Silently he watched them watch the images inside the skull. The strangest thing was that from his perspective, he could see the couple seated on the ground through the side of the skull, but when he focused on looking into the skull's interior through the eye sockets, all he saw was empty space.

How could that be?

Suddenly, the woman opened her eyes.

Emerald green eyes, the color of a priestess.

Cameron gasped.

~o~

Nimri stared at the skull. Was it a trick of the light or did she see a face mushed against the inside of the skull? She blinked, but the only thing that changed was that beyond the flattened nose, which might – or might not – be part of a human face, she recognized GEA-4's eyes. Stranger still, off to the side of the skull a pair of brown eyes watched.

Did this mean the meditation had worked?

Or was her imagination going haywire?

"Larwin," she said softly, "do you see any difference in the skull?"

His eyes opened and turned his head, until he was looking at the back of the sun-bathed skull, as its vacant eyes gazed at Sacred Mountain. Two creases appeared in Larwin's forehead, then he leaned slightly toward the skull and squinted. "Is there something in there?"

"So you see them, too? It's not a trick of the light?"

"If you mean my sister, GEA-4 and a disembodied pair of eyes, yes."

Nimri blinked several times, then studied the flattened face. She had never imagined that Larwin's sister would have a mushed-in-looking face, but since he immediately recognized her, this must be how she looked.

"If she appears in there," Larwin paused to swallow, "does that mean she's dead?"

"I wish I knew," Nimri admitted, as she studied the poor woman who had apparently gone through life with a wide, flat nose. Had that affliction been something she was born with or due to some accident? She chewed her lower lip for a moment. "Did Thunder mention a third person?"

"Beg pardon?"

"He said Tem-aki and GEA-4 were missing, but who belongs to those other eyes?" Gooseflesh rippled over her arms. "It looks like the third person is watching her, and I was wondering if Thunder told you about a third person, or what the meaning of the eyes might be."

"He didn't mention anyone else to me." Larwin scowled. "You were the one he told about meeting her, first. I just learned about that a bit ago." He studied the distant image. "Do you think that other one is a threat?"

"I have no idea," she admitted. "Worse, if they are still alive and in danger, how can we help?"

"You've already begun to help."

"How so?

He gestured toward the skull. "Your guess about myst power seems to have opened some sort of communication link."

Nimri rubbed the tense muscles at the back of her neck. "I guess it is a start." But she wished she knew how she'd done this and how she could use it to find the information they needed to find Tem-aki and GEA-4 – hopefully alive and well. Unfortunately, since their images were inside an emblem of the dead, Nimri didn't have much hope of that.

"At least we now know they are alive and well," Larwin said.

Nimri turned to him, mouth half-open in surprise. Had she said something aloud? Snapping her jaws shut, she swallowed, then asked, "How can you know that?"

Larwin pointed beyond Tem-aki's shoulder to the lumpy black box in GEA-4's hands. "One, I don't think deactivated 'droids would end up in the same place as humans. And two, I suspect they might be seeing our images somehow, because Tem-aki is obviously staring at something and GEA-4 is using her tricorder to analyze something."

Could he be right? Nimri studied the vague images and was surprised to notice that now there were two pairs of disembodied eyes in the background. Four eyes! Despite the fact that one pair of eyes appeared chocolate brown, and the other blueish, they reminded her of the cold, golden gaze the guardians of the Star Bridge had fixed on her when she had guided Larwin to their world. Nimri shivered at the memory and looked for a tell-tale golden glint. But, if the original dark eyes had any color, it was more like a warm chocolate-brown and the newer eyes, had a familiar green glint that looked a lot like Thunder's eyes.

She was almost positive that Thunder could not have died and passed to the next life, since she'd seen him. So, assuming he was alive, why was his image in the skull? Nimri rubbed her aching neck, as she asked Larwin if he thought the eyes looked like Thunder's.

"Could be." He looked deep into her own eyes, then back at the skull. "Same green, so probably."

"But how?"

"He's got a skull in his bedroom, doesn't he?" She nodded. "Then his theory about these things being for communication could be on track."

Nimri assumed that 'on track' meant correct. Larwin frequently made strange little remarks like that, which reminded her that he'd had a whole different life and other-worldly experiences before he came to her world.

She sighed and turned her attention to the skull, which needed to be understood if answers could ever be found.

Another question popped into her mind: if or when they found Tem-aki could she heal the poor woman's face?

And would it be rude to try?

For all she knew, big flat noses were considered beautiful on Guerreterre and nice, normal noses, like her own and Larwin's were considered homely.

Chapter 16

The scent of night flowers was beginning to perfume the air with their heady sweet scents when Thunder and Raine arrived. Nimri and Larwin were sitting in their garden, watching the sun's dying rays put a halo around the top of the stately sequoia their home was built around, when she heard them talking. It was Nimri's favorite time of day, but rather than relax and enjoy it, she hopped up to meet their unexpected guests. Before he said a word, Nimri knew Thunder had returned because of the skull's strange images. What she didn't understand was why he had brought Raine.

Just as Nimri hugged them both in greeting, Mica wailed from his basket under the gingko tree. Raine's eyes went wide with excitement. "May I?" She nodded toward Mica.

"Of course," Nimri said. Raine didn't need to be told twice. As she rushed toward Mica's spot in the shade, Nimri looked at Thunder and said, "She loves babies."

"I noticed." His eyes softened, as he watched Raine pick Mica up. Immediately, the baby's cries stopped. "Now, they are both happy."

Nimri nodded. "But you didn't bring her over here for baby cuddles, did you?"

"Not totally." He smiled. "Have you and Larwin observed anything unusual in your skull?"

"You know we have, because that's why you're here."

He nodded. "Tem-aki and GEA-4 were with you. When did they return?"

"They haven't."

"Then why were they with you?"

"From my perspective, you were with them."

"Seriously?" Nimri nodded. Thunder frowned. "How could that be?"

"Well, GEA-4 is amazing, perhaps she managed it."

"Is that what Larwin thinks?"

Nimri bit her lip as she shook her head.

Thunder lowered his voice to a whisper, "Does he think what I think? That they are dead?"

Nimri shrugged. "I don't think anyone knows what to think, even Kazza seems fascinated by this."

Looking thoughtful, Thunder scratched his head. "Maybe he is the ideal one to figure it out." Nimri felt her eyes open wide. "What? You don't think so?" Thunder put his hands on his hips. "Have you thought about the fact that it is a skull from one of his long-lost kin, and not a human?"

Nimri put her hand over her mouth, as she gasped at his logic. "Why didn't I think of that?"

Thunder shrugged.

~o~

Tem-aki perched precariously on the ledge of a boulder and stared into the calm water of the peaceful pool. At dawn, when she'd walked along this beach, the water had lapped much closer to the ten-story-tall vertical stone wall that imprisoned the thin sandy beach next to the bay. She wasn't exactly sure why the water was lower, now or why the pool with the colorful fish and strange pincushion creatures seemed peaceful, but GEA-4 had shrugged off her comments with one word. 'Tide.' For now, Tem-aki was just happy to have found a seat where she could look into the water and watch the fish.

Who would ever have thought that something, which she had always thought of as an exotic food, could be so colorful or interesting to watch?

Or live in an environment which smelled like something was decaying nearby?

Some yellow-green fish with bright blue freckles and half-closed olive-colored eyes, had been half buried in the sand under the warm clear turquoise water but five of them were now moving around like some form of strange birds, as they navigated around a purple fan like plant, their one foot wingspans banking like a plane as they made the tight turn.

Suddenly, an orange and white snaky thing lunged out of a hole near the base of the fan and all the flying ones darted away. The patch of pretty flowers nearby snapped shut and vanished into straw-like holes. Tem-aki gasped as she leaned forward.

Suddenly off balance, she shrieked as she threw herself back against the boulder. Her spine hit the solid rock with a thud. It hurt, enough for her eyes to water, but falling into something without oxygen could have been deadly.

Heart pounding and eyes closed, she leaned back against the safety of the solid rock, until her pulse calmed. When she opened her eyes, she was looking skyward into Saphera's questioning gaze.

Tem-aki jerked in surprise and nearly launched herself into the water. She dug her bare toes and fingers into the rough rock and told herself that Cameron would not allow the cat into his house, if it was dangerous. That didn't calm her slamming heart, but she did manage a ragged breath.

When she dared to look back up, Saphera was lying down, chin on crossed paws with ears pointed forward as she stared down. Tem-aki gulped. "Are you happy?"

Saphera cocked her head to one side.

"Are you going to lie there and stare?"

Saphera blinked.

"You are, aren't you?" If she hadn't been afraid that launching herself into the water meant death, she wouldn't feel so threatened. Still the creature's body language didn't appear menacing. But that didn't mean she was any less trapped. "Why am I even trying to talk to a dumb beast?"

With a snort of disgust, Saphera lunged to her massive paws, dove over Tem-aki's head and landed in the water. She then casually paddled toward shore.

Tem-aki held tight to the rock so she wouldn't fall in after the cat.

When her heart finally stopped slamming against its imprisoning ribs, her fingertips were slick with blood. Carefully, she climbed back up the massive side of the rock and made her way toward shore. Once on the other side of the massive rock, she saw that the dry sand she had walked over to reach the boulder was now awash with water.

She stared at the shifting, rippling water.

How deep was it?

If she hopped down, would it suck her feet down, like the shallow water she toyed with most mornings?

Tem-aki swallowed her fear, but the lump in her throat remained.

Was it her imagination, or was the water traveling farther up the beach with each wave?

Brow furrowed in concentration, she remembered that today was the first time she had ever noticed that dry sand touched this particular lump of granite, as she walked the beach.

Worse, the water seemed to be rising minute by minute.

If she didn't move, now, she might be stuck here. Standing up, she hiked up the robe's voluminous fabric and leaped as far as possible, then ignoring the sucking sand, she ran for her life.

~o~

Cameron watched a moray eel stick its head out of a yellow coral head, and at the same time, avoid a cloud of small, bell-shaped jelly fish, which were transparent except for the four purple circles each of them had in the middle of their bodies. Closer, a school of orange, purple and pink fairy basslets reminded him of sparks from a fire, as they darted and swirled among the coral.

Hearing a splash, he looked up and saw Tem-aki, robe hiked up to her waist, exposing beautiful, long legs, running from the boulder, where she had been observing life in the tidal pool.

As she sprinted past, he noticed panic etched on her normally calm face. Cameron stood up and prepared to confront whoever had frightened her. But no one seemed to be in pursuit.

More splashing in the tidal pool drew his attention away from the beach, but it was only Saphera toying with the moray eel. Cameron sighed and wondered if he would ever be able to convince her to leave it alone. It had been seven years, since he had noticed Saphera harass the moray the first time. He had felt choking fear when he saw her jaws so close to the eel's poisonous flesh, yet he had managed to shake off the horror of what might be and shout at her to leave the thing alone.

Of course, Saphera had ignored him then as well and the hundred other times he had warned her about touching the creature.

The strange part was that, even on the occasions when her jaws clamped onto a moray and she tossed it out of the water, she never appeared to show any signs of poisoning.

Not seeing anything unusual chasing Tem-aki, Cameron jumped down from the boulder and headed toward the stairway to the cloister. Despite Tem-aki's tendency to avoid speaking, she did say an occasional word or two, and if she was as upset as he suspected, perhaps she would finally talk to him.

Feet mounting each step with determination, he climbed the tall, steep stairway, which was anchored in a crevice of the sheer rock wall. On the patio, the novices were working on decorations and entertainment for the forth-coming Summer Solstice Ceremony, which would begin at Dragon Ridge with the next moon cycle.

A nasty-sounding laugh echoed among the other voices. Recognizing Varlet's tone, Cameron paused to listen to what the misfit, who only seemed to like people, who were either exactly like him or those who tried to curry his favor, was laughing about. Since a major premise of their faction was to accept others and treat everyone as they wanted others to treat them, Cameron had been surprised when Varlet passed his initial training phase.

He was even more surprised that in the months since Varlet had been under his own supervision, the initiate had not done anything which was punishable by expulsion. Varlet had come close to the line, yet he had never actually crossed it.

Hearing no more laughter or derogatory comments, Cameron resumed climbing the steep stairs. Now, instead of wondering why Tem-aki had looked so terrified, he wondered if Varlet or his syncopates had done something to terrify her. Much as Cameron would like to believe her haste to return to his home had something to do with wanting to watch their solstice preparations, in his heart, he knew she did not have any interest in the most important project any draco could ever be assigned to oversee.

In the 1066 years since his ancestors came through the Star Bridge, each eighty-two year-cycle end had been a special time. Had Tem-aki and GEA-4 arrived because this year's Summer Solstice marked the end of thirteenth cycle and the beginning of the fourteenth?

For the first time in his life, Cameron wondered if being in charge of officiating at the celebration would be good or bad.

Whatever it was, it was his responsibility.

As the preparations on the patio came into view, Cameron's gaze sought Tem-aki, but he only saw Varlet. The typical group surrounded the tall, wide-shouldered man. If Varlet didn't have shifty eyes and thin, angry lips, he would be handsome and if he had a more caring heart, he would eventually be a good draco. Unfortunately, Cameron doubted that Varlet would ever become a good draco and realized that as long as the man kept just inside the regulations, there would never be just cause to dismiss him. Perhaps it would be wise to think of a reason for him to resign.

~o~

"Shine a light from the back, so the light comes out of the eyes," GEA-4 said as she held the candle to the back of the crystal-quartz skull. When the interior of the skull began to glow, she added, "It activates the power."

Tem-aki frowned. "What is the purpose?"

"I believe it might act as a dimensional door."

"You think we passed through to a different dimension?" The high-pitched note hurt her own ears, almost as much as the thought that she might have ended up somewhere from which she could never leave.

"It is a possibility."

Tem-aki stared at the crystal-quartz skull. On other worlds, it would be viewed as a masterpiece of art, with no special powers, except its ability to captivate the viewer's interest.

Could it be a way to communicate with her brother, even if he was in another dimension?

If so, it was a miracle that she should use, not complain about because this form of communication was not exactly what she wanted.

So what if Larwin wasn't in front of her and she couldn't speak to him? So what if she didn't know where he was or where she was. She'd spent most of her life not knowing his actual location because, as a Shadow Warrior, his missions were top secret.

She had a way that she could communicate with him, and she needed to figure out how to use it.

Heart pounding, she turned to GEA-4 and told her what they needed to have available the next time the skull connected with Larwin.

Chapter 17

Tem-aki watched Nolan, the kind gray-haired grandfatherly-looking one, instruct Benji, the energetic, young one with freckles, how to chop onions, tomatoes and peppers. Guerreterre's food was processed in factories on whichever world produced it, so she had only seen what the vegetables looked like in pictures and holograms. The reality of cutting onions was not only an eye opening affair, it was an eye watering one, too.

Benji's eyes were watering so badly that he nicked his finger.

Nolan hustled the boy over to the bamboo tube that ran a continual stream of water into a large bowl and washed the injury clean, then applied pressure to the cut flesh. All the while, Nolan calmly spoke to Benji. To Tem-aki's surprise she understood the essence of what he was saying, so apparently GEA-4's most recent additions to the language program were working.

Nolan tied a thin strip of fabric over the cut, then Benji finished cutting the vegetables into small cubes. Once that was done, they moved to the crude iron stove, which they had stocked with twigs, and lit prior to cutting the vegetables.

Benji hoisted a large, shallow black iron pan on top of the hot surface and threw in a glob of yellow goo, which Nolan called butter.

The goo started sizzling and melting. Nolan grasped the pan's crude handles with a thick piece of fabric, then tipped it one direction than the other, as he explained to Benji that the bottom needed to be coated. Tem-aki thought the idea of goo being called a coat was strange, but Benji seemed to accept Nolan's advice. When the liquid was in a thin layer over the bottom, Nolan poured all the cut vegetables into the hot pan. A delicious aroma sizzled into the air.

Tem-aki's mouth watered so much that she had to swallow.

As instructed, Benji used a wooden spoon to spread things evenly, then began breaking eggs into a bowl. Once they were all broken, he added milk and began to energetically beat the mixture. Twice, he stopped beating the egg mixture long enough to stir the cooking vegetables, then when Tem-aki could see air bubbles in the eggy mixture, even from across the room, Benji poured it over the mouth-watering vegetables the pan, plunked a lid on top and grasped the big pan with the thick cloth as he moved it to a cooler part of the stove.

That apparently done, Benji stacked plates and eating sticks on the serving counter while Nolan sliced bread. Without being called, everyone began filing into the large, rustic kitchen. After what Tem-aki calculated to be fifteen minutes, Nolan removed the lid, letting a delicious aroma into the room. He then used the knife to cut the gelled egg and vegetable mixture and began ladling a serving onto each plate.

Cameron didn't need to tell Tem-aki to get in line.

He got in line behind her, and, as he had done so many times, said, "I wish I knew why you came to me."

However, for the first time, Tem-aki understood what he was

saying. She turned to look back at him, surprised that he wanted to know the same thing she did.

Benji put a slice of bread on her plate and Nolan put a big spoonful of the eggy mixture on top of it. As she walked to her place at the table, they did the same thing to Cameron's plate. His words kept circling in her mind. 'I wish I knew why you came to me.'

As he sat in the chair opposite her, Tem-aki softly said, "I wish I knew why, also."

Cameron looked like someone had tasered him. "You spoke!" Staring at her, he sat down hard. "Do you seriously not know why you are here?"

Everyone was staring at her.

Tem-aki gulped and wondered if it was proper to nod or shake her head. "I do not know where here is. I do not know why am here."

All but one of the men looked shocked. She looked from face to face, wondering why they were suddenly looking at her with such strange expressions. Why did Varlet's expression look smug?

"You really don't know why you are here?" Nolan asked, as he sat down on the only empty seat. Turning her attention to him, Tem-aki shook her head.

She swallowed and tried to remember the word for brother. "I try find Larwin."

"What's a Larwin?" Nolan asked.

"Is it a dragon?" another asked.

"Why does she call dragons larkins?" someone else asked.

Cameron simply stared at her, his brown eyes confused.

Tem-aki cleared her throat. "I look for him for three years."

Cameron's forehead furrowed. "Larwin is important to you?"

She smiled and nodded. His frown deepened.

~o~

Cameron shoveled down his breakfast omelet without

pausing to savor it. Conversation ebbed and flowed around him and though he knew that most of it focused on the day's preparations for the upcoming Summer Solstice Ceremony and planning a trek to Dragon Ridge to begin setting up the festivities, his thoughts kept coming back to 'Larwin' and how Tem-aki's face had softened when she'd said the name.

Though she had not said so, he knew from her soft expression that 'Larwin' was a man.

Despite the fact that Nolan's special omelets were his favorite food, breakfast was tasteless and dry. Cameron gulped some coffee to wash it down, and burned his tongue.

Meanwhile, Tem-aki sat across from him eating her food with gusto, and examining several bites, as if she'd never seen food before. Of course, she did that frequently. Was the food here so different from heavenly fare?

And who was 'Larwin' to her?

Furthermore, how could a celestial being lose someone, because that was exactly the impression she had given them about why she was looking for 'Larwin'.

Cameron's teeth ground together.

"You're making Benji feel bad," Nolan whispered.

"Huh?"

Nolan leaned close and spoke softly, so his words did not carry, "The way you're glaring at your plate, stuffing food in your mouth and chewing, as if you don't want to taste it." Nolan sighed. "Benji was so proud to make breakfast, but now..." his words trailed off.

"Sorry," Cameron said. And he genuinely was sorry for making the kid feel badly. "I was thinking of something else."

"I thought as much." Nolan relaxed. "Planning for a major event like this is a burden... and between you and me, knowing this year was the end of the current eighty-two year cycle, is one of the reasons I asked not to be considered for the office of high draco."

Cameron forced his muscles to relax and focused on the conversation. "I wish I had thought ahead, instead of being so honored by the offer, which I immediately accepted." He didn't know why he had assumed the position of high draco would focus on people's individual problems, when with each advancement he had been given, he got further and further from individuals. While he could understand why each promotion became more political and about organization, for some reason, he had assumed that he would still have the satisfaction of helping, and be able to see the results of his time and efforts.

He sighed, as he realized that instead of seeing smiles on the faces of people whose name he knew because of returned health or an improved crop, his results were bags of decorations and canisters of fireworks that would make this cycle ending/beginning a Summer Solstice Ceremony that would be remembered long after he passed onto the next phase of existence.

And, he'd been sure he was in the right place and it was the right time, for him when Tem-aki and GEA-4 had emerged in the Protected Place.

Now, he wasn't so certain.

And now, he wondered who 'Larwin' was and why he was so important to Tem-aki.

Was 'Larwin' the reason why she walked the beaches every morning and stared into the distance some mornings and the depths of tidal pool on others?

Was 'Larwin' more important than the preparations for the coming celebration?

Apparently so, since she never sat down to help with any preparations.

Seeing Nolan watching him, Cameron focused on smiling and relaxing his muscles, then pretended to enjoy breakfast. He doubted that Nolan was ignorant enough to believe his act, but Benji's stiff posture relaxed, so apparently his body language was believable.

Tem-aki ate her last bite, then got up from the table, rinsed her dish, and then headed outside. Presumably to go to the beach and look or wait for 'Larwin'.

~o~

"The tip of the peninsula appears to be an extinct volcano," GEA-4 said.

"You thought that the original place the big boat was at was the site of one, too," Tem-aki said.

"That is true. However, the area under the original site is still heated." GEA-4 made a very human gesture as she pointed at the distant dark brown mountain, which stood in stark contrast to the cloudless blue sky. "While that is not."

The dark, cone-shaped hill overlooked the narrow entrance, which protected the vast harbor-area from the white-topped waves of pounding water beyond.

"I can't see any of those strange hexagonal stones over there. It's a shame that I don't have access to my lab, that data would probably be fascinating. In fact, it might even be a new form of mineral."

"What about the life signs? Do you believe it is possible for a mineral to be a life-form?"

Tem-aki shrugged. "I think anything is possible, until its scientific properties are proven or disproven."

Staring across the calm water, she studied the cone. Volcanoes were fascinating places, particularly the cool ones, which were often excellent sources of gem-stones and other minerals. However, there was no easy way that she could see to get over to the extinct volcano, so there was little hope of finding out any answers to that mystery.

But then again, she could analyze the pools that appeared when the water level went down. Each pool seemed like it was an entire eco-system full-throttle in an explosion of life, yet when the water returned, each one became visually inseparable from the bay.

"Will you finish processing the slate and calcite by this afternoon?"

"The project should be finished in three hours."

"Excellent, we can test it after lunch.... Let us hope the idea works."

GEA-4 gave a curt nod, then turned her attention back to polishing the slab of slate.

Unwilling to think of the hundreds of things which could go wrong with her communication plan, Tem-aki hiked her robe up to her thighs, took out her tricorder, waded into the water and focused on the black-spiked things scuttling in the sea grass closest to her. Shortly after morning meal, she had watched the three youngest yellow-robed boys laughing and splashing in the shallow water, as they played a game with the spiny creatures. Using odd spoon-shaped sticks, the boys had expertly scooped up the bristly balls and tossed them into a basket on shore.

She expected them to dump them back, once their game was over, instead two of them grabbed the basket's handles, while the third had carried the three scooper-sticks toward the stairs.

Did they want those creatures for their pins?

Her tricorder showed that the spiny balls were poisonous. Tem-aki inched backwards, toward shore.

Obviously, the boys had collected the oddly pretty balls because they were trying to make the shore safe.

A large shadow passed overhead. Tem-aki looked up in surprise. Seeing the belly of a bloated, golden beast, she gasped and jumped backward.

Her foot landed on a spiny ball, driving the barbs in deep. With a shriek of fright and pain, Tem-aki fell backward into the knee-deep surf. Water surged over her head and into her nose and mouth.

Flailing screaming, and choking, she fought against the water and the sudden dragging weight of the golden robe. All thought of the thing in the sky was temporarily lost, as she struggled to breathe.

Suddenly, hands grasped her under the arm pits and she was pulled upright. Blinking water out of her face, she saw GEA-4 tow her the short distance to dry shore.

"Thank you for saving me."

"All you needed to do was stand up."

Tem-aki pointed to the three spines protruding from the sole of her foot. "Those are why I fell."

GEA-4 picked up her foot with one hand and expertly extracted the spines with the other.

It felt like fire was moving from the sole of her foot to her knee, then the flames licked higher. Tem-aki closed her eyes and gritted her teeth against the screams of pain, which welled in her throat.

~o~

Cameron hummed a cleansing mantra as he sharpened the tiny, curved blade on the special stone, then, washed the small knife in hot, soapy water to sterilize it. Switching to a preparation chant, he grasped the first sea urchin with a pair of eating tongs and cut a round opening in its top with the knife, then he passed it to Emmet.

Picking up the mantra, Emmet grasped the dangerous spines with his own pair on tongs, and began to scoop out the tongues of sea urchin with a small bone spoon. As quickly as Emmet disgorged a succulent morsel, Tristan rinsed it in the stream of cold, fresh water, then put the cleaned bit into the heavy red ceramic bowl. Meanwhile

Benji added minced onions and chopped cilantro to the bowl. Nolan sliced bread, while he watched them.

Cameron frowned, wondering what was missing, then put down the tiny knife and looked for Varlet. He spotted him outside, leaning over the railing, laugh lines obvious on his face. "Varlet, you need to add the olive oil and lemon juice," he called.

Varlet whirled from the railing and stomped inside. Cameron clamped his jaws together and focused on cutting circular holes in the tops of the urchins. While he could quiet his tongue, even though he was chanting the cleansing mantra, he could not seem to quiet his negative thoughts about Varlet.

Why had the guy joined their order, when he obviously wanted others to serve him, instead of serve others?

"Add some of the fermented apple-mint, too," Nolan told Varlet.

Varlet's eyes flashed a brief look of defiance, but he complied. Then, he went back outside and resumed watching whatever had captured his interest on the beach. Even without looking, Cameron knew Varlet was watching Tem-aki. The question was why he seemed to be laughing at her.

In her pale way, Tem-aki was a beautiful woman, but that didn't explain why Varlet constantly spied on her. In fact, the only good thing about Varlet's apparent obsession with the celestial pair was that he didn't disappear as frequently when it was time to share chores.

Of course, he still only volunteered for the easiest bits. Emmet, Benji and Tristan had spent nearly two hours collecting the urchins, and were now happily helping in the preparation of the special treat. Varlet had barely spared two minutes, as he added the liquids to the marinade.

"Having problems remembering the tune?" Nolan asked.

"Sorry," Cameron said. "I was preoccupied."

"Which is something you do not want to be, when dealing with urchins," Nolan said. "Get pricked and you will be in pain for a long time. That is why we chant during preparation."

"I know." Cameron tried to clear his thoughts, and focus on cutting the small holes.

As the onion, cilantro and urchin mixture marinated, Nolan brushed olive oil on the slices of bread and began toasting them. After both sides were golden-tan, he put them on a serving platter.

As Nolan rang the luncheon gong, Benji placed a large platter of sliced cheese and fruit at the center of the table, then he poured fresh water into the goblets. Meanwhile, Tristan and Emmet spread the sea urchin mixture on top of the toasted slices and arranged them on two smaller platters.

Finally, everyone except Tem-aki was seated. Since urchin was a special treat to commemorate the test flight of the hot air dragon-shaped balloon Annosha's faction had just flown, Cameron gave the blessing, so everyone could begin eating. Though he wondered where Tem-aki was and what Varlet had been laughing about, he had learned it was wise to choose his battles carefully, and never, ever enter one without all the facts.

So, the only thing Cameron did was load Tem-aki's plate, to assure that the boys did not eat her portion.

As they were clearing the table, he kept glancing out the window. It was not like Tem-aki to be late for a meal. Cameron decided that as soon as he could do so, without being obvious, he would go to where Varlet had been standing. But, before he got a chance, he noticed Tem-aki, who was leaning on GEA-4, appear on the stairs. Her wet hair and the robes clinging to her curves, proclaimed that she had endured a thorough dunking.

Odd, aside from the first moment he'd met her, she seemed to avoid getting wet.

As her bare feet touched the stone surface of the patio, he realized she was limping badly. Rushing to her, he asked, "What happened?"

Was her misfortune what Varlet had found so humorous? After all, he had been looking at something down on the beach, instead of admiring Annosha's gigantic golden masterpiece as it flew its maiden voyage over the harbor.

Tem-aki sank onto a nearby bench, raised her left foot and pointed to the tell-tale punctures. Grasping her foot, he inspected the injury. "You did a good job getting the spines out, but you need to soak this in vinegar." He called for Tristan to bring the shallow pan, then noticed Varlet snickering behind the lemon tree.

What was wrong with the man?

Did he think that laughing at the misfortune of another person was proper behavior for a potential draco?

Chapter 18

Bryta's scream startled Nimri. She and Kazza raced across the garden toward the door. Another scream helped her pinpoint the sound as coming from above.

Was Mica hurt?

Worse?

Kazza passed her and she heard his paws thudding halfway up the stairs by the time she was inside the kitchen door. "Bryta, what's wrong?"

But Bryta's screams continued without answer. Nimri took the stairs two steps at a time, arriving at her bedchamber's door, she heard Mica's crying, too.

What had happened to him?

Dashing into her room, she ignored Bryta, who was looking out the window, leaped over Kazza's slashing tail and scooped Mica up out of his basket.

Hugging him tight, Nimri soothed her son and herself. By the time her heart stopped slamming against the confining ribs, she was sure that whatever had terrified Bryta had nothing to do with Mica's health, and he had only been upset because of her screaming.

What had Bryta seen out the window that caused her to put the household into a panic? Taking a deep, cleansing breath, Nimri pivoted toward Bryta, whose screams had reduced to sobs, as she collapsed in a heap next to Kazza, who sat, tail now just twitching with interest, as he stared out the window.

From the back, she couldn't see what they were looking at, but obviously, no one needed help, because they weren't running to aid anyone. Aside from blood, and destruction, what could have caused such excessive emotion?

Edging around Kazza's massive form, she realized his attention was on the skull.

What was going on with it, this time?

Moving closer, she recognized Thunder and Raine's faces. This time, Thunder's face was much clearer, though she only really recognized Raine because of her pale, shoulder-length hair. However, she could make out some leaves behind them. Nimri focused on the vegetation, certain she had seen those leaves recently.

Mica turned his head toward Kazza, then reached for the cat he adored.

"Bryta, why were you screaming?" Nimri kept her tone calm, so she would not upset Mica.

Instead of an answer, Bryta sobbed harder.

"Surely you aren't upset by the skull?"

Bryta turned toward her so fast that one of the braids, she wore meticulously positioned around her head, like a halo, whipped free. "You don't think there is a problem with your brother being in the Skull of Doom?"

"Why do you call it that?"

"It represents death." Bryta began to sob harder.

"Did Rolf tell you that?"

"Everyone knew."

"Except me."

Bryta mopped her face with her apron. "Those who are seen there are gone, never to be seen, again."

"Really?" Bryta nodded. Nimri knelt next to her. "Thunder and I believe it is a communication device. We've both seen each other in there."

Bryta's face went white. "It cursed both of you?"

"I don't think so." Nimri glanced back at the skull. "Now, more than ever, I think it is some sort of communication device, and I wonder if Thunder brought his own skull when he came, last night." Nimri stood up. "I am going to prove this thing is not an evil death device. Would you like to come with me?"

Bryta blinked at her.

"Or not. In fact, it would probably be more helpful if you stayed here. In about five or ten minutes, look at this skull and see if I am in it."

Bryta gasped.

Nimri grabbed her arm. "I am serious. This is not some crazy death curse. I am almost positive Thunder is using his skull to somehow put his face in this one. "And I figure I can prove it. So, please, just watch this skull."

Bryta shook her head. Kazza wrapped his tail around Nimri's waist and winked. "Okay, then Kazza will do it."

With that, Nimri settled Mica back in his basket, then headed down the stairs, out the door and on to the path down to the swimming hole, at the base of the waterfall.

She found Raine and Thunder sitting on a wide, flat sunbaked boulder near the pale sand, staring into Thunder's crystal skull. "I thought I'd find you here."

Thunder glanced back at her. "For some reason, today, the skull shows Kazza."

"Because he is staring into the one in my bedchamber."

"Seriously?"

Nimri nodded. "Bryta screamed loud enough to wake the dead and in fact, she seems to think anyone whose image shows up in the skull is doomed."

"I never heard her," Raine said.

"How could you, with the drumming of the falls?" Nimri asked.

"The falls are why I chose this place," Thunder said.

"That makes sense," Nimri said. "I've always felt this was a place of power. Your image is much clearer than it was, before."

Thunder got up, "Tell you what, you take my place and I'll go up and look in your skull."

"Sounds like a plan. I just hope that Bryta doesn't faint or do anything dramatic."

Thunder laughed. "She wouldn't be Bryta if she didn't over-react." With that, he hopped off the rock and headed for the steep trail to the garden. As he began to climb the steep trail to the house, he called, "Prepare your myst energy."

With a nod, Nimri gracefully hopped onto the rock and sank into hatha position, next to Raine, where Thunder had just been.

Raine gave her a tentative smile. "So it was working?"

"It seems so."

"But you only saw Thunder in the other skull." Nimri shook her head. "You were there, but very dim."

Raine sighed. "I fear I am not capable of learning this myst thing you do."

"If you believe you cannot, then you never will. If you believe that you can, it becomes possible."

"You say that because it is easy for you."

"I say that because I, too, thought I could never learn to use myst power, so I merely went through the motions of trying... And I could never grasp it, at least not as long as I believed I could not."

"What changed?"

"Larwin made me realize that my thoughts were wrong, so I changed what he calls 'my internal dialogue'."

"And that is?"

"My thoughts."

"How did you do that?"

"I needed to pay attention to what I was thinking and had to force myself to change wrong thinking to right thinking. Basically, I changed thinking 'I can't' to 'I can'."

"You're making this up."

Nimri shook her head. "It is the honest truth and someday I will tell you the whole story, but right now, I need to prepare to test this skull." With that, Nimri closed her eyes, relaxed her muscles and began the mantra. Before she zoned into myst, she heard Raine's voice join her in the mantra.

Though she knew the process of separating myst from body appeared nearly instantaneous to observers, from Nimri's perspective, the detachment process took hours. Thunder, who had more practice separating body and spirit, was already watching her from the back of the skull, when she released her myst-energy.

So, he had been correct, the skulls could be used for some form of communication. But why would the skulls only share visual? "Can you hear me?" She asked.

Thunder tapped his ear, while shaking his head.

Nimri sighed and shrugged.

Abruptly, Kazza nudged Thunder aside and she realized that she could hear him purring over the sound of the nearby waterfall. She frowned. How could she hear Kazza, if Thunder couldn't hear her? Before she could formulate an answer to that question, Kazza's myst form leaped out of the back of the skull and landed behind her. Nimri whirled around so fast that she came face to face with her flesh and blood body.

With a gasp, she jumped backward. Suddenly, she was on her bedchamber's floor and Thunder was staring at her as if he had seen a ghost.

"How did you do that?" he asked.

"I have no idea," she admitted, "but Kazza seemed to just jump through." They both turned their attention back to the skull, where they could see Kazza's myst form standing close to Raine, whose image gave an occasional strong shimmer of myst-energy.

"I think we were wrong about this being for communication," Thunder said.

"Are you sure?" Nimri raised a brow, "Seems like you and I are doing exactly that and Kazza seems to be attempting to communicate with Raine." As if in response to her words, Raine shimmered strong and long.

"She's making progress," Thunder tilted his head toward Raine. "Do you think something like GEA-4 has myst-energy?"

"Larwin doesn't seem to think so, but he also admits that he doesn't know how androids are actually made."

"Tem-aki obviously does," Thunder said.

Nimri nodded. "Larwin didn't understand her, when he came to us."

"True." Thunder's brow furrowed. "So how come we could see her in the skull?"

Nimri shrugged. "Perhaps for the same reason we can see Raine, but I don't know what that is." Nimri chewed her lower lip. "If we see her in there, again, do you think we can jump to wherever she is?"

"It's probably the best chance we have of finding her." Thunder looked from her to the skull. "But before I do that, it is probably wise to test this jump thing." With that, Thunder raised his arms, as if to dive into water, and plunged into the skull. Less than a blink later, his body passed over Kazza and Raine and he landed in a rolling summersault on the sandy beach. Nimri suspected his jump was more dignified than her own had been.

A whimper came from behind her. Nimri looked over Thunder and Kazza's relaxed bodies to a tell-tale shimmer in Mica's basket. At less than a month old, was her son already learning to control his myst-energy? Nimri swallowed hard, as she rushed to him. Kneeling next to his basket, she recalled her great-grandfather's scornful tone, as he berated her for trying to learn to use her own myst-energy and telling her she was too young, when she had been at least two years older than Mica. How different might her life have been if she had been encouraged, when she felt those first tender stirrings of power, instead of being ridiculed?

How much anguish had she endured over Rolf's words, which made her feel as if she could not learn things? Nimri vowed that she would teach Mica, as she had tried to teach Raine minutes before. Even as she made the vow, she realized that protecting and raising a myst- empowered-baby, would be a challenge. Still, it had to be easier than growing up with the fear that she was not capable of doing her born-duty and protect her tribe. Leaning close to Mica's basket, she whispered, "If you believe you can't, then you never will. If you believe that you can, it becomes possible." A shimmer of myst-energy answered her.

~o~

Though Tem-aki kept getting whiffs of the mild acid, which Cameron had insisted she soak her foot in, lunch tasted fabulous. The meat and herb mix topping the toasted bread made her want to keep eating and eating and eating. Unfortunately, since she had arrived late, the only food available was on the plate Cameron had kept for her.

She suspected that, if he hadn't been kind enough to keep it, she would have had to settle for eating one of the eye-watering purple balls. Tem-aki shivered at the thought.

After her initial hunger abated, she took the time to aim her tricorder at the amazing taste-mixture and was surprised to learn that, except for the poison, the whitish bits matched the chemical structure of the spiny ball she had stepped on. How had they known those horrid things were food? Delicious food? She frowned and looked around the rustic room. Where did they get the technology to make a gourmet treat from something poisonous?

Perhaps there was more to these strange people than she suspected and the potential technologies of the skull were normal. Perhaps these people used natural power sources by choice, instead of necessity.

Most of them seemed happier than the average Guerreterre citizen. For certain, they ate better.

Chapter 19

Nimri, Larwin and Thunder silently ate their evening meal, while Raine cooed and giggled with Mica.

"How certain are you that jumping to wherever Tem-aki is would be safe?" Larwin asked.

Thunder shrugged.

Nimri swallowed before she spoke. "How can we ever be sure about anything?" She frowned at both Larwin and Thunder. "I mean did any of us know if the Star Bridge would be safe before we stepped in?"

"I didn't realize that was what I was doing," Larwin said. "I mean, how could I have?"

"Well, it's good that you did," Thunder said. "Otherwise, I'm pretty sure you'd have died a long time ago."

Larwin nodded in agreement. "True, but this situation is different. In this one, we know we are making a choice and we aren't sure if we can backtrack."

"You're worried that if Bryta's theory that Tem-aki is dead is true, then a jump to wherever she is would be one way," Thunder said. Larwin nodded, again. "That is a valid fear, at least in some ways, but we already tested jumping between our own two skulls and had no problem. The fact that we see her in our skulls suggests that Tem-aki is also in possession of a skull and there is nothing to suggest that a jump to her location would be any different."

"My concerns aren't over the 'to' part, they're over the 'and back again' potential." Larwin cracked his knuckles. "Don't get me wrong, I would love to see my sister alive and well, but not at the cost of losing one of you." He covered her hand. "Nimri, until I met you, I didn't really know what a lot of things meant." He cleared his throat. "I thought I knew what things like unconditional love, home and family meant, but I didn't. Not really."

The sincerity in his gaze was so overwhelming that her vision blurred. Nimri put her hand on top of his. "I understand how you feel. Believe me, I never got that from my great grand-father, either." She squeezed his hand. "You, Larwin, are the love of my life. You are my family and you are my home and I don't want to do anything to jeopardize that." She cleared her throat. "But Tem-aki is family, too, and if there is any way to bring her here, as Thunder started to do, I think it's worth looking into."

He stared at her long and hard. "So you are determined."

Nimri nodded.

Thunder cleared his throat. "I will jump first and if I can't jump right back -" He shrugged.

Raine sobbed, then a moment later, Mica began wailing.

"No, I will go," Nimri said. "Larwin is my family, which means Tem-aki is, as well."

Thunder squared his shoulders and looked her straight in the eye. "By that definition, she is also my family." He cocked a thumb at Mica. "Now, you – we – have others to worry about, too. And don't forget I was the one who lost her. Plus, you not only have responsibilities to family, you also need to protect your tribe. Trust me, if I thought there was any real danger, I would not go."

Nimri laughed. "Since when do you avoid dangerous situations?"

"As of when I lost Tem-aki." Not knowing what to say to that, Nimri swallowed hard. "I lost her. It is my responsibility to find her. End of subject."

Raine carefully settled the somewhat calmer Mica into his carry-basket, stood up, then sprinted toward the stairs.

Larwin's fingers tightened on her hand, so the only thing Nimri could do was watch her go.

~o~

As the sun set and the boys headed for their hammocks, Cameron watched Tem-aki and GEA-4 continue to hover over the skull.

What was their fascination with it?

Why did GEA-4 spend nearly all her waking hours next to it?

And had he actually seen shadowy figures in it, or had that been his imagination? He squinted at the skull, nearly certain that he saw more figures in it. Moving across the room, for a better look, he heard Tem-aki say, "Thunder."

GEA-4 said, "And Nimri."

Cameron wished they trusted him enough to speak the common language, but at least they had begun making a few comments. Nothing that he could predict the future on, but those few words were a beginning. As he had that thought, the larger figure inside the skull lay down on the floor, as if sleeping and he felt a chill pass over him.

Strange that he didn't feel a breeze, but then the weather this time of year could change in moments. He looked out the window to the cloudless sky and decided that he didn't need to secure the shutters against a storm, though it might be a good idea to have an extra blanket near his hammock, if the temperature dropped during the night.

~o~

Nimri kept half her attention on her skull because Thunder's myst form had just leaped to wherever Tem-aki and GEA-4 were. Turning, she looked at his corporal form. Seeing his chest rise and fall, she exhaled a breath she hadn't even known she was holding.

Had she expected him to die, as his myst passed?

Apparently so.

When Thunder moved out of sight, Nimri glanced back at Larwin, Mica and Raine, who had insisted on being present during the experiment. Larwin and Raine were seated on the floor, their backs to the bed, and pretending to show Mica her favorite fairytale book. The golden dragon on the cover twinkled as it passed through a stream of sunlight, but Mica was the only one whose attention was on the picture.

Raine touched Thunder's wrist, then visibly relaxed. Raine gave Larwin a genuine smile.

Larwin raised a brow. "The pulse is good?"

"Very strong, so I guess I should have trusted him instead of worry."

"It is almost impossible not to worry over a leap into the unknown."

Raine nodded in agreement, then turning her attention back to Mica and the book, she began telling him about how she used to be a Dragon Shepherd.

Kazza strolled into the room and lay down next to Thunder.

Nimri, who had already heard the dragon-herder story, turned her attention back to the skull and was surprised to see GEA-4 hold up a smooth dark surface, with chalky words written on it. Tem-aki was staring at her, as if willing her to respond.

"'Is Larwin there?'"

She turned back in time to see Larwin hand Mica to Raine. A moment later, he was next to her, standing with his hand on her shoulder.

Tem-aki's smile turned radiant, then she quickly washed the words off the dark surface with the rag, grasped a chunky whitish cylinder and began writing down a meaningless series of letters and numbers.

Larwin grabbed the lumpy black box he kept on his belt and started poking it. A glance told Nimri that he was putting in the same strange phrase that Tem-aki had written, so obviously it meant something to him.

Once he had them recorded, he smiled at the skull and put both his thumbs up. Tem-aki jumped for joy, while GEA-4 calmly put down the gray board.

After what seemed forever, but was only about a half hour, Thunder's myst-energy returned.

Nimri said, "That's your idea of 'just hop over and right back'?"

"Sorry, I got distracted."

"Couldn't you have popped back, to assure me it wasn't a one-way trip before you 'got distracted'?"

"Sorry."

"Well, what 'distracted' you?"

"First it was the water running." Nimri blinked as he looked over her shoulder, then softly smiled. "I don't think you're the only one who was concerned. Let's rejoin our bodies, so I only need to tell what I've seen once."

It was quicker to reconnect than disconnect. But what Nimri hadn't anticipated was Raine's reaction. Upon seeing Thunder sit up, she burst into tears, and a split second later threw her arms around him, as if she'd thought she would never see him, again.

Eyebrow raised, Larwin looked at her. Nimri shrugged, but knew they were both wondering if Thunder and Raine realized that their friendship seemed to be headed for a deeper level. But that wasn't the most important thing at the moment. Tem-aki was.

When Raine's sobbing quieted, Thunder continued to hold her close to his side, as he began to explain why he had taken so long. "First thing I saw when I popped over was water running."

Larwin scowled. "Why did that distract you? We see that every day."

Thunder nodded in agreement, then said, "But this was coming out of a golden tube and pouring into a bowl, which never overflowed. It was magic I hadn't seen, before, except that when I looked closely, I realized it wasn't magic, because there was another tube in the bottom of the bowl that the water ran into."

"How long did it take you to figure that out?" Larwin asked.

"Not long, but when I turned back to the skull, I looked out the window and saw that there was only a bit of land before what looked like water that stretched as far as I could see."

"That sounds like the place I've been seeing in my dreams," Nimri said.

"Exactly," Thunder said. "So, I wanted to make sure."

"And did you?" Larwin asked.

"I think so." Thunder tightened his arm around Raine. "On one side, some steep stairs go down to a narrow strip of sand between waves of beating water and a sheer cliff and up the stairs that was on the other side of the place where Tem-aki is, there is a sort of public place."

"What was that like?"

"Some sort of permanent market, with shops selling things, but they were all closed." Thunder frowned. "It seemed like it was just before sunrise there. Or at least it was sometime in the night, but the stars were not fully out and there was a vague gleam, on one horizon, as if the sun might be either coming or going." He glanced out the window, where the sun was high in the sky.

Larwin cleared his throat. "So, assuming she is on this

planet, she is nowhere near us."

"And the only way we can get to her is by air or boat," Raine said. "It won't be easy, but at least it is doable."

"Doable?" Larwin blinked. "On Kalamar, no doubt, but with the technology of this planet?" Mouth flat, he shook his head.

Raine nodded. "This planet has a lot more resources for building a boat than Kalamar does."

Nimri cleared her throat. "The little boats we have to convey produce and wares to market wouldn't be sturdy enough to cross all that water, would they?" Memories of the two times she'd been in a boat made it difficult to breathe. She reminded herself that the second boat had not capsized and she had not faced drowning. Even better, she now knew how to swim.

"They might be big enough, but we will need something bigger, so we can carry enough food to get there." Raine frowned. "Maybe even enough to get back, if wherever she is does not have adequate food."

Seeing her expression, Larwin pulled her close and began to whisper encouragement.

Raine tilted her head to one side and glanced at Thunder, who answered her unspoken question. "Other than on your world, the only time I've ever been in a boat, a storm came up and it was sunk. I barely survived. My parents didn't."

Raine's hand went to her throat. "Oh, I'm so sorry!"

Thunder nodded. Raine looked from him to Nimri, another unspoken question in her eyes, which Thunder understood, and answered, "I don't know how she made it. She didn't even know how to swim."

Nimri found her voice. "Kazza swam for us both, but I really don't want to think about that." She shivered. "Do you really think that we have materials to build something that could get us there safely?"

"First, we need to be sure where 'there' is," Larwin said.

"True," Raine agreed. "That will be the most difficult part."

"Not really." Larwin held up his lumpy black box and pointed to the numbers and letters he had copied down. "These are the coordinates of where they are, so all I need to do is compare these to the coordinates where we are." He snapped his fingers.

Raine grinned in delight.

Nimri shivered with dread. Even though she wished that it could be that easy to find Tem-aki, she knew the location of Sacred Mountain's Peak was in sight and known, but that did not make the journey there and back any easier. Or safer.

Maybe they should be happy having found a way to communicate with them. What they actually needed to do was find something they could write on, then wash off, so they would have a two-way dialogue.

Yes, that was what they needed, not a boat, or some endless trip across water to an unknown place.

Larwin hooked his free arm around his knee and looked at Thunder. "You were gone a long time. Other than running water, time of day and water to the horizon, did you discover anything else about where she is?"

"Due to the time of day, I couldn't be positive, but it appears to be an island. A really big island, but still an island."

"How could you tell?" Nimri asked.

He raised a brow. "How to you think?"

"You soared."

He nodded.

"Could you see Sacred Mountain?"

He shook his head.

Nimri scratched her head. "How can that be? Everyone can see it."

"Everyone that you know has lived in this same place for

generations," Larwin said. "Your laws made leaving this known area a virtual death sentence. I've never understood why those were made."

"Why?" Raine asked. "Because Guerreterre's main mission seems to be finding other worlds and plundering them?"

Larwin reddened beneath his tan. "Are you saying you understand why a culture would confine itself or are you saying that I can't understand because of the values I was raised with?"

"Both."

"Huh." Larwin frowned.

Thunder said, "Why we each think like we do is not important. Nor is why we choose to live in one place, but if you are interested, it is my understanding that we all live in this area because when our ancestors came here, this is the area where the planet's citizens allowed them to settle. My parents taught me that we humans were allowed here, so we could survive, but this world still belongs to the original ones."

"Have you ever met one of them? Raine asked. "Do you know if any still live?"

Thunder and Nimri both looked at Kazza.

Chapter 20

"What a time for this to malfunction." Tem-aki smacked the side of her tricorder.

GEA-4 said, "If you are referring to the energy spike, I believe it was myst-energy."

"Seriously?" Tem-aki smacked her tricorder, again.

"Yes. I have recorded this phenomena many times. The only anomaly this time was that the surge appeared to come from the skull, and then eighteen-point-nine minutes later, it returned to the skull."

"And where was it in between?"

"Unknown." GEA-4 made an oddly human gesture toward the food preparation area. "It initially went to the basin, then appeared to return to the skull, but went past, presumably to the beach. I could theorize that it displayed an attraction to water."

Tem-aki nodded in agreement. "So, after going to the beach, the energy returned to the skull."

"Yes and no. If it had come directly from the water, I would assume it would come from that direction." GEA-4 gestured toward the window, then turned her attention upward. "Instead, it came from above."

"What is up there?"

"Other than the town, which we walked through, as we moved from the Sirocco to here, I have no idea."

"Perhaps you need to research that."

"My time is occupied with this skull, which seems to offer the best chance to find Colonel Atano."

"True," Tem-aki said. "Do you think he understood the coordinates?"

"Affirmative. The more perplexing question is if he can find transportation here. The Chosen and The Lost only have small, rudimentary water craft, similar to the thing that Draco Cameron calls dory. It would be impossible for such a craft to travel here."

Tem-aki swallowed hard. "Am I correct in believing that The Sirocco could make the trip?"

"Possibly, but I do not have a global image of this planet, so have no idea what type of terrain separates us. There was no ocean, sea, or even a lake visible from where they live. There is only a river. While it is a very large river, I do not know where it goes or if it is navigable. Furthermore, I do not have enough data on the type of vessel The Sirocco is to know its capability."

"So, the one thing we need to do is find out what my brother's coordinates are." She swallowed, again, but the lump of fear in her throat remained.

"And find out if they have more maps than those we have already reviewed," GEA-4 said.

"Good idea." Tem-aki looked at the sky and recalled the balloon, which had startled her. "Maybe we should consider other types of transport, like that big yellow dragon-ballon." She took a deep breath. "Do you think something like that would be easier?"

"Negative."

"Why not?"

"Would you really want to put yourself in a position to be

blown whichever direction the wind blew?"

"But there are usually standardized circulatory patterns on every world."

"True, but I do not have that data for Chatterre. Do you?"

"No," Tem-aki admitted in defeat.

A deep rumbling sound came from near her feet, and the next thing she knew, Saphera was pressed against her side, rubbing the side of her furry cheek, against her ear. It was all Tem-aki could do to remain upright. Worse, GEA-4's attention remained on the skull, and worthless android that she was, GEA-4 did nothing to protect her from the onslaught.

"A little help here!" Tem-aki gasped

GEA-4 looked at her. "Lean toward her and put more weight on your right leg."

"That's your idea of help?"

"Did you wish something other than to retain your balance?"

Tem-aki blinked in shock. Saphera pressed until her left hip was jammed against the table the skull was displayed on and the rumbling sound grew in volume.

With no other option, Tem-aki tried to take GEA-4's advice. The moment she did, she felt less vulnerable.

"Good," GEA-4 said, without looking up. "Now, take your hand and gently, but firmly run in from the top of cat's head, toward its tail. Gently... like a caress.... Yes, that's it... Repeat... Again. I have nearly isolated the variances in the frequency."

The frequency of what?

"Purring."

Tem-aki blinked rapidly. What possible difference did the sound the cat was making have? As she pondered that question, she kept repeating the stroking motion, but the images inside the skull became indistinct and the light faded to a dull, vaguely pulsating glow.

~o~

Cameron hurried down the moonlit path, mind full of Annosha's worries about the Summer Solstice Ceremony and her dire predictions that terrible things would happen. Why had she seemed so certain? And what 'dire things' did she expect to happen? When he had pressed her for details, all she would tell him was, "The ending and beginning of a cycle is a particularly special time." Somehow, she had made the word 'special' sound ominous. And then, she had presented him with an emerald green khata-scarf. While a khata-scarf was a versatile gift, it was something one received publicly, not privately. When presented at festive occasions, the khata-scarf signified that the giver wished to give the receiver tashi delek. What did it mean when given privately? Aside from the obvious, was she telling him that she wished him anything besides good luck, but could not do so publicly?

Why did she feel the need to gift him with her emerald green khata-scarf more than two weeks prior to the Summer Solstice?

Did she foresee problems prior to then? If so, had she heard rumors or had she had a precognition?

Cameron clutched the silk scarf in his sweaty palm as he hurried home. Though he had tried not to show his worry to Annosha, now that there were only stars to see, and he didn't need to pretend to be strong, he dared to let down his guard.

First, Tem-aki and GEA-4 had come to him, but they refused to explain why.

Now Annosha gave him this token of luck.

What did they know that he did not?

Saphera seemed frightened of Tem-aki and GEA-4. Could he be wrong about where they had come from and why they were here?

Might they have come to tear apart the order of Shaka-uma?

Did he have demons in his home? Under his protection?

Or, were they sent from above, as was his first thought?

Mouth dry, Cameron hurried down the steep steps to his patio, glad that most had already turned in for the night and that he would be able to 'sleep on his thoughts' before seeing others. At least, he hoped he could sleep.

A vague, pulsating light came from the salon. Who had forgotten to blow out the candles, before going to bed? Had they also forgotten to put water in the shallow dish under it? He hurried forward, glad that he had gotten home in time to deal with the neglect.

Was this why he'd been given the scarf?

He rushed through the dragon door and into the salon, where he saw Saphera leaning adoringly against Tem-aki, who was petting her, while staring at the skull.

What was this?

When had Saphera claimed them?

How long had they been able to touch her? Saphera still wouldn't allow some of the boys to pet her, though she had never run from them, as she had from Tem-aki and GEA-4.

Other than being given the scarf, what had changed, since he had gone up the cliff to speak to Annosha?

Stranger still, there was no candle and the odd, dull light was coming from the skull. Clutching the scarf, as if it was a life-line, he stumbled backward, unwilling for them to see how confused and useless he felt.

~o~

"If my calculations are correct," Larwin said, as he smacked his tricorder, "and I believe they are," Larwin cleared his throat, "then GEA-4 and Tem-aki's location seems to be on the opposite side of this planet."

Nimri looked to her right at Thunder and Raine, who looked

as confused as she felt. "Does that give you a clue how they got there or how they can come back?

He shook his head.

"What is the surface of this planet like?" Raine asked. "I mean, obviously, it is very different from Kalamar."

Larwin looked at Thunder. "You didn't go high enough to see Sacred Mountain, but did you go high enough to get an idea of how many land masses there might be between here and there?"

It was Thunder's turn to clear his throat. "As I said, all I saw was the one island in the center of water as far as I could see. Assuming you are correct and they are on this planet, I have no idea which direction I could have gone to return here without the skull."

"Interesting," Larwin said.

Yes, 'interesting' was the word, Nimri thought.

Larwin closed his eyes in thought for a moment. "Okay, how about this: next time the skull allows us, one of you crosses over there, then soars upward from there, while the other one soars from here. Once you get high enough, you should be able to see each other."

"Like the view from my ship," Raine said with a nod. "He's right, if you can go high enough you should eventually be able to see one another." She frowned and looked from one to the other. "Can you really go that high without a spaceship?"

"You saw Kazza," Thunder said.

"Well, yes, but -"

"He is a cat?" Nimri asked. Raine nodded. "His flesh and blood body breathes air, just like you and me. And, like us, his myst-form doesn't need that, nor does gravity hold it." She turned her attention to Larwin. "I am willing to do this."

"As am I," Thunder said, with a decisive nod.

~o~

"Our body, mind and spirit continue to move toward balance, yet we often have too much outer stimulus and noise and not enough time to dedicate to ourselves, which prevents us from achieving a better state of harmony," Annosha told Cameron, as she arranged her flowing emerald robe, so it would not flutter in the strengthening breeze, which caressed her patio.

Cameron nodded in agreement. "Sound helps get to the inner peace we all desire." Annosha smiled and nodded.

He took a breath to continue, but Annosha launched into a seemingly endless monologue about sound, which was something every initiate began learning on day one. He leaned back against the railing overlooking the harbor and his own patio. From this perspective, the novices looked like industrious golden bees. Cameron politely pretended to listen to her, as he tried to think of a valid reason to escape.

"Sound therapy treatment can be either passive or participatory. The passive aspect is that you become more relaxed by lying down and slowing your breath. By doing this, you prepare yourself to become the receiver of sound."

"I agree!" Cameron said, as he jumped to his feet, "but right now, I need to help with the preparations. Can we continue this discussion later?" He finally needed to pause for breath.

"Of course, of course, I need to oversee the balloon, too." Annosha rose to her feet, and though she continued speaking, she began walking toward her temple.

Cameron fled.

Dodging through the market, he glimpsed a familiar shade of gold. He abruptly turned toward the stall, intent upon finding out who was shirking their duty. If it was Varlet, he might have something practical that he could use to begin dismissal proceedings. For certain, he would look like a fool if the only tangible things he could point out were shifty eyes and thin, angry lips. It was infuriating how individuals, who were obviously unfit for leadership, still often managed to worm their way into positions of authority.

Late afternoon shoppers rushed to complete purchases, and he didn't catch another glimpse of gold for several paces. When he did, the individual's cowl covered its head and while he couldn't see the face, he realized whoever it was didn't appear to have overly wide shoulders, as Varlet did, nor was he tall or bony enough to be the chauvinist. Afraid that he might stumble on something that could implicate otherwise good novices like Emmet, Tristan or Benji, he started to leave. Just then, the figure turned and he recognized Tem-aki's profile.

Why had she come here?

This time of day, she always liked to head down to the beach. Come to think of it, she spent most of every day, rain or shine, down there.

The afternoon he'd seen her standing on the patio in the wind-driven rain, she had stared at the dark, rolling clouds as if the downpour was a miracle.

She had come from the water, too.

And, onboard the Sirocco, she had spent most of her time on deck, staring at the harbor.

Upon arrival at his home, she had made a beeline to the kitchen and stared at the running water system.

Was it his imagination, or was she focused on water?

Yet, now, as he watched her move from stall to stall, she didn't seem interested in anything offered for sale, with the possible exception of some inferior block prints depicting Khaleesi, who some believed was the Mother of Dragons. Cameron frowned and wondered if Tem-aki did not speak of anything important because he had always been taught the dragon-mother was Shaka-uma, not Khaleesi. She wouldn't close him out for such a trivial technicality! Would she?

Was the dragon-mother's name actually Khaleesi?

Had the dragons abandoned them and stopped nurturing the fields because somewhere back in time, someone used the wrong name?

Cameron swallowed and admitted to himself that he too might be offended if someone called him by another name. But surely, he wouldn't shun the person... unless, due to the incorrect name, he hadn't realized someone was addressing him.

Perspiration broke out on his brow and he vowed that at next prayer, he would use both names.

Tem-aki put aside the inferior print and picked up a map of their island.

Chapter 21

"If you believe you can't, then you never will. If you believe that you can, it becomes possible," Nimri yawned, as she murmured encouragement to herself. They had spent hours working out how they could try and locate Tem-aki's location, so between that and Mica's middle-of-the-night feeding, she was so tired that she was afraid she would fall asleep, as soon as she relaxed enough to free her myst-energy. "If you believe you can't, then you never will. If you believe that you can, it becomes possible," she whispered to herself, again, as she relaxed, so she could launch her myst-energy straight up into the morning sky.

Thunder had gone inside moments before, and would soon begin his part of the project.

She yawned so hard that her ears popped. And, she continued to yawn. Hopping up, she dashed over to her Ashwagandha plants and plucked several bright red berries. Nose wrinkled at their flavor, she quickly ate them, then grabbed a mint leaf to chew.

Feeling more energized, already, she wondered if the raw berries had actually worked that quickly or if she simply felt better because she had moved.

She suspected the latter, however, she didn't know how to

harness myst-energy when she was moving, so she sat down in the hatha position and again, began to relax her body. Though another yawn threatened, she was able to get beyond the desire, so soon her exhausted body had relaxed enough for the separation.

A glance at the window, far above her, assured her that the skull was still glowing, which would allow Thunder to make his jump. So, with no reason to stay, and every reason to get the information they needed, she allowed her myst-form to move straight upward.

The higher she rose, the cooler it got. Eventually, it was downright cold. And then, it got colder than she would have ever believed possible. Had she needed to breathe air into her lungs, she suspected she would have frozen from the inside out. She looked down and around, but only had a hint that the river was meeting something that might – or might not – be something other than land.

So, she moved even higher.

Then higher.

And higher.

Finally, she was so high, that she could no longer distinguish Sacred Mountain from the long range of mountains it stood in, and the river was only a thin dark line, which appeared to begin at an enormous, deep blue lake. But she knew the water flowed toward the big body of water, so obviously this was where all the water had actually gone, not where it was coming from.

How very curious.

And how extremely cold!

She looked for Thunder, but couldn't see him. Since she couldn't distinguish Sacred Mountain, this didn't surprise her. Nimri realized that her home-world now looked like a brown, green, white and blue ball suspended in black ink. It was a view of her home-world that she had not expected, but something that Larwin, Thunder and Raine had all seemed to expect her to see.

Looking down, Nimri followed their instructions and memorized how all the greens, browns and whites were shaped against the blues. Then, before she could lose the mental picture, she told herself, "Wake up."

The taste of mint infused her mouth and another yawn threatened, but before she could forget any of the information she had collected, she grabbed paper and ink and began drawing. When she was finished, she went inside to compare what she had seen to Thunder's observations.

To her dismay, aside from being round on the exterior, his drawing looked nothing like hers. In fact, if he'd gotten his colors correct, most of what he had seen was a glob of brownish green in the middle of what appeared to be mainly blue, while what she had seen had been more of an equal distribution of colors.

Seeing her expression, Thunder grinned, then grabbed one of Kazza's play-balls and began duplicating his sketch on its hard, wooden surface.

"Didn't you see any white?" she asked.

"Sure. Mostly here, and some here." He pointed to opposite sides of the ball. "Of course, there were also areas of cloud-cover, and those were mainly white, but since those are always changing, I didn't bother to put them down."

"Clouds?" Nimri blinked. "How could you tell they were clouds?"

He opened his mouth to answer, then got a strange look on his face. "I'm not sure, but I think that one might be a cloud." He pointed to a big, lumpy white crescent, which intersected all the other colors. "When you saw that, did you have the feeling that it was on top of the other colors?"

"Now that you mention it, yes." She quickly put a few dotted lines in, connecting the 'lower' colors. Then, she did the same with three other lumpy white areas. Soon, her sketch began to have a more defined feeling.

Larwin and Raine entered the dining room. He put four large mugs of rose-hip tea on the table, and sat down, while Raine, who had Mica in her arms, stayed on her feet. She moved to where she could look at the drawings and said, "So this confirms it, she is on this planet."

Nimri looked from her sketch to Thunder's. "It does?"

Raine nodded and using her free hand pointed. "See here and here?" Nimri nodded. "That is the same area, but it was drawn from the opposite perspective... Kinda like if two people painted you, but one person was looking at you from your right side and the other one was on your left... or, in this case, sort of half-way between facing you straight on and your left side."

Nimri narrowed her eyes and studied the two areas Raine had pointed at. Even though Larwin was nodding in agreement, she could not see how the two drawings were of the same area. Fortunately, she didn't need to understand this part, so she leaned back in her chair, sipped her tea and listened to the other three share ideas on how to get to where Tem-aki was. Raine referred to the location as an island. Larwin's finger frequently hovered over the large blue portions of Thunder's drawing. Nimri wondered if he was fascinated by the abundance of water in Tem-aki's location or if he was as bothered as she was by the difficulty of getting to her.

~o~

Cameron waited until Tem-aki left the shop, then, before it closed, dashed in for a closer look at that map that had held her attention. Frowning, he realized it wasn't even an accurate depiction of the land and currents, but then this map was designed more as a work of art than anything to navigate by.

When Cameron left without making a purchase, the proprietor closed the shop door with unnecessary force.

For a moment, he began following Tem-aki, then he thought about her apparent interest in maps, so he veered toward the harbor and took his dory out to The Sirocco, where he collected several charts of their land's surrounding water and one that was an accurate representation of their land. In fact, the only area where the map maker had put more emphasis on art than accuracy was Dragon Ridge, which looked more like a dragon sleeping, than the sheer escarpment that it was. Of course, since one of his order had made the map, Cameron understood why this one had been drawn that way. Making Dragon Ridge special was understandable, while drawing houses, fish, poultry and orchards on the one for sale was simply silly. So was the oversize boat drawn in the harbor.

Cameron paused by the deck's railing to look over the peaceful harbor-area. The dying rays of sunlight shimmered in a soft glow, but the water close to the cliff was already in shadow, so the homes and shops, which had been carved into the rock, already had candlelight shining from several windows, so the darker water was striped with many thin, bright, elongated reflections.

He never tired of this peaceful view, nor the sun's gentle benediction on another day.

Still, unless he decided to sleep aboard the Sirocco, he needed to paddle back to shore.

Cameron went to the kitchen area, where he securely wrapped the precious maps in oiled cloth, then he swung down the boarding ladder.

When he got back to shore, the market was closed, as were the doors for homes. He didn't see another person for a good quarter mile, and then, he heard the sound of rushed footsteps and saw a glimpse of dark robe rounding the corner of a mud-brick apartment building.

Shadows were deep when he passed an open window of the building, and though there was no candlelight inside, voices were raised. "Are we going to keep tolerating this?" a familiar voice demanded.

Cameron paused to listen.

"How much longer are we going to waste our time worshiping a figment of some historical figure's imagination?" Varlet demanded. Cameron's teeth clenched. "Do you know how desperate the dracos are to keep control?" Several voices made negative sounds. "Desperate enough for Draco O'Ryan to pretend to discover Draco Shakura's staff of power!" He paused dramatically, as a confusion of voices expressed outrage. "And that isn't all. While the brotherhood and I were preparing the ridge for the upcoming ceremony, he also discovered two females, which he wants us to believe are some form of divine beings."

There was another surge of noise, where Cameron could not identify individual speakers' voices or what they were saying, but the message was clear. Varlet needed to be cut from the order, and for a reason everyone could understand. Somehow, they also needed to find proof that the beliefs his brotherhood had followed for more than a thousand years were true. Obviously, his discovery of Tem-aki, GEA-4 and the staff were not enough to renew faltering faith, but having an initiate publicly state what Varlet had was equivalent to a wound developing a life-threatening infection.

Though Varlet was obviously speaking to a group, on some level, they knew they were wrong. Why else hadn't they lit candles? If they'd known they spoke the truth, they would do so in the light of day where they could see each other's faces.

Read the truth or lies in each other's body language.

Tempting as it was to march into the building and confront Varlet, he knew that accusing Varlet right now would be a bad choice.

And calling a hearing about this wouldn't work, either. Varlet Bledgood was nasty, but he wasn't stupid, so he would undoubtedly have one or more people who would give evidence and testimony in his favor and perhaps even claim that he, Cameron O'ryan, was making malicious accusations about Varlet.

For a moment, Cameron considered rushing to get Nolan and bring him back, but common sense told him that any tarring of reputation would work just as well for two as it did for one. He didn't need what would amount to hearsay, he needed tangible evidence.

Yet Varlet could even twist solid evidence, like Tem-aki, GEA-4 and the staff to create doubt. Though how the initiate had managed to turn those hopeful things against their order was something Cameron knew he would never understand.

There had to be a way to get the man to leave their order without creating more disruption. But how?

~o~

Tem-aki and GEA-4 stood side by side at the long table and watched Cameron roll out several old-fashioned charts, which looked worthy of a museum. When the ends tried to curl, he calmly weighed the woven paper down with two candles, a bowl of sweet beige granuals and finally, with nothing else nearby, the palm of his hand.

Then, with his free hand, he pointed at a spot of the chart, made sure they looked where he was pointing, then, he pointed at the floor.

Tem-aki nodded in understanding, despite the rough texture of the paper, and the fact that she could see how long, thin individual leaves had been woven to create the paper, she could also understand the simplistic lines of the coastline. In fact, the only surprising thing was the fact that Cameron's chart showed that water was on all sides of the landmass.

Confident that they understood him, Cameron went over to the cooking area, broke off a small piece of twig, then returned to the table and insinuated himself, so he was standing between them. Tem-aki put her right palm down to hold the corner he had abandoned, while he ceremoniously placed the small stick in the middle of the harbor-area. "Sirocco." He tapped the stick and pointed out the window to where she knew the actual boat was sitting in the harbor. "Sirocco."

She dutifully nodded, even though she wondered why he was explaining this as if he was speaking to a two-year-old.

Cameron smiled, and seemed to gain confidence. Then, he slowly moved the piece of wood out through the harbor entrance, which she knew was overlooked by the extinct volcano, then he continued moving it about a third of the way around the land mass, and into a smaller, almost perfectly round harbor. He started talking and gesturing far too fast for her to understand the words, but Tem-aki had the distinct impression he was talking about the harbor where she had first seen his boat. As if he had read her mind and wanted to make certain she understood him, Cameron began to walk backwards around the table.

"Do you know if he is trying to make a point?"

"Probabilities indicate affirmative, but I am uncertain what his objective is," GEA-4 said.

"He is talking about our voyage from the first place to here, right?"

"Probably."

Cameron stopped on the opposite side of the table and stared at them. "Why do you refuse to speak to me?" he asked, enunciating each syllable distinctly enough to Tem-aki to understand.

"Speak slower," she said, drawing out each word, as he had just done.

His brows shot up and he leaned forward. "Youthinkl speak toofast?" His words jumbled.

Tem-aki nodded.

"Sorry," he said slowly and carefully. Tem-aki smiled encouragement.

"Speak new language difficult," she admitted. "Am to learn." Cameron beamed at her, as if by simply talking to him, she had given him a wonderful gift. If that was all it took to make him happy, she would talk to him more often. Well, at least more often when the others were not around. Though they all dressed alike, their personalities were not the same, in fact, while she liked Cameron and felt that he was a very good and honorable person, some of his flock – or whatever they were called – were downright shifty.

As the wicks of the two candles burned lower, Cameron pointed to several parts of the chart and talked as much as the one called Annosha. Several times, he seemed to get excited about his topic and every time he did, his words would come out faster and faster. However, he also kept an eye on her expression, and apparently something in her face showed when she could no longer understand, so Cameron would stop talking for a moment, pause and begin speaking at a noticeably slower rate, only to pick up speed a few minutes later.

The outer door opened causing the candles to flicker. They all turned toward the foyer. Though Tem-aki was surprised to learn that anyone was out so late, she noticed that though Cameron's mouth flattened, he didn't seem surprised. Cameron straightened his spine and looked at the archway separating the eating area and the foyer. As three of the group passed it, on their way to the sleeping room, he said, "Varlet, Dirk, Malin... you're out late."

The tall thin one that despised her turned toward them. "What business is it of yours?"

"None whatsoever, as long as you are fit to perform your duty. I was merely making an observation," Cameron said.

The short one with acne and stringy hair, tried to hide behind the muscle-bound wide one that didn't look like he had a neck.

The tall one nodded, as if he'd proven something. It looked like he would continue on, then, his eyes narrowed and he moved toward them. "Why do you have the maps here?"

"Simply conferring with Tem-aki and GEA-4 about a few things. Since they are unfamiliar with our land, it was easier to explain things using the map."

"Those belong on The Sirocco."

"When we're under sail, yes, but there is no regulation stating they must stay there at all times." Cameron folded his arms across his stomach and tilted his head as he looked at the tall, nasty man. "Why do you seem so upset by this?"

"They disgust me."

"Why?"

"They're female."

"So is your mother."

Tem-aki wasn't sure what Cameron had said, but it made the angry one furious and the other two snicker.

"Leave my mother out of this."

"Fine, that still leaves half of the followers we minister to being female. You simply cannot ignore a gender."

"Then how come our faction has never had any female members? The females always join Annosha's sect and become priestesses. They should, too." The man was so enraged that he was spitting out each word. Worse, he kept glaring at her and GEA-4.

"If that is their choice, they are welcome to, but for some reason the creators sent them to me." Cameron put his hands palms upward and shrugged. "Would you have me defy the creators by rejecting their emissaries?"

The man was going to have a stroke if he got any angrier. Apparently, he realized that, because he turned on his heel and stormed out of sight. His two companions trailed after him like tails of a kite.

"Well, that was interesting," GEA-4 said. "Looks like they didn't like being put in their place."

"Did you understand what that was all about?" Tem-aki asked.

"Not completely, but it had to do with them not wanting us here."

"That is no surprise," Tem-aki said, "the tall one seemed to hate me on first sight."

"Varlet seems to hate all females and I suspect anyone in authority."

"Do you think his mother was a domineering woman?"

"One can only speculate," GEA-4 said.

Cameron cleared his throat, so they turned back to him and tried to follow his explanation for some plans he seemed to have for the madrox, which was drawn on the map.

Aside from Kalamar, she had never known anyone so obsessed with the vile creatures. Yet, on her first solo mission, both cultures she had encountered seemed obsessed with madrox. What hadn't her professors taught her about the beasts?

Chapter 22

Nimri stood at the window of her childhood room, which overlooked the distant river and used Larwin's magic binoculars to see how Raine's boat adaptation project was progressing.

Thus far, it didn't look very impressive.

In fact, Nimri wondered if Raine knew half as much about boats and boat building as she claimed. Did she really think that she could take two of the long, thin cargo canoes, which were used to carry loads of milk, cheese, butter and leather to market and build some sort of hut over them, which they could travel in to Tem-aki's island?

As she watched, two mules led by Larwin and Thunder pulled a cart load of the kind of giant bamboo, used to build barns, into the clearing and they began to unload it. Some of the townspeople used it for sheds, and while it was a lovely golden color, Nimri wondered why Raine would choose barn material.

If they managed to build a boat, she suspected it would sink before they got to the blue water, which would be upsetting, but survivable. If it sank in the blue water, it would probably mean sure death.

She shivered.

Bryta bustled into the room. "Oh, you surprised me. I thought you'd gone with the others."

Nimri turned from the window and shook her head. "No, my part of the project is collecting fabric and sewing a sail." She gestured to the pile of sheets by the chair.

"Do you need help with that?" Bryta asked.

Nimri gratefully nodded. "Always, you know how incompetent I am with a needle."

Though she could see how tempted Bryta was to comment on that, instead, she picked up the sheets she had begun sewing together.

"Raine said that a triangle shape is easiest to hold and control the wind."

Bryta's eyebrows both rose. "You plan to command the wind?"

Nimri shrugged. "I'm just quoting Raine." She gestured to the sketch and the length of yarn Raine had measured. "She color coded the drawing, so the longer up-down part needs to be finished the exact length of the red yarn and the blue yarn is what the bottom must be."

Bryta snorted. "Exactly?"

"It's what she said." Nimri put down the binoculars. "She also said the easiest way to get the high-pot-ten-use correct would be to sew a rectangle half the length of the red yarn on one side and the exact length of the blue one." Bryta's brows rose higher. Nimri shrugged. "I don't know what she meant, but Larwin seemed to think it was good advice, so what I've got so far is the blue, but I'm still working up to the red."

"Why half the length for the red?"

"Apparently, once that is done, I will need to measure halfway across one of the blue sides, down to one corner and then cut." She made a frustrated gesture. "It doesn't make sense."

"Perhaps it does, if you then sew the two pieces together."
Nimri frowned. Had Raine said anything about that?
Bryta's mouth puckered as she looked at Nimri's seam.
"Would you be offended if I added a few stitches?"
"Not at all." She'd been worrying about the gaps, too and
was grateful that Bryta cared enough to help. "In fact, I will
have a lot more faith in this working if you sewed it."

~o~

After morning meal, Cameron watched Tem-aki casually
move past the work tables on the patio, but today, instead
of heading down the stairs to the beach, she was going
toward the stairs to the town.
This was the second day in a row, that her pattern changed.
Had something that he was unaware of changed? Cameron
frowned, as he wondered why her destination bothered him.
Why did he feel the need to know where she was and what
she was doing?
"She's a beautiful woman," Nolan said quietly.
"That she is,"Cameron agreed.
"Traditionally, dracos were married, celibacy only became
popular in the past century."
"I know." Cameron turned to fully face his friend. "As you
know, my grandfather was a draco, as were several of my
ancestors. If they had not also been married with families, I
would not be here, today." He clasped his hands behind his
back. "Is there any reason why you feel the need to speak
about marriage?" Cameron arched a brow. "Are you
considering a relationship with one of our visitors?"
Nolan's eyes widened so much that the irises were
surrounded by white. "Me? No! I am quite happy with my
life." He lowered his voice, so no one else could hear. "But if
your family line is to continue having members in the order,
it might be something for you to consider."
Cameron took an involuntary step backward as he looked

left and right to make sure no one else was nearby. What he actually saw was Varlet following Tem-aki. He tilted his head toward the stairs, "Perhaps I'm not the one you should mention that to."

"You think he's interested in her?" Nolan shook his head. "Varlet has no interest in females."

"At least that is what he would have us believe."

Nolan laughed. "You think it's an act?"

"Would it be so unheard of for someone to pretend one thing, when the opposite is true?"

"Sadly, it would be quite typical, which is why our job is so difficult." Nolan ran his fingers through his thinning hair. "However, in this case, I am quite sure that he has no tender feelings for her. And I know for a fact that you are the only one her eyes search for."

Upon hearing those words, a warm feeling exploded in his core and a sense of buoyant optimism began to tickle his senses.

"Wonder why Varlet is following her," Nolan said.

"You think he is?"

"Don't you?" Nolan turned to face him, his expression grim. "That boy has a bad core."

Cameron nodded, "But he doesn't do anything we can actually dismiss him for." He signed. "Believe me, I've been looking for just cause to dismiss him and his two syncopates."

Nolan looked around the patio and his expression became perplexed.

"What's wrong?" Cameron asked.

"How often does Varlet do anything without Dirk and Malin there to bolster his confidence?"

"Never."

Nolan nodded. "Exactly."

Cameron turned his head so quickly that he felt a sharp

twinge in his neck. Nolan was correct, Malin and Dirk were each quietly painting an eye of the giant paper-mâché dragon head, which would be attached to a flexible, fabric body. Once done, the dragon would lead the parade, which began the Summer Solstice Ceremony.

"Without Varlet around, those two are decent workers," Nolan said.

"Always?"

Nolan shrugged. "This is the first time I've seen them without him around to influence them toward veiled contempt."

"That's exactly what he does, isn't it?"

Nolan nodded, then turned his attention toward the stairs to the town. "Are you going to follow them?"

"Do you think I need to for some reason?"

"He hates her. What if he decides to attack her?"

"Then I would pity him," Cameron said. Nolan blinked in surprise. "Remember me telling you that GEA-4 tossed me in the drink? Those two emissaries, or whatever they are, are much stronger than I am."

Nolan shook his head.

Cameron nodded.

~o~

Tem-aki felt a prickle at her back, as if someone was watching her. She tried to appear casual, as she entered the closest shop on her right. Once in, she quickly stepped into the darkest clump of shadows and turned, to look out the open doorway. Less than a minute later, the surly one hurried by, looking from left to right, as if searching for something.

Or someone.

Why was he following her?

The one called Varlet turned in a quick circle, his gaze searching the shadows and shop interiors. Ah, so he had just realized he'd lost track of her. Tem-aki forced herself to stand still. Few things attracted a predator's attention quicker than movement, so even when it felt as if his gaze was raking her, the only thing she did was close her eyes to slits, so light could not reflect off them.

He spun around two more times before heading in the original direction she had been wandering in.

She counted to fifty before she dared move a muscle. Turning, she realized that an ancient-looking woman was seated on a three-legged stool in the rear corner of the shop. Her tan, wrinkled face, knobby knuckles along with her worn fingernails suggested that most of her life had been spent doing hard, manual work outdoors, yet now, she was using her work-worn hands and a delicate hook to fashion ivory thread into beautiful lace. Actually looking around the shop for the first time, Tem-aki realized that all the items in it appeared to have been created in the same manner.

Fascinated, she watched the old woman's hands move, as if they were an expert dancer, meticulously performing a ballet. As if by magic, whatever the piece she was making grew in length.

She was creating something beautiful, with only the odd hook-thingy and thread.

Again, Tem-aki looked around the shop's interior and admired the flawless construction.

To think that these scarfs, shawls and blankets could actually be made without a factory!

She took a few steps closer and knelt down to better watch the amazing hands create the intricate-looking piece. The old woman's head raised and Tem-aki was given a beautiful smile and word of greeting. In that brief moment, she realized the old woman's eyes were white. Though she'd never actually seen cataracts, she'd studied about them in medical history.

Still, it was startling to actually see someone who suffered from the affliction.

If the old woman could create flawless beauty out of nearly nothing, and not even be able to see it, then she, Tem-aki Atano could and would find her brother by using the resources she had available. At the moment, that was GEA-4, the strange skull, a slate slab and a stick of homemade chalk, but those all gave Larwin information to come to her.

Was she some silly female that needed to be rescued?

No!

She was the female that had set out to rescue her brother, not vice-versa.

Tem-aki grimaced, then admitted to herself that she simply had not expected to actually find him alive, much less have so much water involved.

Was GEA-4 correct that Larwin could be at least two-thousand miles away?

Even if she learned to swim or found a way to replenish the air in her suit, she was sure she could neither swim nor walk that distance.

The pattern the old woman was making in the center of the scarf, or whatever she was making, reminded Tem-aki of the round wheel Cameron had used to steer Sirocco. As she stared at it, she realized that her best option for reaching Larwin was to learn to speak Cameron's language well enough to ask for his help.

Choice made, she rose to her feet, adjusted her robe and went to the door. After a careful check, during which she didn't see any golden robe, she turned back toward Cameron's home, determined to learn to communicate with him as quickly as possible.

~o~

Nimri watched Raine and Thunder position a grid of the

large structural bamboo over the two long canoes so the entire project became a long rectangle, which had canoe-type foundations on the long sides. Then, they began laying thin, sturdy reeds on top of this, which apparently would be a floor.

Instead of having the sides of a boat to hang onto, did they expect passengers to ride on top of that flat surface, where they would bake in the sun and get soaked with rain? And just how did they plan to use the fabric they had entrusted her to sew? Was her part of the project even necessary?

She turned the binoculars to Larwin's face, and saw barely veiled excitement and anticipation. When you loved someone, it wasn't easy to accept some of the things they wanted. While Nimri applauded and supported his desire to be reunited with his sister, she didn't know if she would ever be happy about the proposed method of getting to her.

Mica began to fuss. Nimri put down Larwin's magical glasses and picked up her son. "Did you think you were being ignored?"

Mica gurgled and kicked his feet.

"I'm sorry you felt that way. I love you and always hope to be here for you. Your daddy loves you, too... He also loves his sister, that's your Aunt Tem-aki. Do you realize how special love is? Did you know that distance doesn't matter if you really love someone?... What matters is trust for that relationship to work out."

Mica cooed, as if he understood. Unfortunately, he didn't understand how dangerous the thing was that his father wanted to do. Yes, Larwin might find his sister, but what if he couldn't find his way home, afterward?

Nimri's eyes swam with tears.

Until this moment, she had considered making the trip with them, but now, she realized it would be impossible to take Mica on such a journey, and, to be honest, she dreaded the thought of being on a boat, particularly for the length of time it would probably take to get to wherever Tem-aki was at.

She also dreaded the thought of being separated from Larwin and the reality that if something happened to the flimsy wood and bamboo boat, she could lose not only her mate, but her brother. Her arms tightened protectively around Mica.

She wasn't sure what she could do to protect them on what Larwin called a mission and Thunder called an adventure, but if there was a way to protect them, and still protect Mica, she vowed to find it.

Chapter 23

Understanding poured into Tem-aki's mind, then GEA-4 removed her hands and the mind-meld was abruptly over.

Tem-aki straightened. "Let us hope this update is enough to finally begin serious conversation."

"I will continue to monitor their speech patterns and add to the program."

"Thank you." She wiped her damp palms on her robe, then headed out the door to test her new vocabulary on Cameron. Tem-aki found him watching the group that had been making paper bags. To her surprise, instead of putting things in the bags, they were using string to tie a small candle onto each bag's open end. As she watched, the freckled one lit a candle, while another carefully held the bag open, so that the heat and smoke went into it.

Why in the world were they doing that?

As she watched, the bag seemed to fill out. Cameron nodded to the one holding the bag and he let go. There was a chorus of 'ohs' as the bag hovered in the air, then began to drift toward the sky.

Heat rose, while cold settled, so on the physics front, what she'd just watched made sense. But it certainly didn't make any logical sense. Why in the world did they want empty bags in the air?

Tem-aki moved next to Cameron, whose attention was on what she could only call a poor excuse for a balloon. Still, she had to admit that it did look rather pretty as it sailed out over the harbor-area.

When Cameron noticed her, he smiled. "Can you imagine when we release hundreds at midnight?"

She blinked, half surprised by his question and half because she had understood it. Apparently, GEA-4 had finally figured out the language.

Tem-aki smiled. "Beautiful."

Cameron looked like she had given him a medal. "I'm so glad you approve. At first, I wondered why you were not participating in making the decorations, then I realized that you were here to see how well we would do, not do it for us."

Tem-aki understood the words, but not his meaning. Who did he think she was? Did the women supervise the men on this world? Was that what Annosha did, when she came to visit? Tem-aki focused on the word decorations, which seemed to mean that all this activity was about creating ornamental things. On Guerreterre, that sort of thing was mainly used for special ceremonies, which made sense, and could explain what he had tried to explain to her using the old-fashioned maps. She cleared her throat and asked, "These are for dragon ridge?"

"Absolutely! And, I assure you that everything will be ready to take there by the end of the week."

She smiled and nodded. "This is very special?"

He took her hand and squeezed it. "You know it is and your presence makes it more so."

That was nice of him to say. And it felt nice to hold his hand, too. "Tell me about all your plans."

"Again?"

Ah, so he had told her, before. She'd suspected as much. "Yes, please, but while you do, can we walk by the water, or do you need to be here?"

He waved to the nice gray haired man. "Nolan, you're in charge." He caressed her palm with his thumb. "I'm all yours."

She liked the sound of that so much that she couldn't help smiling, even though she knew he didn't mean it the way her daydreams wanted to take it. When they reached the top of the stairs, he let go of her fingers. Was that reluctance she had felt? Regardless, they both needed their hands to hold onto the rails, as they descended the steep steps.

They were silent while they went downward, but once they reached the sand and kicked off their sandals, his fingers found hers. "What do you want to know that requires such privacy?"

"I simply prefer to be here. But please tell me about your Summer Solstice Ceremony and why you go halfway across your island for this celebration."

"Don't you know?"

"I would prefer to hear what you think."

For a moment, Cameron seemed to be at a loss for words, then, as they slowly strolled along the still-wet sand, he began to speak. "As you know, we revere the dragons, partly because they represent fire." With his free hand, he gestured toward the cone-shaped mountain at the harbor entrance. "Fire built this island. Now, fire protects us when it burns out poisons and fire feeds us when we are hungry... Is there something you think we should worship instead?"

"Not at all. I just wanted to hear your thoughts in your own words."

"Do you worship fire?"

She blinked in surprise. "Not really."

"Dragons?"

She shook her head.

He stopped dead in his tracks. "Then what do you worship?"

Her gaze traveled across the harbor, to where the Sirocco was moored. "I don't know if worship is the correct word, but family is the most important thing to me."

"Family is a good thing." He seemed to be thinking hard. She waited, and after several moments he asked, "Do you not participate in the Solstice preparations because you believe our beliefs are wrong?"

"What is important to you is important to you, and that is good." She tilted her head to look up at him. "If something feels right in your heart, do you always ask others to confirm its value?"

"Others do not come from the creators."

"I beg your pardon?"

"Others do not come from the creators." She motioned him to continue. "Never before, in the entire history of my faction, have the creators sent an emissary, yet they sent you and GEA-4 to me while I was in the Protected Place. And, so there could be no mistake about who you were, you brought the lost Staff of Power." He raised his hand and touched her hair. "Of course, with your golden hair, I would have known."

"You think I'm a creator?" She shook her head. "I am as human as you are."

He paused for a moment, then shrugged. "At least you were sent by them."

If creators existed and one had sent her here, would he or she have explained it to her, or would they decide this was where she needed to be and send her plummeting through whatever she had fallen through to get her where they wanted her? She swallowed. "Tell me about how you got here."

"I was born here."

"Okay, tell me how your people got here." Had they, too felt as if the floor gave way beneath them and were hurled through solid rock, only to land at the bottom of an unknown sea?

"Our history began on Solterre," he began.

Tem-aki felt her eyes widen in surprise to learn his people came from the same world hers had. "How long ago?"

"Summer Solstice is in ten days and that will mark the end of the thirteenth eighty-two-year cycle."

"So 1066 years."

"Since Draco Shakura and his followers came through the Star Bridge, yes." His eyes narrowed. "Are you testing me? It is well known that the end/beginning of a cycle is a particularly special time, but never have the creators sent an emissary before."

Again, he was back to the creator thing. Though Tem-aki's tongue itched to correct him, she also needed his help to find Larwin, and it seemed much more likely that he would do what she asked, if he continued to believe she was some sort of supernatural being. Though why something as powerful as a creator would need the help of a man, was a question she didn't think it was wise to ask. Tem-aki bit her tongue.

"We were forced to leave because the dragons, which we worshiped, had overpopulated Sanyima and this made it unstable."

Though she had never heard of Sanyima, the rest of his story sounded somewhat familiar. "And the ones who came here were dracos?" She went over to a big rock and sat down so she was looking out to sea.

"Our group was part of many faiths, but soon after coming through the magical portal, Shaka-uma, who you might call

Khaleesi, followed." Cameron frowned. "When the other faiths tried to kill Shaka-uma and her mate, they fled and we followed."

"Your people followed dragons?" She asked, certain that she had misunderstood, but he nodded. Tem-aki was glad that she was already sitting down.

How many cultures, aside from Cameron's and Raine's, didn't have the sense to run away from the toxic things? She could understand how Raine had become a dragon herder to harvest a resource, but she was still uncertain how their scientists had discovered that madrox had anything worth harvesting.

And now, Cameron was sitting next to her, looking and acting sensible, while telling her that his people had worshiped the things for over a millennium.

Tem-aki licked the salt from her lips and wondered what to say.

~o~

"If you believe that you can, it becomes possible," Larwin said, as he entered the kitchen. Though he looked sweaty and windblown, there was a bounce in his step. "Thunder and Raine believed we could build a boat to get to the coordinates, and we have."

"But you only began two days ago," Nimri said. While she was pleased that Larwin had apparently adopted one of her pet phrases, she wondered how they could have the project done so quickly. The first day all they had managed to do was make a plan and begin collecting things. Yesterday, they had assembled a floor over two old boats. And now the project was done?

Impossible.

Larwin nodded. "Once word got out about Tem-aki and the project, everyone pitched in. Last night, Reed and some others spent the entire night making the hulls water-tight and adding the mast, as well as a retractable keel and rudder." Nimri blinked rapidly and wondered what those things were. "This morning, when we got there, we could hardly believe how far they'd gotten. And if that wasn't great enough, a group from this side heard that Reed and some others had come over to help, so this side of the river decided they had to pitch in, too." He shook his head in wonder. "It was amazing! When I rounded the corner, the boat wasn't there. It was floating at the dock and a wall was being raised by one group and Raine was rigging Bryta's sail." He snagged an oatmeal-raisin cookie. Before popping it in his mouth, he added, "Now, all that needs doing is to load supplies, but somehow I suspect that might be done by morning, so we might be able to leave first thing."

Nimri sat down with a thump. "Tomorrow?" She winced as she heard the tell-tale squeak of fear. "You leave tomorrow?"

He gave her a confused look. "Yes, I think we should be able to leave tomorrow. So after dinner, we need to pack the things we'll need. Aside from bedding and at least one change of clothes, I think it would be wise to bring the skull and the staff. What do you think?"

"I think this sounds dangerous. And I'm not sure I want to go." Tears threatened to choke her. "I am also afraid not to go. Who will protect you, if I'm not there? But who will protect Mica if I leave him here?" A tear rolled down her cheek.

"Oh, honey!" Larwin said as he wrapped her in a hug. "I love you too, but you don't need to choose between me and Mica. You both can come."

And have their entire family drown? Nightmare memories from her childhood, when her family had tried something similar – and lost – filled her mind. She cried harder. "I'm afraid."

"And you have every right to be." Larwin hugged her tight. "I am too and I promise that if it looks too dangerous when we get to where the river becomes the ocean, I will turn back."

"Seriously? You promise?" She leaned back to look him in the eye.

Larwin solemnly nodded. "Cross my heart and hope-"

Nimri put her fingers over his mouth. "I don't know why you like that phrase, but please do not say it, especially when there is a very real possibility that you could drown."

He kissed her fingertips. "Bryta and Coral had begun packing the craft when I left. That's why I figure we can leave first thing in the morning."

"And you promise me that if I come and if it looks too dangerous when we get to the big water, we will come back." Larwin nodded. Nimri took a deep breath, then exhaled. "Okay, I will go to the big water before I decide." She wiped her eyes. "You really think it is safe to bring Mica?"

Larwin nodded. "Perhaps not if he was walking, and he could fall overboard, but this age, yes."

"If he was old enough to walk, he'd be old enough to know how to swim to shore, if the boat sank," Nimri said defensively. Her heart slammed against her ribs, as if it was a wild beast trying to break free of a trap.

"Rolf is not here to brew up a storm to attack us." He took her hand and traced her palm with his thumb. "What happened to your parents is past. Don't let it affect you."

"That is easy for you to say. You've had years and years of training that taught you how to handle all sorts of things." She sniffed.

"True, but I admit that I'm afraid of this. Guerreterre didn't have a lot of water, so while I love being able to swim, I'm also a little afraid."

"Seriously?" He nodded. Somehow, knowing she wasn't the

only one with fears made it easier. "Fine, we'll protect each other."

"And we'll both protect Mica."

She wrapped her arms around him in a crushing hug. "If things go as well as Raine seems to think, we'll be able to rescue Tem-aki and that would be wonderful." Silently, she reminded herself to keep her thoughts positive. If I believe I can, it becomes possible. Surely, with the support of Larwin and Thunder, and the Staff of Power, they would be able to rescue Tem-aki, so she needed to begin thinking about how wonderful it would be for Larwin to have his sister nearby.

Chapter 24

Tem-aki and Cameron sat on the rock until the moon rose and the water began to lap against their toes. Cameron looked up at the sky, where stars were beginning to shine. "I think we missed evening meal." He stood up and stretched. "We'd better get back before anyone misses us, or starts rumors about where we've been and what we've been doing."

It took her a moment to understand that he was suggesting that the others might suspect they were having some sort of romantic liaison, instead of sitting on a rock, in view of anyone who wanted to look down at the beach. He hadn't held her hand as they told each other about their families and shared their beliefs, but now, he reached for her hand and helped steady her as they walked to the stairs. Then, he motioned her to go first.

Halfway up, it felt as if the entire stairway heaved and rolled. With a startled shriek, she dug her fingernails into the railing and held on tight. Behind her, Cameron was beseeching someone to protect them.

As suddenly as it began, the movement quit.

Heart slamming, Tem-aki turned to look down at Cameron. "I should have realized this island was seismically active."

"What?"

Forcing herself to relax her grip, she gestured to the distant cone-shaped mountain. "Volcanoes are generally found near fault lines, which are known to be unstable."

Cameron stared up at her. "Volcanoes? Fault lines? Seismically active?" He shook his head. "I don't understand, but can we get off these stairs?"

"Of course." Tem-aki turned and hurried upward. "I should have remembered about the aftershocks."

"Aftershocks?"

When she got to the flagstone-covered patio, she rushed to a chair near the center of the open area. After all, an earthquake could destabilize things, so it was best to stay away from the railing overlooking the ocean as well as the sheer cliff-face above the depression Cameron's home was constructed in.

A moment later, GEA-4 came outside. "That was a four point six," she said in Cameron's language. She then focused on him. "How often do you get earthquakes?"

"Never," he said. GEA-4 tilted her head to the side. Cameron shifted his feet, then added, "Not since I was a child."

"Interesting," GEA-4 said.

"Earthquakes tend to occur in groups, as the ground makes large and small moves," Tem-aki said.

"You know about these things?" Cameron asked in surprise. "Never mind, of course you do."

"I am a geologist, which means I study of rocks," Tem-aki said, mixing words from her native speech in with Cameron's language. "Earthquakes happen when rocks move, so while earthquakes have never been a primary interest, they are part of my knowledge-base."

"When I was young, the ground shook several times over four or five days. Many of the mud-brick structures fell down, hurting the people inside."

"Were you injured?"

He shook his head. "We were out in our boat, fishing and didn't even realize anything horrible had happened until we got back to shore."

"Lucky for you."

"Not really. My father is a fisherman, and he goes out for days at a time."

"That's why you said your father was never around much." Cameron nodded.

"Pressure in the earth can build up over a long time..." She felt her feet tremble and knew she was feeling an aftershock. "And right now, is a fine example of what I meant about how there is usually a series of earthquakes. The first one is usually a reaction to pressure – either increased pressure or decreased pressure – which causes some rocks to move."

"All earthquakes are a reaction to pressure," GEA-4 said. "But after the first, many consider the later ones to be reactions to the reaction. Another type of reaction is a tsunami."

"Right, I read about that," Tem-aki said.

"What is a sue-nom-eee?" Cameron asked.

"A tidal wave, which can be created when water displaces ground," GEA-4 said.

"So the second ones are always less," Cameron said.

"Not always, but usually," Tem-aki said.

"Too bad we don't know which area had changes."

"On the map, you called the epicenter Dragon Ridge," GEA-4 said.

"How could you know that?" Cameron said, then looked at the stars. "Never mind, I understand."

"Isn't that the area your group was working at, when we met?" Tem-aki asked. Cameron nodded. "Could anything they did have caused a pressure change?" She considered the fact that GEA-4 was the only one, who had come outside very suspicious.

"I don't know, but I intend to find out." With that, he turned and stalked inside.

~o~

Cameron tried to control his temper as he entered the sleeping room and realized that everyone was asleep in their hammocks.

How could they have slept through the earth moving?

Even as he wondered, he realized that if the hammocks could minimize the movement Sirocco made in a bad storm, and allow them to rest, the design would also allow undisturbed sleep if the land moved.

He stood in the doorway, wondering what to do. If there was another aftershock, did he want to sleep through it? Even if he tried to get into his hammock to sleep, after the evening he had just had, and the things he had learned, could he relax enough to sleep?

Learning that Larwin was Tem-aki's brother had made his heart leap in delight in much the same way as it had later leapt in dread when he felt the earth beneath his feet move.

Nolan quietly rose, put on his robe, approached him and then whispered, "Can't sleep?"

Cameron shook his head, then gestured for Nolan to accompany him back outside. Once there, they settled onto seats near the middle of the patio, where he had left Tem-aki and GEA-4. One glance assured him that they were now inside, looking into the glowing skull. Turning to Nolan, Cameron told him everything that Tem-aki had told him, then shared how afraid he had felt during the earthquake. He concluded by asking, "You were at Dragon Ridge. Do you think there is any possibility that something we did could have caused the earth to move?"

"All we did was clear the paths, rake the leaves and pile dead branches for the bonfire." Nolan stretched his neck, causing it to crack and pop. "We didn't take any fireworks and even if we had, I don't see how they could make enough of a bang to be felt here."

"That's what I figured, too."

"So what are you really worried about? That it might have shaken down more deadfall or something?"

"Actually, I hadn't thought about that, but obviously, that could have happened." It was difficult to admit, but keeping his worries inside would be even worse. Cameron cleared his throat. "It's the unknown."

"That is always difficult," Nolan agreed. "In fact, it wouldn't surprise me to find out it was everyone's greatest fear."

"Seriously?"

Nolan nodded. "It is a major reason why I refused to accept the blue cowl."

"You would have made a better high draco than me."

"I don't think so."

"I do."

"That is only because you are having doubts and your thoughts are scattered."

"Are they?"

Nolan snorted. "You are trying to organize the Solstice Ceremony, yet; you have idiots like Varlet to worry about and if that isn't bad enough, you are constantly told by some that the old ways should be ignored. They don't realize that profit and possessions aren't particularly valuable things."

"True. If I'd thought about it, I would have passed on the cowl, too."

"Varlet was third in line."

"Why do you think I accepted?"

Nolan leaned back and crossed his ankles. "If he'd been

second, I would have accepted, too. I can't see anyone besides one of us having the faith or temperament to be draco. Can you?"

Cameron shook his head.

"For the sake of the order, I'm glad you accepted." Nolan cleared his throat. "I'm just hoping that the choice is as good for you, as an individual, as it is for the rest of us."

"What is that supposed to mean?"

Nolan gave the window where Tem-aki was leaning close to the skull a pointed look. "I know your thoughts and concerns are scattered, but when you told me who Larwin was to her, your entire demeanor changed. It is possible that the creators sent them to aid all of us, but have you ever thought that she only came here for you?"

If he hadn't already been seated, he would have needed to sit down. Could Nolan be correct? If she was here for him, it explained why she felt 'family' was more important than most anything else. And, it could explain why she seemed to know quite a bit about dragons, yet did not seem to completely understand his obligations as the sect's leader. Strange, though, that she seemed to view reverence for the bringers of fire and fertility as a curious thing to venerate.

Did the creators want him to have a family other than the order?

His fingers touched his palm as he remembered how right it felt to hold her hand.

Nolan might have something with this idea. He would think on this some more, but not now. Now, they needed to decide what to do about GEA-4's prediction that the earthquake's center was at or near Dragon Ridge. "I think we need to send someone to Dragon Ridge to make sure that it didn't damage the area."

"Anyone in particular?" Nolan asked.

"Anyone other than Varlet, Malin or Dirk," Cameron

whispered, worried that one of them might take the opportunity to create problems – assuming the earthquake's cause hadn't been the result of something they had done. He hated to think that about anyone, particularly someone within the order, but that trio kept offering veiled proof that they wanted to undermine the brotherhood.

Nolan nodded in understanding. "Better to keep an eye on them."

~o~

As Larwin helped her aboard the boat, Nimri felt as if a frantic ball of beating wings was in her stomach. But, when she realized that the golden bamboo mat beneath her feet felt as stable as the dock, most of her anxiety vanished. Next, Larwin handed her Mica's basket, then the staff of power and then the summoning skull, which was packed in a carry-basket like Mica. After she put them in the shelter of the structure on the back portion of the strange boat, he directed her to sit on a swing-chair near the long stick, which he had called 'tiller'. Larwin seemed excited about the tall, straight pine trunk, which he called 'mast' and the long horizontal piece attached to it, which he called 'boom'. What interested Nimri about the boom was that the sheets she and Bryta had sewn together were tied to it along with a woven rope, which appeared to come from the top of the mast.

As her gaze wandered over everything they had created in such a short period of time, she noticed more woven ropes going from the top of the mast, to other parts of the boat, but when she asked what they were for, Larwin's reply was, "They are called lines, not ropes and they are to hold the mast steady."

Nimri scratched her head over why ropes needed to have a new name, just because they had designed a new model of boat, but now, when the last bits were being loaded, was not the time to ask. Instead, she did her best to keep out of the way while Larwin and Thunder put bags and baskets of food on the deck for Raine, Coral and Reed to put away. To Nimri's amazement, they picked up several parts of the deck and put the food under the floor, instead of in the sheltered portion near the tiller.

As she watched, she realized that in addition to putting things below the deck, they also seemed to be somehow balancing the weight, which apparently affected how level the deck was. Obviously, those three had a lot more experience doing this than she could have imagined.

Once the last basket was secure, they put the pieces of deck back in place and even though she squinted, she couldn't see where the lids were.

Amazing.

But what was even more amazing, by the time she finished scrutinizing the decking, Thunder was pulling her sail to the top of the mast with the rope and she realized they were already in the middle of the river, moving toward the rising sun.

It didn't feel like they were traveling, but it certainly looked like the banks on either side were moving.

The movement was peaceful.

With surprise, she realized she could learn to like being on a boat. Relaxing on the gently swinging seat, she watched the shore slip by and realized that they actually might be able to rescue Tem-aki.

It would be wonderful to have a sister...

~o~

Tem-aki watched the two nicest ones put on backpacks and head for where GEA-4 had calculated the epicenter of the previous day's quakes to be. She had tried to caution Nolan about the potential for more quakes and how she felt that things should be given time to stabilize, but he had merely smiled at her, as she imagined a loving grand-father would, and patted her hand in an oddly comforting way.

Now, she looked at Cameron, to see if he would stop them, but all he did was wish them safe journey. Her eyes narrowed and her tongue itched to say something, but then she remembered all the years when family month was over and they all had to part to resume their individual roles. Was what Nolan and the boys were doing that much different than the way things functioned on Guerreterre?

She sighed and realized that aside from rustic clothing and lack of technology, they were very similar and each of them was doing what he thought he needed to do.

Cameron could accept that.

She needed to accept it, too.

And maybe, she needed to learn to accept Larwin's loss. Learn to be grateful that she could occasionally catch hazy glimpses of him in the skull. After all, he had lived far longer than most in his graduating class, and one of her most vivid memories from her childhood was overhearing her parents talk about how grateful they were that her talents had been in the area of science, not warfare. For a long time, she had secretly thought she was better than her brother, but as she grew older and realized how dangerous being a Stardust Warrior was, she understood that her parents were relieved to know she was safer.

Yet in a way, being a geologist had landed her in the same situation as her warrior brother. What were the odds of that happening?

Tem-aki followed Cameron outside and listened to him direct the novices. "Work fast, but still take as much time as you need to do it right the first time." He concluded, "Everything must be ready in ten days."

"Is there anything I can do to help?" she asked.

His gaze raked the tables before he shook his head.

"Sorry."

She nodded in understanding.

Just as she had turned to head for the beach, she heard a familiar voice call, "Good Morning Draco Cameron."

His hand closed on her upper arm. "On second thought, could you keep Annosha occupied?"

"Of course." With a smile of welcome pasted on her lips, Tem-aki reversed direction and went to meet the woman she had often wondered about.

Chapter 25

Until she set foot on the stable deck of the craft Raine had designed, Nimri had felt sorry for her having to spend the majority of her life living on Kalamar. Now, she realized that with ingenuity and a bit of work, even living on water could be comfortable.

In fact, sailing down the river was not only interesting, it was peaceful.

Kazza sprawled on the open front deck, which Raine called 'the bow' and promptly went to sleep.

Though she had imagined taking a boat on this large downriver would be a lot of hard work, with everyone paddling and working hard to make any progress, very little work seemed to be involved. At least as long as they were moving with the current and had a bit of a boost by the wind.

For the first time since she'd set foot on board, Nimri wondered if it would be possible to get the boat back upstream. Clearing her throat, she asked Raine.

"It would be faster and easier with a motor, but it's possible using only wind power."

Since she seemed confident, Nimri was able to relax. "Thanks. I'm wary of boats."

"Because of when you were young." Raine nodded. "Thunder told me." She visibly shivered. "I can't imagine how horrible that was, or having to grow up with some horrid old man."

Nimri swallowed and wondered how much Thunder had told Raine, then realized that it didn't matter. Both of their tribes knew what Rolf had done, why shouldn't Raine, who was probably going to become Thunder's mate, know?

~o~

A hand clamped around Cameron's bicep and spun him around. Instinctively, he went into a defensive posture.

"Relax," Nolan said, "And walk with me."

"I didn't expect you back until tomorrow."

"We wouldn't have been, if we could have taken care of everything by ourselves."

Cameron stopped walking. "How bad is it?"

"Do you know the clearing where we always hold the ceremonies?"

"Of course." Cameron narrowed his eyes. "Why wouldn't I know that? Everyone knows where the top of Shaka-uma's head is where we hold the ceremonies."

"Well, it's no longer there."

"What do you mean, 'it's no longer there'?"

"Exactly that. In fact, most of Dragon Ridge has collapsed into a crevasse."

"That's impossible."

Nolan shook his head. "The facts say differently." He looked around the patio, then pulled Cameron over to the bench overlooking the sea. "We don't have enough manpower to clear it before the solstice. So, we need to consider alternatives."

"Like what?"

"Like maybe at the shore. There was minimal damage there." Nolan looked earnest as he rested his elbows on his knees. "Since this is a special year, we could claim it needed to be held at a special place... as close as possible to where Shaka-uma originally nested."

"Do you really think it's a good idea to have a crowd that includes non-believers that close to the Protected Place?"

"No, and I'm not so sure about having them that close to the hot, thin areas, either, but I figured that if three or four of us started tomorrow, we would have time to rope off the dangerous areas and somehow camouflage the Protected Place."

"If you think that's our best option, then do it." Cameron glanced around the patio. "To haul that much rope, you'll either need pack mules or to load The Sirocco."

Nolan's expression brightened. "Four of us could manage The Sirocco, but are you sure about that?"

"Can you think of a better option to meet the deadline?"

Nolan shook his head. "No one but the high draco has ever captained it."

"Have we ever been forced to relocate where the festival would take place?" Nolan shook his head. Cameron raised a brow. "I cannot be in two places at once, and we'll be doing good to move all the supplies necessary and get set up if you take the ship... Do you think we could meet the schedule if you didn't take her?" Again, Nolan shook his head. Cameron nodded. "It isn't as if you don't know how to handle her, so why should I be the only one allowed. It isn't as if you would be taking her just for the fun of it."

"Fine, I'll do it, but realize, people will talk."

"They always do."

Nolan rose, "Well, I'd better get started collecting and loading materials." He rushed away.

Voices were raised at one of the tables. A glance verified that Varlet was trying to bully them into doing things his way. Cameron sighed. Sooner or later, he needed to find a solution for the problem Varlet's attitude was causing, but right now, Tem-aki was moving toward him with a purposeful attitude. "I need to ask a favor."

Cameron motioned for her to continue.

"You are sending Nolan and some others back to where we were." Cameron inclined his head, as he wondered what she was getting at. "I would like to go with him."

Surprise ricocheted through him. "Why? I didn't think you liked sailing."

She made an odd gesture with her hand. "I don't, but the place interests me. I'm a geologist and there was some really strange stuff there. If you don't think I'd be in the way, I would like to go and study it."

"Who am I to tell you what you may and may not do?"

"So you agree?" She asked, as if she needed the approval of a mere mortal.

Cameron ran his hand through his hair. "Who am I to stop you?"

Tem-aki blinked, as if surprised by the thought. "Well, good, then." She bit her lower lip. "Would you mind if GEA-4 came with me?"

Cameron exhaled in frustration. "I have no say over her, either, so why ask?" Varlet's voice was getting louder and the tone more dictatorial. "Look, do whatever it is you and GEA-4 think you need to do. I have other things I need to deal with." He turned his back on her and hurried over to where Varlet was holding a knife in a menacing way, while Tristan and Emmet stood shoulder to shoulder and glared at him. Malin's eyes shifted to Varlet.

"Is there a problem here?" Cameron asked.

"No!" Varlet snarled.

"Yes," Emmet said.

"Interesting," Cameron said. "But this won't settle anything." He deftly snatched the knife out of Varlet's hand. "Since you aren't having a problem, get back to work on the candles, while I have a chat with this pair." He put a hand on Tristan's shoulder and the other on Emmet's. "Walk with me." Malin snickered as they walked away.

"You shouldn't have interfered," Tristan growled. "That blowfly needs to understand that he isn't the dragon's gift to mankind."

"I am sure he will learn soon enough, but it isn't your job to teach him."

"Then why are you punishing us?"

Emmet silently chewed his upper lip, but apparently he also considered their 'chat' to be punishment. Dealing with Varlet head-on was a waste of time, which he didn't have the luxury to spend. Worse, it was an exercise in frustration, but Cameron couldn't explain that to them. "I need your help with a bigger problem."

"What could possibly be bigger -"

"Or worse," Emmet interrupted.

"- than Varlet?" Tristan concluded.

Cameron told them about the earthquake's destruction and the need for him to split the novices into two groups in order to pull off the celebration. "Nolan is going to need the best help possible. Can you do it?"

They nodded vigorously. "Will Benji be going back with Nolan, too?"

"Yes."

"So you're sending all the best workers there."

Cameron nodded.

"But what if we aren't finished in time?" Tristan asked.

"A few hundred less candles won't make as big a difference as having someone step on a thin crust of lava and fall to their death," Cameron said. Their eyes went round at the thought, but they also seemed to finally understand that they were being asked to do something even more important.

Just then, Nolan, quickly followed by Benji, Tem-aki and GEA-4, carried large baskets toward the stairs. "Better grab supplies and go with them," Cameron said.

Hours later, after the Sirocco had been packed, they hoisted anchor to catch the evening's breeze, and passed through out of the harbor, Cameron went inside and realized that not only were his most trusted allies gone, so were the skull and staff of power.

Even stranger, he couldn't find Saphera.

Was that bad or good?

~o~

Nimri woke from a peaceful sleep to the strangest dawn she had ever imagined. She sat up and rubbed her eyes, but it didn't change the fact that the sun appeared to be rising out of water. In fact, it was difficult to tell where the water stopped and the sky started. She looked from left to right, but could not see the river banks anywhere.

Turning around, she couldn't see any sign of land in the shadows behind them, either.

So much for only going as far as the end of the river. Nimri realized that she wasn't as upset about going along for the entire journey as she imagined she should be.

And it certainly wasn't as frightening.

At least, not at the moment.

Looking closer, she realized that Mica, Larwin, Raine and Thunder were all asleep, so that explained why no one had woken her when she still had a chance to get off.

In fact, Kazza was the only one awake. Though he was still sprawled on the bow, he was staring forward, eyes gleaming and whiskers thrilling in anticipation.

Nimri rubbed her eyes again, then went to sit next to Kazza and watch the sun climb from the sea to warm the day. When she put her arm across his massive shoulders, he began to purr. Though she didn't know why, she was certain that he was excited about this trip and it had very little to do with rescuing Tem-aki.

Though she did not feel any wind and there was nothing but water and sky, she sensed that they were traveling at a high rate of speed. Even as she thought that, she realized it was a ridiculous thought. How could they be moving fast, when there was nothing to either push or pull them?

A groan from above made her look up at the sail, which looked rounded and smooth, but how could it be holding wind when she couldn't feel any? She would have to ask Raine, when she woke.

The sun was completely out of the water by the time Mica awoke. His cries woke the others, who all seemed as surprised as she had been to realize they were in the middle of the unknown.

As Nimri took care of Mica, Thunder and Raine made morning meal for the adults and Larwin checked the sail, then consulted the lumpy black box, which he seemed to think held the answer for just about anything. His posture straightened. "Unbelievable!"

"What is?" Nimri asked.

"We're more than halfway to our destination."

"But you said it would take weeks." She blinked in confusion.

"I know what I predicted with this form of transportation, and I don't know why we seem to be moving so fast."

"I wondered about that, too." She pointed to the sail. "It looks like the wind is pushing us, but I don't feel any breeze."

Larwin frowned. "If we were moving at the same speed as the wind, theoretically we wouldn't feel it."

"I hadn't thought of that," Nimri admitted. Then, after thinking it through, she brightened. "So that means that we

can get home."
"How so?"
"Do you remember what Raine said about tacking being able to zig-zag to get anywhere, as long as there was a good wind?"
"Did she call it tacking?"
Nimri nodded. "If we can go this direction on the wind, surely we can tack our way home."
"Is that why you weren't sure that you wanted to come all the way? The fear that you could never get home?" She nodded. He knelt next to her and kissed her forehead. "We will get home. I promise."
She kissed his bristly cheek. "Thank you."

~o~

As the ship's momentum slowed, Tem-aki looked out the window and saw a golden speck on the horizon. She blinked, certain that it was either her imagination or a trick of the light, but it was still there, when she looked a second time.
She lunged out of her hammock and went to find GEA-4.
Arriving on the upper deck, she found GEA-4 gazing toward the rising sun. "I need you to scan something for me. It will only take a minute."
The eerie silver gaze turned toward her and Tem-aki pointed to the golden speck. "What is that?"
"It is another craft."
Not a madrox! She heaved a sigh of relief. "Thanks, GEA-4, I was worried that it might be a dragon, after all, these people seem to worship them."
"Not a problem." The silver eyes were already locked on the first rays of dawn.
Nolan and the rest were adjusting the sails and seemed to be waiting for something. Had they come all this way to meet the other boat? She had thought they were returning

to the original harbor-area, and she would have a chance to examine the strange hexagonal structures. A look around confirmed that they were standing off outside of an opening, so perhaps she had misunderstood their destination. Or, perhaps they were just waiting for the other ship because more than one was going.

The sails began to fill and The Sirocco groaned as she picked up speed toward the narrow passageway into the circular harbor.

A glance back, showed that the golden speck had gotten noticeably larger. Large enough, so that Saphera was sitting on the stern, tail twitching in excitement, eyes shining and ears tipped forward watching the other craft.

Okay, so the other boat was expected if the cat knew about it.

Tem-aki found herself a place where she was out of the way, but could still watch how they positioned the ropes to get The Sirocco to go where they wanted. As they passed through the narrow mouth to the harbor, she looked backward and realized that the other ship was even closer and coming fast.

How could something so primitive and with one sail move at such speed?

The strangest thing about the other vessel was that a large cat, which looked a lot like a golden version of Saphera, was sitting on the bow of the on-coming vessel and that Saphera seemed to be quivering with excitement.

What were the odds that two vessels randomly meeting each had a super-sized cat aboard?

Not likely.

So, for whatever reason, this meeting was obviously planned.

Chapter 26

Nimri stood behind Kazza and stared at the land, which was getting larger by the minute.

The great cat sat still as a statue. Nimri didn't know if he was mesmerized by the scenery or what, but he certainly was not acting normal.

Despite the fact that she wanted to get to the new land, the speed at which they were approaching alarmed her. Apparently, it alarmed Raine too, because she tied down a portion of the sail. Then, she looked from the sail to the approaching land, as if surprised.

Nimri asked, "The speed didn't change, did it?"

"I don't think so." She cleared her throat. "In fact, if I'm any judge of this, we've picked up speed."

"I was afraid of that." Nimri wet her lips. "What is moving us? A current in the water?"

Raine gave a helpless shrug and pointed to the glaze-smooth water. "Judging by the surface of the water, there isn't a current, at least not one on the surface. I suppose there could be one under the surface, which our hulls are actually being moved by.... Once we get close enough to swim to shore, prepare to jump."

"Why?" Nimri asked, startled.

"The survival options would be better than crashing." Raine blinked back tears. "I'm so sorry that I talked you into this, but I had no idea how strange the physics were on your planet."

Strange? Larwin had always said that he thought the physics were the same between Guerreterre and Chatterre, why would Raine's world be so different? Nimri's eyes narrowed as she looked past Raine, to where Larwin was playing peek-a-boo with Mica and Thunder appeared to be asleep. Was Thunder actually asleep or in myst-mode? With that thought in mind, she looked at Kazza, whose concentration made her suspect that if anything was different between Kalamar and Chatterre, it was probably myst-energy.

Moving over to Larwin, she knelt down and asked, "How far off course has this wind or current, or whatever is moving us, taken us?"

Larwin took out his bumpy black box and poked at it for a moment. "We're on a fairly direct course. I'll see once we get there." He gestured to the approaching land. "We know she's on an island, and I wager that is it. Mind you, once we get there, we might still have a good hike to get to wherever she is."

Just as she had suspected, either Kazza or Thunder or maybe both of them working together were using myst-energy to move the boat, which was something Raine obviously still didn't have a grasp of, so it was doubtful that there would be any crash-landing. Nimri tickled Mica's toes. "Soon you'll get to meet your Aunt Tem-aki."

Mica giggled with delight and kicked his feet.

~o~

Once into the harbor, Nolan gave the order to 'doff the sails', which apparently meant to take them down. Even once lowered, The Sirocco continued on a straight line, though it did begin to slow.

As soon as the sails were lowered, Benji and Tristan hurried to the bow and worked together to roll a large donut-shaped rock, which was attached to a long fiber-rope to the edge of the deck, then held it poised, as if waiting for something. Meanwhile Nolan held a rugged round wheel and Emmet used small pieces of rope to tie the sails, so they could not flutter in the breeze.

Tem-aki's attention was divided between admiring how well they all worked together and glancing back to watch the other boat enter the harbor, which was why she and Saphera, whose attention never wavered, were the only eyes to see the low, golden vessel race between the rocky arms of the harbor's mouth much faster than the Sirocco had made the passage and speed directly toward them.

"Now!" Nolan called. There was an immediate splash and a heartbeat later, a tug at the bow yanked the Sirocco to its left.

The other boat continued to speed directly at them, worse, the people, who were barely visible in the shadows of the rustic thatch-roofed shelter, did not seem to be making any effort to be in position to take down their raggedy sail. In fact, the only one, who appeared to be paying attention, was the enormous gold and black striped cat.

Saphera's attention didn't waver, but she began quivering. Tem-aki swallowed hard, wondering if she should shout a warning, but before she could get the words out, she realized the cat wasn't acting fearful, she was acting as if she was brimming with excitement.

Tem-aki moved to the center of Sirocco and wrapped her arms around the mast, expecting the other ship to T-bone them. Instead, at the very last moment, the other ship made a sharp ninety-degree turn and abruptly stopped.

With a howl of delight, that got the attention of Nolan and

the others, Saphera leaped over the rail, onto the deck of the new arrival. Shouts of surprise made her realize that either the other ship had not been seen, or it was unexpected.

Legs shaking, Tem-aki walked to the rail and looked down three feet to see the two huge cats ecstatically greeting each other. They were beautiful together, and though her companions seemed mystified, obviously the cats knew each other very well. Their purrs were loud as massive generators.

Nolan, looking as shaken as she felt over the near-miss, joined her at the railing, but instead of his full attention being on Saphera and her friend, he looked from them to her, as if she were responsible for the unknown craft floating peacefully an inch from the Sirocco's steep side.

"I had no idea Kazza and Saphera knew each other," GEA-4 said.

Kazza? Tem-aki blinked in surprise and studied the massive cat's markings. Yes, he might be the same animal she'd seen the ghostly image of, but this huge cat was no ghost. A second after that realization, she realized that if Kazza was here, he should know where Larwin was.

And another second later, she recognized Raine, who was securing the sails, much as Emmet had.

If she was here... she moved so she could see under the thatched roof and was certain she recognized Thunder and the woman she had seen in the skull and, yes, she recognized those broad shoulders, too! "Larwin!" she screamed.

He whipped around and was on his feet in a flash. She met him halfway by leaping over the railing. The welcoming hug was everything she had hoped for and all she had never truly believed possible.

~o~

Cameron spotted Benji stumble-jogging toward him, his red hair unmistakable in the sunlight, even at this distance.

Why was he there?

Had there been a shipwreck?

Where were the others? Even as Cameron took off at a run to meet Benji, his gaze raked the trail for signs of the others.

When Benji saw him, he seemed to gain strength.

Cameron engulfed the boy's trembling body in his arms. "What happened?"

"Boat."

Dread choked Cameron, as he imagined the worst. Had his callous disregard for tradition sunk The Sirocco and killed his best friend and the others who meant so much to him? "But you survived?"

"Yes, I didn't think I'd make it.... I've been running for two days to get here, but Nolan said you needed to be told."

Nolan was alive? Hope sprouted. "How bad was it?"

"It was totally unexpected. One moment we were dropping the anchor and next they were suddenly there."

Cameron frowned in confusion. "So you made it to the harbor?"

"Of course, that's where they showed up."

"Who showed up?"

"That's what I told you, the boat showed up just as we were dropping the anchor. I've never seen anything so bizarre, and I understand how you must have felt when Tem-aki and GEA-4 came to you."

Cameron scratched his head, suspicious that he had missed a crucial bit of information about what had happened that inspired Benji to spend two days running cross-country. "Okay, let's take this slowly and start from the beginning." Cameron's pace slowed to match his calm words.

Benji nodded.

"So, as you were dropping the anchor, something unexpected happened to The Sirocco."

Benji shook his head. "No, the other boat was just suddenly there."

Cameron blinked in confusion. "What other boat?

Benji shrugged. "We still aren't sure where it came from, it was suddenly just there. First thing we knew about it was when Saphera and Tem-aki jumped over the rail. I mean that was startling, but I guess it was good, because the way Tem-aki was hugging the guy, you could tell that it wasn't some sort of attack or anything."

Tem-aki had hugged another man? Cameron swallowed twice before he could say, "Go on."

Benji began describing the oddly constructed golden boat, but all Cameron could think of was the image of Tem-aki in the arms of another man.

"And then GEA-4 started talking." Benji's brow furrowed. "She is really strange and it's more than just her eyes, but she really does have amazing vision, because when I ran here, the path gave me a good view of Dragon Ridge and I'm pretty sure she was right."

Benji would have continued on, but Cameron held up his hand, to stop the confusing babble. "Let's take this a bit slower. What exactly did GEA-4 say?"

"Oh, I forgot you weren't there to hear her." Benji's speed was picking up, again, so Cameron motioned for him to slow down. "Sorry." Speaking slowly and carefully, be said, "She was looking at Dragon Ridge, instead of at the new boat, and said, 'the dragon moved, that's probably what caused the earthquake'." Then she tilted her head, like she was scanning the area and I didn't know if I should wait for her to continue or watch Saphera wrestling with the other cat-"

"What other cat?"

"Kazza, the one that came with the other boat."

"And Saphera was fighting with it?"

"No, more like the friendly wrestling I do with my little brothers."

Cameron blinked at that unexpected and confusing image. "So Saphera acted like this other cat was a friend and Tem-aki was hugging some stranger and GEA-4 was just looking at the coastline."

"Yeah, that's pretty-much how it was. Of course, once things settled down, and they all climbed aboard the Sirocco, it was easier to keep track of everything. Well, I mean not everyone got aboard the Sirocco, the cats swam to shore and explored the area that GEA-4 said was where she thought 'the madrox', which Tem-aki says is who we call Shaka-uma, dove through the thin crust to the magma."

Cameron gripped Benji's arm, "Are you saying that Shaka-uma is alive?"

"Yeah, Raine's best guess is that she was hibernating, but she's never really seen that happen, though she'd read about as what she called a 'historical footnote'."

"Raine?" Cameron asked, as he wondered if he would ever sort out Benji's story.

"Yeah, she has hair sort of like Larwin and Tem-aki, but she is shorter and says her job was being a 'dragon herder'."

"Larwin? Was he the one Tem-aki hugged?" Benji nodded. Relief flooded through Cameron, as he realized that Tem-aki had been hugging her brother. "Anyone else on that other boat?"

"Just Raine, Thunder, Nimri, Larwin, the cat, Kazza, and the baby."

"Was the cat the size of Saphera?"

"A bit bigger and gold stripes, instead of white."

"So the boat was big as Sirocco. Strange that you didn't see it before it was suddenly there."

Benji nodded in agreement. "Strange group, but Tem-aki seemed to know everyone except the woman with the baby. And it was a really little one, probably less than a month old."

"And they bought it on this other boat?"

Benji nodded. "Everyone made a big fuss over it. I mean, it is the cutest baby."

"But you didn't run for two days to tell me about the baby."

"Nolan told me to run here to let you know about the other boat's arrival and that Shaka-uma might still be alive and in the magma and he's concerned about what that could mean to the ceremony."

"Well, it would mean that we're right and the ones who worship profit are wrong, when they say that dragons don't exist."

"True, but is it safe to have the ceremony near where she might be nesting?"

"What do you mean?"

"Well the new ones, plus Tem-aki and GEA-4 seem to think dragons are dangerous and need to be killed."

"Sacrilege!"

"Nolan knows how busy you are here, but he really needs you." Benji stopped walking and turned to face him. As he cleared his throat, Cameron could feel the boy's anxiety. "Everyone thinks we need to cancel this year's ceremony."

He didn't know what he'd expected Benji to say, but it wasn't something that hit him in the stomach like a hammer. It took a few moments to get his breath back. "Totally cancel everything?"

Benji's eyes looked like green islands in white seas. "At very least, the pilgrimage portion."

"That's the most important part!" Benji nodded in agreement. Without the annual pilgrimage to honor the dragons, this would barely differ from any of their other events. "Do YOU think it would be that dangerous?"

Benji's forehead furrowed. "I'm not sure. I mean, GEA-4 was talking about all sorts of strange things she called statistics, which make it sound like a bad idea to have followers there, but the new ones kept talking about how dragons – they actually call them madrox – consume something called myst-energy, which apparently kills humans when they eat it." Benji swallowed hard. "Have you ever heard about anything like that? I know there are fairy tales where dragon's burned unbelievers, but I've never met anyone who'd seen a real dragon. At least I hadn't until the others arrived and supposedly all of them have, yet none of them seemed to think dragons should be worshiped, they just want to kill Shaka-uma." Tears threatened to spill down Benji's cheeks, and he blinked hard. "We need you."

"And I will go there, but it will be faster by boat."

"But The Siroc-"

"Fishing boat," Cameron specified.

Chapter 27

As Nimri, Larwin, Tem-aki, Raine and Thunder waited for GEA-4 to finish her analysis of the area, Thunder watched Raine playing peek-a-boo with Mica. His tender expression could not totally distract her from GEA-4's shocking statement that a dragon had been hibernating on the appropriately named Dragon Ridge and that it was now warming in the deep, hidden lava pool, which lay close to where they were anchored.

The only solace was that it was doubtful that the beast would attack them as long as they stayed on their boat.

Raine's initial disbelief to the news still bothered Nimri and she wondered if she was focusing her attention on baby games as a way to avoid dealing with the potential danger. Or maybe, she was just distracting herself from worrying while GEA-4 conducted her 'assessment via long-range scanners'. Whatever that meant. For certain, she had only moved from her position on the bigger ship's deck when the breeze changed and the big ship shifted on its anchor rope and their smaller boat mirrored the movement.

Kazza was acting very strange. If he had been human, Nimri would have suspected a love interest in Saphera, who seemed like a very nice, if shy cat.

Larwin and Tem-aki were seated on the bamboo deck and both seemed to be quietly talking at once. They frequently touched each other's hand or arm, as if assuring themselves they had actually found each other.

And Nimri continued to wait for GEA-4 to tell her that she had taken her son from a place of safety to danger and potential death. Periodically, one of the gold-garbed males would move into her line of sight, but mainly, they stayed away from their ship and appeared to be building a rock wall in front of a cave-type opening on the hill.

GEA-4 finally came to the railing of the taller ship and hopped down to join the rest of them.

Larwin was immediately on his feet. "Well?" he demanded.

"Four," GEA-4 said.

"Four what?"

"Four madrox." Nimri gasped at GEA-4's statement. "The adult mother and three more, which I believe will soon hatch."

Raine held Mica close to her chest and stared at GEA-4 over the top of his head. "Our scientists could never predict that. How can you tell?"

"Temperature variance and the fact that two of the young are clawing at the inside of their rocky shell, as if trying to break free, much like a hatching bird does."

"You can detect a temperature variance inside the lava?" Raine asked.

"The ova are not in the lava." GEA-4 pointed to the shore where vast vegetation-free hectares of massive octagon-shaped objects, shimmered in the sunlight.

Larwin cleared his throat. "But only three are alive?" GEA-4 inclined her head in agreement. "Well, I guess that is lucky."

"Cameron told me that ancient tales claimed that a mighty mountain with a lava-lake at its summit once stood where this harbor is, now." Tem-aki rubbed her temples, then continued, "He said that over a millennium before, his ancestors followed the great dragon-mother, which they called Shaka-uma and watched her lay her eggs in the lava-lake, which somehow makes this place a historically important area. If that old story is true, I guess that's how those madrox eggs got all over the beach, and it would explain why the followers of Shaka-uma still make annual pilgrimages here."

"It is not safe with one dragon, let alone four," Thunder said.

"I agree," Raine said. "In truth, I really can't understand why anyone would build a sort of religion around them."

"This from the person whose culture built an industry around them," Thunder said with a laugh.

"They were profitable," Raine said.

"And dangerous," Tem-aki said. "Their behavior nearly pushed Vilecom into Kalamar and destroyed your entire planet."

"That was the Reclamation Unit's fault." Raine said, as she raised her chin.

Larwin made a dramatic gesture. "Fine, but none of this is relevant to our situation."

"True," Nimri agreed.

"Do you know what I don't understand?" Thunder asked, then added, "I thought that they needed heat to survive. So, how could that mother-shaka-whatever survive in normal rock for centuries and how come three of those egg-things still have live ones getting ready to hatch?"

"Unknown," GEA-4 said, "but I suspect she could have a special gene that allowed her to adapt instead of die."

"And obviously, she passed it on to three of her larva or whatever an infant madrox is called," Larwin said.

"Are you suggesting that they might not be as vulnerable to cold?" Tem-aki asked.

"I'm saying that what we know about the species might not apply."

Nimri sighed. "They were difficult enough to deal with when we knew their weak spots."

Tem-aki and Raine shared a worried look. Raine was the first to turn to Nimri and ask, "How could you deal with them if you didn't have properly equipped craft?"

"Water," Nimri said.

Raine relaxed and nodded. "Nambaba's main defense and control mechanism was her hydro-blaster. Plenty of water around here to supply us."

~o~

Tem-aki watched the man, who claimed to be Larwin, tickle Mica's feet. He was the same height and had shoulders the same width that she recalled her brother having, but his skin was darker, his hair, longer and lightened by the sun. This man dressed in hand-woven fabrics and sandals instead of black, form-fitting battle-gear, but the difference between the brother she remembered and the man in front of her went far deeper.

Mica's peals of laughter were answered by a deep, warm chuckle. "Like that, don't you?" Larwin's well-known voice said.

Amazing, this man's eyes glinted with happiness and laughter tinged his words. Previously, she had only seen determination in his eyes and she had never imagined him laughing.

Could anyone really change this much?

Could anyone really be as happy as he seemed in a world, which didn't seem to operate on power and profit?

At face-value, it seemed so, but this was something that she would have to watch and try to understand.

Granted, she understood how someone like Cameron, who didn't know any different, could be happy without luxuries and the technologies that a powerful society could offer. Cameron simply didn't know what he was missing.

But Larwin knew what was available, so why had he let Thunder use his environmental suit to try to close off any option of escape instead of use it to repair his ship?

Nimri settled down next to Larwin and touched his wrist. For a moment, they smiled into each other's eyes in a way that reminded Tem-aki of the way her parents looked at each other.

And it looked as genuine as Mica.

Had her brother left everything and everyone from his past behind because of a woman? Tem-aki's hands clenched into fists, but she didn't know if she wanted to lash out at Larwin for abandoning her or Nimri for luring him away.

And because of her blind devotion to her brother, now she too had lost everything and everyone that was important to her.

~o~

Cameron held tight to the tiller as his grandfather's small fishing boat beat its way through the waves. As uncomfortable as his stomach felt, he had the satisfaction of watching Varlet and Malin hanging precariously over the rail as they emptied their stomachs for the umpteenth time.

Perhaps a rogue wave would sweep the rail clean and two-thirds of his problem people would vanish.

But, instead of a wave solving that problem, the small boat rounded the point and the raging seas calmed. Gradually, Malin and Varlet moved a pace away from the railing and sat down on the slick deck.

Once free of the confused seas, the boat began to make serious progress.

Varlet turned a glowering, green-tinged face to him. "We should have walked."

"It would have taken too long," Cameron said. "If GEA-4 is

correct about Shaka-uma awakening, we needed to be there yesterday."

Malin's dark, oily hair clung to his acned face. "I never realized the seas could be so rough."

"They only seem that way," Cameron said, "because The Sirocco is much larger and you aren't sleeping in your hammock." Cameron glanced back at the area that sailors referred to as 'the cats and dogs' because in that section the waves always seemed to be fighting.

"If you say so," Malin said. "Don't know why you chose us for this trip. If we had to go in such an unstable thing, I'd think you'd choose one of the novices from the lower ranks."

Cameron bit his tongue so he couldn't waste more breath trying to explain that being the son of a fisherman was equal, if not better than being the son of a money-lender. And, for the millionth time, he wondered if Malin's family had urged him to become an initiate, so his beliefs would act like a cancer, harming their order from the inside.

If so, then the plan might be working on Dirk, but then his attitudes were already so skewed by Varlet, that it probably didn't matter when Malin made his snide little status comments.

Varlet, who had demanded that he, Malin and Dirk be allowed to come on this 'momentous trip', lay down on the deck and closed his eyes. If his reason for traveling along had held any sinister plans to take over the order, at least for the moment he was too ill to execute them.

Cameron settled down for the second half of the journey and hoped that without Varlet and syncopates there to distract them, that the rest could finish preparations. Though Benji had wanted to come along, too, he had understood that once he rested, his help was needed at the main base. Besides, the small, old boat really wasn't large enough for five grown men. In fact, having four adults aboard was double its normal capacity.

~o~

"Now, all three are clawing," GEA-4 said. "And the first two are nearly through the exterior."

Nimri shivered. Glancing at Mica, who Raine held protectively in her arms, she wondered if being aboard a boat, would protect her son from the impending danger of young madrox.

Would they be like infant poisonous snakes, which were more deadly than the adults, because they had not learned control?

Or, would they be like Mica and require a mother's attention? Involuntarily, she looked at the thin portion of lava, which GEA-4 claimed the mother was under. Had Shaka-whatever woken from her sleep because of the impending hatch?

Was that a ripple of movement in the crust?

Nimri swallowed three times before the lump of fear stopped choking her.

GEA-4 pointed to the ovum on the right. "And it is through."

Raine stared at the tiny hole in the rock. "So they hatch like birds... I've always wondered."

"Why?" Larwin asked in surprise. "I thought you said you worked with them every day."

"I did, but never knew how they procreated." Raine shrugged. "My job was to keep them near Vilecom and not let them stray away." She gave Thunder a warm look. "Obviously, I wasn't always successful."

"But you did get it back to the herd and save me in the process," Thunder said.

"So, you do have experience with the young ones," Larwin said. Raine nodded. "Aside from presumably being smaller than an adult, is there any major difference between how you need to handle them?"

Raine raised her face to the heavens. "Yes." She sighed and looked at Thunder. "I met you because a juvenile escaped and I had to get it back to Vilecom." She turned her attention to Larwin. "The adults are too well-trained to escape like that."

Nimri frowned. "As I understand it, your people have herded them for decades."

Raine nodded in agreement."Since before I was born."

"Did you ever hear anyone say anything that would make you think that herding, instead of getting older, might change their behavior?"

Raine's eyes widened. "No, but you're right, being trained to couple with the reclamation units and react to the herders might have changed how they acted."

"And since the ones we need to deal with have never encountered Kalamaran ships, it is safe to say that none of us really knows how they will act," Larwin said.

"I think it is a safe bet to predict that they will go after myst-energy," Thunder said.

Nimri nodded in agreement.

Mica wailed and Raine held him close, as if frail human arms could protect anything from a powerful, primitive madrox attack.

"The second has broken through," GEA-4 said, as she pointed to the ovum farthest from the shore.

"Too bad there isn't a way to pump their ova full of water and drown them before they ever hatch," Larwin said.

Nimri nodded in agreement. In this case, the miraculous machines and amazing things he occasionally told her about would be very handy and could save lives. Her gaze went to Mica.

~o~

Tem-aki listened to Larwin talking with Thunder and Nimri

as if he seriously was planning to stay here and fight the hatching madrox in hand-to-hand combat, even though he, like all other pilots were taught that the proper way to deal with the destructive beasts was to run. Even though how fast or far could one run with these primitive boats, was doubtful. Running was certainly a wiser alternative than sitting here watching the things hatch.

In fact, since they were stuck with such primitive transportation, they should have left as soon as GEA-4 let them know there was danger.

Had her brother suffered some sort of head trauma when he crashed?

Was that why he looked and acted so different from the brother she knew?

Knowing that they did not have time to waste, talking and planning, she knelt down near Larwin and took his hand. "We need to leave here."

He stared at her. "Why?"

Tem-aki swallowed twice. "It's too dangerous to stay."

"It is more dangerous to leave," Nimri said. "Unless we deal with them here and now, they will remain a threat."

Tem-aki clenched her teeth together as she slowly turned to face the woman who had brainwashed her brother. "That is the dumbest thing I've ever heard."

Nimri stared at her as if no one had ever had the nerve to disagree with her. Tem-aki narrowed her eyes at the arrogant woman. "At the moment, they are trapped in those rock shells. We need to leave now, while we can." The more Tem-aki spoke, the surer she felt that she was right.

Nimri gave her a sad smile. "Larwin thought that, too, but then he learned that Guerreterre has different ways of doing things than Chatterre. We have no fast ships, so there is no escape. If we run, now, then the threat will always be here. Worse, the baby madrox would have time to grown into a bigger threat."

"She's right," Larwin said. "I know you don't understand this, but if we don't take care of this now, it will only get worse."

Tem-aki squared her shoulders. "But not today, and probably not tomorrow."

"Maybe not even for the next hundred years," Larwin agreed.

"So you understand why you need to be sensible and do what we were always taught to do."

Larwin gave her a sad smile, then shook his head. "Just because we were taught something since we were old enough to focus our eyes does not mean it is right." He cracked his knuckles. "Fortunately, I lived long enough to learn that."

Nimri's hand covered his hands with her own. "We survived the first one. We can survive this, too."

Right, like they'd done hand to hand combat with a dragon. Tem-aki took a deep breath and tried, again, "Can you understand why I question this choice? When you captained a star-fighter that had the fire-power to blow up a planet, you always ran. Didn't you?"

"Of course," Larwin said. "And can you understand that I now have a family to protect?" He took Nimri's hand in his.

Tem-aki gritted her teeth and nodded. "Still, this is impossible to do, so you need to leave."

"If you believe something is impossible, then you never will be able to do it, but if you believe that you can do something, the impossible becomes possible," Nimri said. "I learned that when we faced the first one." She took Thunder's hand in her free one. "It took all of us working together to win, and it will take all of us this time, too. If you're afraid, then you and your negativity need to run away."

Fingers itching to slap Nimri, Tem-aki clenched her fist. "I have gone places you never imagined and taken assignments no one else would, while I tried to find out what happened to my brother." She glared at Nimri. "And now you tell me to leave?" When Mica wailed, Tem-aki realized she was shouting. With force of will, she lowered her voice. "I found him and I will die with him, so I'm afraid you'll just need to get used to having a reality check around. And if by some miracle you survive this and I don't, remember that I told you so."

Chapter 28

As the prow dipped into the rolling waves, Cameron lined his grandfather's old fishing boat up with the harbor's entrance and then waited for the on-shore breeze. If it hadn't been an emergency situation, which forced him to travel with the worst three in the order, he would feel excited, instead, he felt tense. But what else could he do? He certainly couldn't leave Varlet, Malin and Dirk behind. And they had insisted on coming.

Feeling the first stirrings of wind, Cameron flexed his fingers, then wrapped them around the tiller and made the final adjustment, so the sail caught the wind and the tiny craft leaped toward the opening between the jagged rocks that protected the harbor-area.

"What are you doing?" Varlet bellowed.

"Isn't it obvious?" Cameron asked.

"We're pointed at the rocks." Malin snarled, as he lunged toward him. "He's planning to kill us!"

Dirk grabbed Malin a fraction of a moment before he got to him. After wrestling him to the deck, Dirk sat on Malin's chest and held his wrists down. "It's safer with his hand on the tiller than no one guiding us."

Malin hissed a reply, but the fight went out of him and Dirk was able to go back to his spot by the rail. Malin crawled to the other railing.

"If I wanted to kill any of you, do you think I would put myself in a position where it was three to one?" Cameron raised his brow at Varlet, then, when the only response he made was a reddening face, Cameron turned his full attention back to guiding them through the passage.

The rocks had looked wicked from the deck of the Sirocco, but from a smaller boat, they looked lethal. Years of navigating the passage gave him the knowledge that the sides of the passageway were like those of the harbor-area and were nearly vertical, thus, Cameron gently altered course, so that the knife-edged rocks were close to Malin's side of the boat.

Malin turned white and closed his eyes.

Cameron pretended not to notice, but inside, he was dancing in silent glee at finally finding something that could unnerve the annoying initiate.

As they rounded the last boulder, he saw the golden vessel Benji had mentioned floating next to the Sirocco. Though he couldn't see anyone aboard his ship, there seemed to be several people sitting in the shade of a thatch-roofed shack on the deck of the smaller ship.

Not knowing what to expect, he guided the old fishing boat to The Sirocco's other side and tied it where they usually secured the dory, which had been pulled up on the shore.

~o~

Tem-aki watched Cameron pilot a small, scruffy boat into the harbor. He'd come! Her heart skipped a beat, then, realizing that he wasn't coming directly toward her, she rudely turned away from Nimri, climbed back aboard the Sirocco and rushed across the deck to see where he was going.

As she looked down, Saphera and Kazza joined her at the

rail. Looking down, she realized that the three nastiest novices were with him and a lot of her happiness fizzled.

Still, as Cameron looked up, into her eyes and his face broke into a look of delight, her heart skipped another beat as she smiled back.

"You came," she said.

He nodded. "We did."

"So Benji made it." Tem-aki bit her tongue and told herself that stating the obvious was stupid. Varlet and his two buddies scrambled up the ladder and made a bee-line for the galley. Tem-aki swallowed then added something Cameron didn't know. "You're just in time to see the dragon eggs hatch."

"What?" He frowned in confusion. "Benji told me that Shaka-uma might be alive. What's this about eggs?"

"GEA-4 says the madrox you call Shaka-uma is warming herself in the lava, and that three of her eggs are getting ready to hatch."

"You're telling me that after having no dragons for over a century, that we'll have four?" Cameron's face looked like he'd just won the greatest lottery prize in ten galaxies.

"That's about it, but why are you happy about this? Don't you realize how destructive dragons are?"

"Do you mean fire?" Cameron asked, looking confused.

"Well, since the old world burnt to a crisp, which would be one reason why people can't understand why you'd want to welcome destruction."

"Yes, fire can destroy, but it also built this island, it can protect us and it can burn out poisons and feed us safe food."

"Larwin believes that your dragons feed on some humans. How can you think that is good?"

Cameron blinked in surprise. "Is that what you believe?"

She gave a cautious nod.

Cameron inhaled deeply and stroked Saphera's flank. "What about the fertility they bring? Isn't this just another example of how one thing is both good and bad? And, when you think about it, isn't that true of most things?"

"I don't know, but I think you need to speak to Larwin, Raine and Thunder, because they are making plans to kill those dragons."

Cameron's eyes widened in shock. "How can they even consider that?"

"Ask them," Tem-aki said, then ushered him to the strange boat and introduced him to everyone. She watched with interest as cultures collided over the question of whether it was right to kill the dragons to possibly save lives or if the correct thing to do was leave them alone and hope Cameron was correct about the dragons making the land more fertile, and thus save lives from starvation.

Thunder cleared his throat, then said, "Until you brought up the subject, I hadn't thought about it, but our crops are doing especially good this year." He looked at Nimri. "Do you think that is coincidence or might the madrox have done something to enrich the soil?"

For the first time since she'd met the woman with the ridiculously long black braid, Nimri didn't seem to know what to say. Tem-aki clamped her teeth together to hold in the bubbling laughter over her confused expression. So, she wasn't as perfect as she thought. Good!

"Now that I think about it," Raine said, "The fields, which were downwind from the storage sheds, were our most productive." Her forehead wrinkled in thought. "I don't know how the broken bits being stored there could affect fertility, though."

"Strange coincidence," Larwin said. "And while I would love to say, fine, they might have a valid use, so let's quit trying to figure out a way to deal with them before they become a major issue'. Unfortunately, I'm not exactly willing to trade a slightly larger crop of vegetables for my son's life." Larwin put his hands on his hips and looked Cameron in the eye. "Mica is already showing a talent to use myst-energy, but he's a baby and too young to control it."

"Or to protect himself," Thunder added.

"And myst-energy attracts madrox better than anything else," Nimri said. She leaned forward and placed her palm on Cameron's forearm. Tem-aki's hands clenched into fists as Nimri sincerely told Cameron, "I need to protect my son and the best way I know how to do that is kill the madrox."

Larwin nodded. "You first said that you needed the madrox to assure your followers that mad-er-dragons exist. Surely a dead carcass is proof."

Nimri and Thunder eagerly nodded, but Tem-aki noticed that Raine remained noncommittal. Apparently Cameron noticed that, too, because he asked, "Raine, what do you think?"

Her eyes widened at being singled out. "I'm not sure, but then I've never had to deal with one without Nambaba – that is the name of my herder-ship. She was built to deal with the beasts. If I hadn't seen the proof with my own eyes, I wouldn't have thought it was possible to deal with them bare handed."

"But we did, so we know it's possible," Larwin said.

GEA-4, who was standing on the bow, broke the lengthening silence, "The first madrox is hatching."

Calling for Varlet, Dirk and Malin, Cameron scrambled onto the Sirocco's deck.

Telling herself that the higher vantage point would have a better view of the hatching, Tem-aki followed him.

~o~

Larwin's fingers wrapped hers in a strong, comforting grip which gave Nimri confidence, even though she knew that physical strength alone would not solve their problem.

Even Mica, now cradled protectively in Larwin's other arm, seemed to be silently watching the distant shore. As the sharp beak emerged from the break, Nimri noticed that the yellow-robed men, who had gone ashore, had crossed the lava-field and were on their knees in front of the cracking rock. Her fingers tightened around Larwin's. "Do you think they will be okay?"

"I have no idea," Larwin said.

"No one has ever seen anything like this," Raine said, "so there is no way to know how a hatchling will behave."

Thunder wrapped a protective arm around Raine's shoulders and pulled her against his side.

With a loud crack, the hexagonal rock split and a soggy gold ball of ooze, which had a dragon head appeared to roll onto the harsh black ground.

The three gold-clad men threw themselves face-down on the ground, arms reaching forward toward the disgusting looking hatchling.

"Maybe Cameron will change his mind about wanting to keep the things alive, when he sees that just being close to the things kills people," Thunder said.

"They are not dead," GEA-4 said, "I believe they are expressing reverence."

Nimri looked at the higher deck and realized that the four yellow-clad men around Tem-aki were doing the same thing as the trio on the shore. She nudged Larwin, and tilted her head toward them. "Looks like GEA-4 is correct."

Larwin grunted in agreement.

Now that his sister wasn't glaring at her, and her attention was focused on the shore, Nimri had a chance to study the woman that meant so much to Larwin and wonder why she seemed to hate her. Nimri's eyes began to water as she remembered the barbed comments and anger she had forced herself to ignore. Did Tem-aki hold her responsible for being trapped here? If so, she needed to remember that she could have returned to Kalamar aboard Nambaba and it had been her choice to stay with Thunder and Raine. Thunder had been very specific when telling them that Tem-aki had made the choice in hopes of joining Larwin.

If she was going to blame someone, she needed a reality check and to take a good close look at her own choices.

"Is it my imagination, or do they look wet?" Larwin asked.

Nimri's attention snapped back to the newly-hatched dragon. Indeed, it looked wet, but how could that be? Didn't water kill the young ones?

Now that she thought about it, how had the larva – or whatever young madrox were called – survived incubation in a cool area?

A chill ran down Nimri's spine, as she realized that the three surviving larva, as well as the mother-dragon were obviously somehow different from the one she had dealt with.

"How can we kill them if they can survive being wet?" she whispered.

Raine turned so quickly that she broke free of Thunder's protective arm. "That IS what we're seeing, isn't it?" Her face turned white. "Do you think any of the ones on Vilecom can survive water, too?"

Thunder gathered Raine against his body and wrapped both arms around her. "If you're worried about your family," he said, "don't be." She tried to turn to face him, but he held her firm. "Remember that they have a fleet of herder-ships to protect them."

Raine visibly relaxed as a bright red spot of color formed on each cheek. "How could I have forgotten that?" she murmured.

Nimri leaned forward and touched Raine's hand. "I'm sure

your family will be fine."

Raine nodded. "I am, too." She straightened and gave the shore a significant look. "If we can't kill them with a quick-cooling in water, how can we kill them?"

Nimri wished she knew the answer to that question.

~o~

Tem-aki's jaw clenched as she listened to Raine and the horrible Nimri discussing how to murder the madrox, even though Cameron had made it plain to them that he wanted to protect them. How dare they show up here and begin telling people, who had lived here for generations how things needed to be done?

What right did they have to kill the madrox?

She looked down at Cameron's prostrate form and wondered why he didn't get up and tell them to leave.

But if he did that, he wouldn't be the man she had come to admire. Tem-aki went to the mast and sat down near Saphera and Kazza, who were intently watching the shore. Leaning against the mast's solid strength for support, she wondered how she had gotten in the middle of what two people she cared about wanted. What should she do?

If she supported Cameron, then by definition, she was against her own brother and his family.

Yet if she supported Larwin, she was doing what the parasitic Nimri wanted, and while she could understand the argument about protecting her son, who after all, was her very own nephew, how much of a threat could the golden blob on the shore be? Only the head looked like a madrox, the rest of the long, lumpy form looked more like slimy scrambled eggs, which were not quite done.

As she watched, the creature moved. Squinting, she thought she could identify a leg. The stubby little thing reminded her of a hologram she's once seen of a new-born puppy. How dangerous could it be?

Convinced that Nimri was being overly-dramatic and using her child's health and well-being as an excuse to get them to do what she wanted, Tem-aki made the decision that she would support Cameron's wish to protect the madrox. While this put her at odds with Larwin, it wasn't as if he still seemed to be the brother she knew and loved.

Choice made, she began stroking Saphera's silky fur.

~o~

Cameron tried to focus his thoughts on the miracle on the shore, but his mind kept going back to the tears that had shimmered in Nimri's vivid green eyes when she told him that madrox fed on myst. While he had never heard of myst-energy, it sounded remarkably like a soul.

Was myst-energy their word for soul? And was his lack of understanding this concept due to some vocabulary omission in GEA-4's odd way of teaching language?

Saphera began purring. Glancing back, he blinked in surprise when he realized the skittish cat was, again, leaning against Tem-aki. He had often wondered if Draco Hern had jinxed her when he chose a name with 'fear' in the middle. Now, sitting between Tem-aki and the big golden cat, she appeared confident and happy.

Did her new calmness have to do with the baby dragon or was it due to Kazza's arrival?

Was it plan or coincidence that the new ones had arrived just in time for the hatching?

Either way, was Nimri correct about the dragons being a threat or could he continue to rely on what he had been taught since birth?

Would he be questioning his beliefs if Nimri's eyes were not the color only a priestess could wear and Kazza wasn't the color of a celestial dragon?

Rising to his feet, he went to kneel next to Tem-aki. Surely she would tell him what to do.

Chapter 29

Tem-aki stared at Cameron. "I can't tell you what to think or do," she cleared her throat, "but I will support whatever you choose," she said as softly as he was speaking.

His sincere brown gaze looked like he was trying to read her soul. "Do you think they are right about the dragons bringing death instead of life?"

While she would have liked to disagree with Nimri, everything Tem-aki had ever been taught told her that, at least on this topic, the woman was correct. "I have always avoided contact with them," she said truthfully.

Cameron's mouth flattened. "In that case, it probably isn't wise for Nolan's group to be so close."

"I would have run the other direction," she admitted.

With a decisive nod, Cameron sat back on his heels, put two fingers between his lips and emitted a sharp, distinctive whistle. The three novices on the deck and the three on the shore all jerked upright. Cameron motioned the ones on shore to return.

Was her opinion so important to him that he would disrupt everyone because of her advice? Warmth suffused her and she couldn't help but smile.

The three on shore headed toward the dory.

Saphera purred louder, but Varlet scowled at her. Tearing her gaze from his hate-filled eyes, she realized Malin and Dirk were looking at her as if she was the worst person alive. Tem-aki lifted her chin as she turned her attention back to Saphera and stroking her amazingly soft fur.

As Nolan climbed aboard, he asked Cameron, "Why did you tell us to return?"

Cameron looked at her, then turned to Nolan and said, "I have it on good authority that being close to dragons can be harmful." He smiled as he patted Nolan's shoulder. "Better to be safe than sorry."

Cameron nodded. "Besides, we can eat sandwiches while we all watch the hatchling dry, together."

Emmet clapped, but Dirk growled, "Did I understand you correctly? Did they have to come back from worshipping the first dragon seen in a hundred lifetimes because she said it wasn't safe?" In his fury, Dirk spit globs with each S.

"You could say that," Cameron said, "but-"

"Forget your buts," Varlet roared, "I, for one, refuse to act like a baby listening to what some woman says. And if you're doing as she says, I will no longer listen to you." With that, he swung over the railing and climbed down to the dory. Malin and Dirk looked from Varlet to Cameron for a moment, then quickly turned and followed Varlet.

Nolan and Cameron looked at each other and shrugged.

Tristan looked at Emmet and said, "More for us." Then, they headed toward to galley.

When they were out of earshot, Tem-aki said, "Cameron, while I'm honored that you are willing to pay attention when I tell you what I know about madrox, I don't want to make problems for you."

"The problem existed long before you walked into my life... They are just using you as an excuse."

While she knew that what he said was probably true, it still made her feel uncomfortable. "If -" she realized she didn't know what to say, so she shut her mouth.

Cameron seemed to understand. He ran his knuckles down her cheek and smiled.

Nolan leaned against the railing and watched Dirk and Malin row the dinghy toward the shore. And Cameron tried to watch everyone. Once on shore, Varlet hiked with determination toward the drying hatchling. Instead of dropping into a reverent pose, as Nolan, Emmet and Tristan had done, at a respectful distance, the three continued directly to the baby dragon and only stopped when they were near enough to reach out and touch it.

Emmet and Tristan brought a heaping tray of sandwiches, a bowl of fresh fruit and a ceramic pitcher of herbal tea outside. After setting everything down, Emmet returned to the galley and Tristan went to the other rail, where he invited Larwin and his friends to join them.

By the time everyone was seated legs crossed on the deck, Emmet returned with dishes and cups.

Thunder couldn't seem to take his eyes off the ones on the shore. Face pale, he asked, "Do they realize how dangerous madrox are?"

Cameron and Nolan nodded.

Tem-aki said, "They chose to ignore the advice to keep a safe distance."

"In fact," Nolan added, "I suspect they made sure to get as close as possible as a sort of rebellion."

"Whatever their reason, it's dangerous." Thunder said.

Tem-aki said, "Those three don't have any respect for my opinion."

Emmet snickered.

"They scorn all females," Tristan said.

Tem-aki felt her eyebrows rise, yet realized that she should have figured that out.

"Sad thing is that consistency is the nicest thing I can say about them," Tristan concluded.

"Ignore the malcontents," Nolan said, "and enjoy your lunch."

A companionable conversation moved and shifted from the topic of fruits that Larwin and his friends had never seen to the experience they'd had with madrox. As Tristan told them how he had made the green-tinged spread he'd used on the vegetable, cheese and meat sandwiches, there was a loud cracking sound. Everyone stopped eating and stared toward the shore, but the only difference was that Varlet appeared to be touching the baby's head. "That probably isn't smart," Emmet said.

"Sacrilegious," Tristan agreed, then he returned to his explanation about how to make guacamole. A moment later, he hopped up and returned to the galley. He was back in a flash, four big fat brown ovals in his hands. Handing them to Nimri, he advised her how to plant the avocado seeds.

What was it with that woman and how did she manage to beguile males? And why did Larwin look pleased about the fact that Tristan was obviously trying to make an impression on the mother of his child?

Tem-aki glanced from Larwin to Nimri and, for the first time, wondered if they were as tightly bonded as they had led her to believe.

Another crack, loud as if thunder were splitting the clouds directly overhead, reverberated over the harbor. This time, when she looked toward shore, Tem-aki saw that the smooth black lava had fractured and she could see hot orange magma bubbling beneath the thin crust.

"The mother madrox is breaking free," GEA-4 said. "They should move away from the young one."

Cameron put his fingers to his mouth and emitted the same whistle, which had told Nolan and the others to return to safety. But instead of returning, Varlet raised his hand in a rude gesture, then turned back to the hatchling.

A moment later, as the third boom blasted their ears, she saw something coming out of the lava. A heartbeat later, she identified the nose of a madrox. Suddenly several things happened at once. Cameron whistled, again, Nolan, Emmet and Tristan shouted, Nimri screamed and clutched Mica to her chest and Kazza howled.

By the time the madrox's immense body was free of the lava, Varlet and the other two began running back to the dory. Malin was slightly faster than the other two. The mother madrox's wings beat the air. Blue lightning shot from her mouth with a shrill shriek so piercing it felt as if the sound had torn off Tem-aki's ears, even though her hands covered them. The shriek came again and again. So did the whipping blue lightning and the writhing madrox seemed to get larger and larger.

Malin made a bee-line for the harbor, instead of running to the more distant boat, which Dirk and Varlet were sprinting for. Reaching the water's edge, Malin ran straight in, until the water suddenly closed over his head. Nimri gasped. Mica howled. Tem-aki didn't realize that she'd been holding her breath until she saw Malin's head pop back up.

She gasped for breath.

Several heartbeats later, she realized that the madrox's bright blue tongue was no longer lashing out and it seemed to be heading toward the hatchling, which had raised its head.

Motherly love. Who would have thought that an energy-devouring beast like a madrox was capable of that?

Malin swam as fast as he could toward the Sirocco.

"Where are Dirk and Varlet?" Emmet asked.

With a start, Tem-aki realized that she couldn't see them anywhere and the dory was still lying untouched on the beach.

"They were consumed," Nolan said.

"No!" Emmet said. Cameron, Larwin and Raine nodded. "Dragons don't eat people!" he protested.

"Apparently, they do," Cameron said. He looked her in the eye. "And they were warned."

White faced, Emmet gulped, while Tristan began to sob. "I've never seen anyone die before."

"Now do you understand why we said they were dangerous?" Nimri asked Cameron.

~o~

Cameron stared into Nimri's vivid green eyes and saw sympathy. When he didn't immediately answer, she added, "I'm sorry that you lost your friends." And he saw sincerity. "I wish there had been another way for you to learn that dragons aren't all good. Everything seems to have some sort of bad aspect, to someone, somewhere. I guess that you need to ask yourself if fertile fields are important enough to pay with the lives of your friends."

Cameron held up his hand for her to stop speaking. "Before you continue, the two that were lost were part of my order, but I would never refer to them as friends."

Tristan snickered. "That's the truth. The only friends they were, was to each other."

Nimri frowned in confusion. "They were bullies," Emmet told her. "If the dragon was going to eat someone, they were the best choice possible."

"But they won't be the last," Thunder said, "and you might not like who they consume next time."

"Cameron told you to leave them alone," Tem-aki said. "Yes, they might be a threat, but this isn't your island and it certainly isn't your place to come here and tell him what to do."

Cameron took Tem-aki's hand in his and patted it. "I

appreciate your support, but I wouldn't be much of a leader if I only listened to people who told me what they thought I wanted to hear."

"But-"

He put a finger to her lips effectively silencing her. "It's fine. Really." When she nodded, he removed his finger, but kept her hand clasped in his. Turning his attention back to the newcomers, he asked, "Is there any way to protect the people and still allow the dragons to fly free to make the land fruitful?"

The four of them looked at each other, then Larwin said, "None that I have ever heard of."

"Or I," said Raine.

Discussion on the topic stopped when there was a clattering at Sirocco's side. Malin, wearing nothing but a soaking, saggy breechcloth was climbing up the ladder as if the dragon was still in pursuit, but a glance at the shore verified that it was coiling itself protectively around its hatchling. As soon as Malin's bare feet hit the deck, he launched himself forward. Cameron dropped Tem-aki's hand and prepared for an assault, but instead, a sobbing Malin threw himself on the deck and began to kiss his sandals.

Reaching down, he pulled the boy to his feet. "It's fine. You're safe now."

Malin blubbered unintelligible things, but Cameron was able to pick out 'should have listened to you' and 'wrong'. While it would have been nice to believe Malin was admitting guilt, it seemed like he was still blaming others, instead of shouldering responsibility for his own choices. Looking over his shoulder, he motioned for Tristan and Emmet to come close. "Take him below."

"To dry?" Tristan asked.

"First wash away his fear," Cameron said.

When the young ones had gone, Cameron returned to the idea of finding a way to save the land and still protect the people. There must be some way to do so. Surely Draco Shakura knew the dangers as well as the benefits when he followed Shaka-uma here. For the first time, he noticed that Larwin was holding Draco Shakura's Staff of Power. Heat quickly followed by ice flowed through him, as he wondered how the man had gotten his hands on the priceless artifact. Cameron took a deep breath, then excused himself and escaped into the galley, where he plopped down on the first available chair, closed his eyes and tried to control his breathing by telling himself that Larwin had a right to hold the sacred artifact, after all his sister was the one who had brought it to him. In fact, the man probably had more of a right to touch it than he did. And perhaps Tem-aki knew that, and it was why she had brought it with her.

Did Larwin know how to use it to control dragons, as Draco Shakura had?

Could the staff of power be the way to save both fields and dragons?

Cameron's eyes shot open and hope soared in his soul. A movement by the window caught his attention. He turned to see that both of the cats were sitting side by side, still as statues, their noses pressed against the back of the ancient skull, which Tem-aki had taken from him.

How strange. Until Tem-aki had arrived, he'd never seen Saphera give the skull a passing glance.

Cameron massaged the bridge of his nose and tried to imagine how Draco Shakura might have used the staff. Prior to seeing the actual size of an adult dragon, he'd assumed the staff of power was used for dragons in much the same way that goatherds used their staffs.

Now, he knew that was impossible.

Before going back outside, Cameron filled a pitcher with

herbal tea, so he could use it as an excuse for his abrupt departure. Turning to go, he saw the staff of power leaning next to the doorway.

When had Larwin returned it?

Why hadn't he heard him?

He looked out the open door at the mysterious man and realized there was also a staff in his hand. Cameron put the pitcher of tea down with such a thump that it sloshed over.

How could there be two staffs?

Was the one Tem-aki had brought actually Draco Shakura's or were they common among her people?

Forcing himself to breath, Cameron got a good grip on the pitcher and went back outside, where he could get answers to his questions.

Chapter 30

Nimri wondered why Cameron was clutching the fat brown jug, as if it was a lifeline and staring at Larwin, as if he was both terrified and infatuated with her mate. Meanwhile, Larwin, oblivious to Cameron, quietly talked with Nolan.

Thunder, who had his arm around Raine, was standing by the rail watching the dragon. Though Raine' was leaning into Thunder's side, her attention seemingly was on whatever Tem-aki was saying. She made several gestures toward shore, so Nimri assumed the topic of conversation was how to deal with the danger, which was what occupied her thoughts, too.

When they had been attacked, there was barely time to defend themselves from the myst-eating monster. If she had been taught that madrox could benefit crops, would she have been so quick to think that defending herself and her tribe was the only option?

Nimri wasn't sure.

But she was sure that she would defend Mica to the death, much as the mother dragon had apparently done. The real question was why Shaka-uma had believed that the mere touch from a human hand could harm the hatchling.

Now, the huge form was coiled around the baby, so the

mother was obviously protecting it with her own body.

Was that any different from what she was willing to do for Mica?

Larwin and Nolan turned to her. Judging by Larwin's expression, he'd discovered something interesting. Nimri joined them and asked Larwin, "What is it?"

He tilted the staff of power back and forth. She felt her forehead furrow in confusion.

"They have one just like this and they call it a staff of power, too. That has to mean something, right?"

Two staffs? What were the odds? Nimri wet her lips, then asked, "Are there any stories associated with yours?"

Nolan eagerly nodded, "Draco Shakura, our sect's founder, used it to control Shaka-uma, as she led us here."

Larwin gave her a significant look and mouthed the word, 'control'. Her great-grandfather had used his staff to control the weather. Could it be called the staff of power because it controlled things? That was a power, wasn't it?

How could there be two staffs?

Was the one Tem-aki had found actually Draco Shakura's or were they common?

~o~

Forcing himself to breathe, Cameron got a good grip on the pitcher and went back outside, as Nolan said, "Our staff had been lost for centuries, but your sister returned it to us."

Larwin turned to Tem-aki. "How did you get it?"

Nolan's eyes widened in surprise. "But you have the same."

"It belongs to my mate's line."

"But they must have come through the Star Bridge together," Nimri said. "I mean it makes sense, doesn't it? Ours arrived with the first Tramontain, and he became our tribe's first keeper of the peace, theirs apparently came with their sect's founder, which I bet isn't much different from what my ancestor was."

"Draco Shakura followed the dragon mother in the first migration," Cameron said, as he joined them. Though he still clutched the brown jug against his stomach, he somehow felt less stressed. "I recognized the staff from a sketch in the ancient journal."

"So you've lived here, with a dragon, for years?"

Nolan frowned. "Yes and no."

"He's trying to say that our faction is based on respect for them, but it has been many generation since one was seen alive," Cameron said.

"In fact, I turned down the offer of becoming high draco, in large part because I didn't want to be the one everyone was looking at when the faction failed," Nolan said.

Cameron raised a brow.

"One thing I don't understand," Larwin said, "is how a full-grown madrox managed to fit through the Star Bridge, previously."

"What do you mean?" Cameron asked.

"Well, when I arrived on this world, this side of the Star Bridge was very much an old cave, but after the madrox broke through, everything was changed."

Nimri nodded. "Broken, melted, then reformed. It looked very different from the old cave."

"Rounded?" Cameron asked. Nimri nodded. "Smooth instead of rough rock?" She nodded, again. "Interesting. That almost sounds like the place our faction considers special."

Larwin turned toward Tem-aki. "Could you join us?"

"What is it?"

"You're our rock expert."

~o~

She nodded, then moved between Larwin and Nolan, who each shifted aside to give her space. "What do you want to know?"

As Larwin explained about the Star Bridge and Cameron reminded her of where they'd met, Nimri had a chance to study Tem-aki without being obvious about it. Without the anger and hatred in her eyes, Tem-aki was actually an attractive woman. And judging by her comments on molten rock, an intelligent one too.

The real question was if understanding how rock could become a liquid could help them solve the madrox problem. If the mother dragon had somehow existed in or on the distant, broken ridge for hundreds of years, then it must have the ability to hibernate.

When bears came out of hibernation, their focus was on feeding. Nimri frowned, as she wondered if that was what the creature had been doing in the lava, or if it had come out of the lava's heat to feed on the myst-energy of the unfortunate two.

"Perhaps both," Larwin said.

Nimri gulped.

~o~

Tem-aki tore her gaze from the motionless madrox and looked back at the murmuring group. Every male in sight was clustered around Nimri, leaning toward her, as if hanging on her every word. Tem-aki's eyes narrowed and her jaw tightened, then she glanced at Raine, wondering why she didn't seem to be bothered about the way Nimri behaved. Didn't she care that the woman was apparently trying to lure her guy away? Tem-aki ground her teeth as she watched the way Nimri smiled at Cameron. The next thing she did was pat Nolan's arm.

Did the woman have any limits?

Wasn't Larwin enough?

How dare she throw herself at every male?

Tem-aki moved over to Raine, who seemed more interested in the madrox. "Doesn't it bother you?"

"What? Learning that they are good mothers?" Raine smiled. "It isn't a total surprise, but I admit that even after years of working with them I've never seen a mother and baby interact." She rubbed the back of her neck. "It sort of makes them seem almost human. At least, it makes me wonder if Cameron's perspective needs to be considered more deeply."

"I'm not talking about that." Tem-aki forced herself to take a deep breath. She jerked her thumb backward. "Doesn't it bother you how she tries to grab every male around?"

Raine's eyes widened in surprise, then she laughed.

Tem-aki's hands clenched so tightly that her fingernails cut into her palms.

"You're serious!" Raine laughed harder. "You only say that because you don't know her well. Yes, she's fun and beautiful and men like to be around her, but she is one-hundred percent devoted to your brother."

"So that's why you don't mind that Thunder spends so much time with her?"

Raine laughed until her eyes watered. "You aren't really worried about that." Raine managed to stop laughing. "You're jealous that Cameron is talking to her."

Was Raine right? Tem-aki shook her head.

Raine nodded. "You can lie to yourself, but we've all seen the way you and Cameron look at each other." Raine looked her in the eye. "Don't worry about Nimri, worry about figuring out how we can protect lives and at the same time help Cameron."

Tem-aki stared at Raine for several moments, but realized she was correct. Right now, dealing with the madrox was the issue, she would deal with Nimri and the way she took her brother for granted later. "Fine, you're right. We need to focus on the madrox and Cameron's issues." Tem-aki leaned forward and rested her forearms on the rail as she studied the coiled madrox. "What would you do?"

"Without Nambaba, I'd get to the middle of the ocean and dive in."

Tem-aki straightened and gave her a startled look. "I would never have thought of that, but you're right, that would do the trick."

At least it would for the short-term.

How long did it take to drown?

As if in some unspoken agreement, they turned back to watch the motionless madrox, which seemed to be radiating heat or something. Both of them leaned on the rail. "That's odd," Raine said.

"What is?"

"I've never seen a dragon shimmer."

Tem-aki squinted at the distant coils. "I've seen steam rise lots of time." She shrugged. "I didn't realize Kalamar was so different."

"I know what steam looks like," Raine said, "that's a shimmer."

Tem-aki narrowed her eyes. Now that Raine mentioned it, it did look more like a translucent shimmer instead of foggy steam. In fact, in a few areas, it was almost like a vague rainbow arched over the coiled beast. "It's sort of pretty."

Raine looked over her shoulder, then gestured to GEA-4.

"Yes?" the android asked.

"I've never seen a shimmer like that, do you know what is causing it?"

GEA-4 turned her eerie silver eyes toward the coiled beast. "Unknown power source, but from this perspective, the phenomena appears to be enclosing the madrox."

Tem-aki's spine snapped her to attention. "If there is energy around it, does that mean it is gaining strength?"

"My scan was inconclusive, however, I did not detect any transfer of energy to or from the madrox."

How very strange.

GEA-4 turned toward the other group. At the next pause in conversation, she asked them if the energy dome was known to the area, but her question was met with surprise. The others joined her at the rail, as if viewing something nearly a mile away was easier if they moved a few feet closer.

"It almost looks like a wind-bow," Thunder said, then explained that sometimes, when the wind blew the clouds into a nearly transparent layer and sunlight was just right, an entire section of sky would look as if someone had painted a huge horizontal rainbow across the sky.

"I've seen those," Nimri said, "but that is different. In fact, it reminds me of the special hat Larwin was wearing when I first saw him."

Larwin chuckled. "You screamed and fainted."

"I meant that it was like a big bubble over your head."

He squinted at the madrox for a short while, then nodded in agreement. "GEA-4, if the heat from the mother was evaporating the hatchling's moisture, would it look like that?"

"Inadequate data, but logically, something like that would mainly emit evaporation over the center portion."

Though the shimmers of color were difficult to see, Tem-aki could see that their distance from the madrox seemed to be about the same on both sides, as well as above the coils. "Could the beast's heat cause that?"

"Unknown," GEA-4 said.

"It looks a lot like an energy barrier," Raine said.

Tem-aki blinked in surprise, realizing that she was correct. But why would there be one? "Do madrox – er – dragons usually put up some form of protection fields around themselves?"

Raine put her hands palms up, as she gave her a perplexed

look. Tem-aki saw Larwin's frowning glance and was glad to know that she wasn't the only one who thought that someone who had spent years caring for the creatures should know a bit more about madrox and their habits than Raine seemed to.

Abruptly, GEA-4's already stiff posture became rigid and she spun toward the shoreline. "Something is moving."

Tem-aki squinted, but didn't see anything move other than the water lapping the shore.

Not even a bird was flying.

She looked at Cameron, then Larwin, Nolan, Thunder and Raine, but they looked as mystified as she felt.

"It is moving higher," GEA-4 said.

Staring at the top of the coils, she spotted a bright yellow-gold glint. Was it movement or her imagination? It came, again. She gasped in air, not having realized she was holding her breath.

Cameron's fingers wrapped around her hand, but otherwise, all his attention seemed to be on shore.

Though the coils didn't appear to move, slowly, the bright yellow-gold glint materialized into the baby madrox's head. Now dry, it clambered onto its mother, a vivid spot against her darker brass-toned body.

"It's so cute," Raine said. "I've never seen one this young."

Thunder put his arm around her shoulders. "I wonder if they're like baby snakes."

"Meaning?" Tem-aki asked.

"Adult snakes have learned to control their energy and poison, but the babies haven't. Add the fact that they are cuter," he gave the top of Raine's head a significant look, "and you now know why more people get hurt by the young."

"It's the same with my tribe," Nimri said.

The baby madrox slid off the top of its mother, and landing

on the ground in a ball, rolled into the shimmering shield, then with a shriek, it leaped backward.

At the same time, the mother dragon uncoiled and her tail hit the rainbow area. Sparks flew and she bellowed.

Cameron cleared his throat, "Something tells me that whatever that is, isn't her creation."

"It looks like whatever it is, has trapped her," Nolan said.

"What kind of energy could do that?" Larwin asked.

"And where did it come from?" Nimri added.

GEA-4's head turned from the shore to the galley door. "I picked up short blips, when the contact was made and was able to confirm that the source is aboard this vessel."

They all rushed toward the galley's door.

Chapter 31

Cameron stopped where he could see through the doorway, and watch the shore at the same time. Tem-aki stayed with him, her fingers still firmly gripping his hand. After the others passed, GEA-4 stood in the doorway, presumably observing something. But there was nothing to see. Saphera and Kazza were still sitting motionless by the skull. In fact, neither of them so much as batted an ear when the other five swarmed into the room.

Nervous as Saphera was, her sudden calmness shocked Cameron into taking a closer look at her.

Was she ill?

Had one of the visitors done something to her? GEA-4 had said Nimri was a healer. Could she have somehow helped her relax? Her own cat, Kazza, certainly didn't exhibit any obvious tendencies toward acting worried. In fact, when Shaka-uma had surged out of her bed of lava, the only reaction he'd displayed was perked ears.

Could Kazza's simple presence calm Saphera that much?

Possibly.

For certain he'd felt more capable of dealing with anything that came his way since Tem-aki arrived. He gave her fingers a gentle squeeze. There was an immediate answering caress.

Cameron smiled.

His gaze traveled to Nolan, who had been a major supporter since he was a child. Another person that made him feel capable of dealing with anything, even initiate-eating-dragons.

Would he have felt as confident if Shaka-uma had consumed Emmet and Tristan?

He suspected not.

In fact, he was certain that if she had devoured one or both of them, he would now be too distracted for rational thought. However, his only reaction to the loss of Varlet and Dirk was that he realized Nimri had a valid point. And as long as he was being totally honest with himself, he admitted that he was actually secretly pleased at having the Varlet problem eliminated.

"The strange energy emission is coming from the skull," GEA-4 said.

While Cameron blinked in surprise, a babble of excited conversation broke out in the galley.

And still, Saphera and Kazza remained motionless.

"So, it does more than simply link myst-energy," Larwin said.

Nimri, who had also been studying Kazza and Saphera, nodded. "It obviously works on feline-energy, which I should have realized years ago. I mean, it is the skull of a cat, after all."

Intrigued by her comment, Cameron went the three steps into the room and asked, "Years ago?" She nodded. "But you just arrived today."

"Thunder and I each have an identical one."

"Impossible!"

Without a word, Thunder left the room and headed back to their strange craft.

Nimri shrugged. "Unlikely, since we thought ours were the only two, but obviously possible." Her attention moved to a place beyond his left shoulder. "I have a staff of power, too."

He already knew that and could see how something like that could be duplicated, whereas it would be impossible to duplicate the skull. For one thing, where would anyone find the material to make another one? And for another, where would they get the tools?

Had Tem-aki brought to him the staff Draco Shakura had used?

She'd never claimed it was Draco Shakura's. He had made that assumption. In fact, now that he thought about it, when Tem-aki arrived, she didn't seem to know anything about Draco Shakura, that dragons were beneficial or even that they deserved to be venerated.

Before he decided what questions he wanted to ask, Thunder returned with a huge translucent skull under each arm. He carefully placed them on the counter, so that the eyes looked out the window.

At a loss for words, Cameron quickly sat down at the table. So did Nolan, who looked as if he would have fallen down if he'd tried to stay on his feet.

Oblivious to his reaction, Larwin said, "Even if they are creating this protective shield, they can't do this indefinitely."

"True," Raine said. "For one thing dragons are very long-lived. If that is in fact the same dragon that Cameron said his ancestors followed here, it's over a thousand years old."

"So, this solution can only be temporary," Nolan said.

Cameron stared at the cats and wondered what would happen when they got hungry or tired.

"We need to figure out a permanent solution," Larwin said.

"She has probably grown a lot since she came through the Star Bridge," Raine said. "That's probably why she fit."

Interesting, but irrelevant.

"We need to figure out a solution that will allow Cameron's land to become more fertile, yet still protect the inhabitants," Tem-aki said.

While he appreciated her loyalty, Cameron didn't think both goals were an option in this case, but he didn't have the heart to tell her so.

~o~

"So what we need to do is figure out how to emulate the vibration that triggers the barrier, except on a larger scale," GEA-4 said.

Amazing how the odd little woman always seemed to make complex problems sound simple, Tem-aki thought.

"I am sure you can figure that part out," Larwin said.

"What about the fertility part?" Tem-aki asked. "How would the agriculture workers get access to that?"

"Good point," Nimri said. "Would it be possible to increase the size of the barrier, so the workers didn't need to get so close to the beast?"

Who would be crazy enough to get inside that barrier? "Why not make it big enough to cover the island's fields, so they don't need to deal with it?" Tem-aki asked, hoping to shut Nimri up.

Nimri's gem-like emerald eyes widened. "Do you think that would be possible?"

GEA-4 said, "Perhaps if we triangulated the skull with the two staffs of power."

Sounds of interest reverberated throughout the room and soon, Cameron was rolling out the maps on the table while Nolan weighted down the corners with crude metal utensils. A lively discussion ensued about the ideal locations to place the skull and two staffs.

What had just happened? How dare they take her sarcastic comment seriously! Despite the fact that she had failed to put down Nimri, Tem-aki couldn't help but feel proud that her remark had had the unintended result of providing a potential solution to their problem.

~o~

Nimri studied Cameron's map as she tried to imagine what the actual land looked like. Larwin and GEA-4 were enthusiastically discussing how they could position the skull and staffs to protect the land, but the long, foreign words they were using confused Nimri. Though tempted to ask them to explain, she realized that she didn't need to understand why certain locations contained 'too many vulnerabilities' or why other spots were considered 'in proximity to a high population density'. What mattered was that this strategy-stuff was something Larwin and GEA-4 knew how to do, so the best thing to do was let them do it.

She was good at healing, she could help, as long as they weren't consumed by the dragon, but seeing the two mouthy ones simply vanish like that had been unsettling. Though for some reason, Tem-aki's obvious dislike for her bothered her more.

A lot more.

Probably because it was aimed at her and no one else.

Larwin's finger stabbed the map. "This is a high spot and therefore, an ideal placement for the skull. It's also near the town, so Cameron, or whoever he designates can go out there and turn off the tricorder when the workers need to go in and tend the fields. BUT," he nearly shouted, "I must stress that they be allowed through the shield and the shield must be turned right back on."

"Field workers should be tested for myst-energy," Nimri said. "It would be irresponsible to allow anyone with myst ability in there."

Nolan nodded, "It would be like waving a red flag at a bull."

Nimri blinked at his description, which made no sense to her.

"I can turn it on and off. At least, I'm sure I can learn how," Cameron sounded confident. "But I don't know how to test anyone for this myst-stuff."

"Nimri and I can do that," Thunder said.

"Excellent," Cameron said. "What still worries me is that with the barrier up, what will happen inside? Won't everything dry out?"

"The harmonics of rain, not to mention the size of the droplets should pass through," GEA-4 said. "However, I am unsure how a lightning storm will affect it, since I have never worked with this particular frequency before and I am unsure how the two forms of energy will interact."

"But the rain will be able to get through to the crops?" Nolan half-asked, half-stated.

"And these locations should be ideal to triangulate the staffs with the skull." Larwin jabbed two other areas, which would give the dragons a large triangular area to roam.

Assuming Larwin and GEA-4 were correct about how the staffs and skull could work together with a tricorder, it sounded like it might work. Still, it all sounded very complicated to Nimri, but when it came to methods like this, Larwin and GEA-4 had always had good advice.

"So, how do we place things so far apart and know when to activate them, or even if they are in the best place?" Cameron asked.

"Since we have three skulls, we should send one of them with each staff-bearer, but first, we should situate a staff and temporary skull here," Larwin tapped the closest area, "and see if Kazza will move there, which will allow us to move the one they are using."

"Why?" Cameron asked.

"So we can communicate with each other via myst-energy. If you really think about it, this is kismet. Have you noticed that we have everything we should need? And better yet, in addition to needing three points, we have three individuals capable of using the skull's frequency?"

Cameron frowned. "Why can't the cats stay where they are?"

Larwin raised a brow. "Okay, let's say we do that." Larwin gave Cameron a piercing look, which he had probably perfected in his years as a Shadow Warrior, but had given up trying to use on her. "How many centuries do you think they can maintain this control?"

"Centuries?" Cameron echoed.

Larwin nodded. "You told us that the mother is over a millennium old and obviously, she's still alive. One hatchling is out and soon there should be two more. How long do you think your cat and Kazza can maintain their concentration?" Larwin gazed at the cats as he cracked his knuckles. "Frankly, I'm impressed that they've managed it this long and even if they could continue this for a few thousand years, do you think this boat would last?"

Cameron crossed his arms over his stomach. "You're right. This is temporary." He cleared his throat. "But how do we know your plan is permanent?"

"We don't. In fact, the only permanent solution is figuring out a way to kill the beasts, but you don't want to consider that, do you?" Cameron shook his head. "Fine. In that case, Thunder, you can head here to set up the other staff." Larwin jabbed his forefinger at the farthest one. "While Nimri and Tem-aki head here." He tapped the closest one. Why was he partnering her with his sister? Her question must have shown on her face because Larwin's expression softened. "She can set up my tricorder to emit the frequency Kazza is using, but you, GEA-4 and Thunder are the only ones who seem capable of reliably using the skulls to communicate."

He had a valid point.

~o~

Tem-aki couldn't believe her ears. Her gaze darted between her brother and the woman, who had obviously brainwashed him. "I would prefer to be part of your team."

Larwin gave her a hard look. "I can handle a tricorder just fine, Nimri can't." Tem-aki opened her mouth to protest, but Larwin raised a warning hand, then said, "If you want this operation to be successful, you will do as I say."

"This is Cameron's island, not yours. Why do you think you get to say who does what?"

Cameron cleared his throat. "Your brother seems to have a plan that could work and obviously has more experience with planning this sort of thing than I do." He gestured toward the map. "I have no problem with what he has proposed or the way it will be executed."

Unbelievable!

"Why should Thunder go on his own?" Tem-aki asked.

"I would be honored to go with him," Nolan said, as he gave Larwin a hopeful look.

Larwin nodded. "If you can keep up." He turned his attention to the tall, dark one, who was so still that the only movement seemed to be the fluttering of the tiny blue feather, which was woven into one of his thin braids. "I know you can carry both the staff and a skull, position the staff, then contact us on the skull." Thunder inclined his head. Larwin turned his attention back to Nolan. "Even with his burdens, Thunder is younger and moves fast, but if you wish to accompany him, it is fine with me."

"The land looks different from the ground than it does in a map." Nolan touched an area about two-thirds of the way between their location and where Larwin wanted the staff planted. "This area is unstable. Many have been lost in the shifting sands. I believe I can help."

Larwin and Thunder both nodded in agreement. Then,

Larwin's attention shifted to Cameron. "I would like you with me to set up the skull, which we will utilize with the two staffs. I know you don't know how to use a tricorder, but since you will be responsible for the shield, you need to learn how to operate it."

Nolan tapped the map with his index finger. "Since the population lives in the town and would need to go to the fields from there, it seems wise to place the controlling skull there."

"Perhaps we could even make the activation of the system part of the Solstice Ceremony," Cameron said.

Tem-aki listened and watched as the remaining plans were made, then she, Nolan, Thunder, Raine, Mica and Nimri moved aboard the strange craft. First, they took Thunder and Nolan to the shore, then they sailed across the harbor to the spot Larwin had deemed most desirable for the other staff to be placed. As Nimri dug a hole to plant her staff, Tem-aki input the code into her tricorder and leaned it against the back of the heavy skull, which was seated on a large, flat rock. It lit up.

Raising the binoculars, which Larwin had loaned her and adjusting the focus, she saw a second, somewhat larger shield shimmer into view.

Shortly after that, the remaining gold-garbed boys hurried to Sirocco's bow and began tugging on a thick rope and Kazza emerged from the galley, leaped overboard and began swimming toward them. As the Sirocco exited the harbor, the staff slipped from Nimri's fingers and went bouncing and rolling down the mountainside.

Tem-aki rushed after it, Nimri on her heels. With a flying leap, Tem-aki grabbed it, but she landed wrong and felt her ankle snap. Despite the jolt of pain, she didn't let go of the staff. How could Nimri have been so clumsy that she dropped it? No wonder her brother had told her she needed to help the incompetent woman.

~o~

Nimri slid to a stop next to Tem-aki, who had the staff clutched so tightly that her knuckles had already turned white. Her face looked white and in pain, too. Had she gotten hurt? Kneeling next to her, Nimri allowed her myst-energy to flow over Tem-aki.

In the distance, Shaka-uma roared.

It didn't take long to learn that the flowing golden robe covered a broken ankle. Lifting the fabric aside, Nimri studied the way the foot lay at an L angle to the leg. Nimri looked into Tem-aki's eyes. "You have a bad break, but I can heal it. Please breathe deeply because the oxygen will help."

"Fine, set it," Tem-aki barely moved her lips to speak.

Nimri firmly took the injured foot between her hands and repositioned it. She didn't need to hear Tem-aki's gasp of pain, to know she'd hurt her, but sometimes doing something painful was the only way to get to the point of healing.

When she glanced back at Tem-aki, her pale face was covered in perspiration. "I'm sorry for hurting you, but that was the worst part. I still need to mend the sinews and bone, but that won't hurt so much." Assurances said, Nimri began to use myst-energy to heal the torn bone and tissue. Though she was concentrating on her task, she also knew that Shaka-uma's bellowing had increased and that the ground even seemed to be trembling.

By the time the last damaged muscle had been mended, the ground seemed to have developed a steady shake.

Nimri sat up and stretched her back to ease the tension, then she looked around. Under the shield, Shaka-uma was lashing her scaly tail and stomping the ground, but now that the healing process was done, she should start calming down.

She didn't.

Tem-aki sat up, dried her face on her sleeve and looked toward shore. "Do you think it finally realized it was trapped?"

"It is reacting to the myst-energy I used to heal your foot."

Tem-aki gave her a look normally reserved for those who had consumed too much fermented juice. What had she ever done to Tem-aki to make her detest her so much that she couldn't even act appreciative after being healed?

Suddenly, there was such a large thud that not only did the earth shake, but small stones began to roll downhill. Nimri twisted to see what Shaka-uma had done. The madrox slashed her tail against the ground again. The earth shook. More rocks bounced downhill.

Worse, the shield began to flicker, as if it had weakened. Then, abruptly, it totally winked out.

A backward glance showed that the skull was no longer illuminated. Nimri gasped, then pulled Tem-aki to her feet, "Quick, grab the staff and run to the boat. You must use it to protect Raine and Mica."

"You expect me to use that against a madrox?"

"The staff is our only hope." Nimri thrust it at her. "Please, protect your brother's son."

"And what are you going to do?"

"Try to fix whatever went wrong with the shield." Tem-aki opened her mouth, but Nimri had had enough talking. "Just go to Raine, both of you hold the staff and maybe you'll survive." With that, Nimri sprinted up the rise to the skull.

The lumpy black box had fallen off the rock and the skull had moved. She grabbed the box, adjusted the alignment of the skull and put the box back where Tem-aki had placed it, but the skull did not glow. Had the box gotten broken or had she arranged things incorrectly?

She bit her lip and looked from the skull to the dragon.

Released from its mother's warmth, the hatchling toddled around the shore, purposefully moving inland, in the same direction the mother had gone.

With a start, Nimri realized the baby dragon was going toward the rock with the large hole in it.

She heaved a sigh of relief, knowing that the hatching of the second one could have been what made the mother frantic.

Perhaps her use of myst-energy had not caused this problem, but it was still her responsibility to make it right.

Chapter 32

Tem-aki sat next to Raine on the deck of the flimsy craft and held onto the staff, as if it was the only thing that could save her. Not because the great and mighty Nimri had told her to do so, but because Cameron had considered it to be so important.

'I wonder where it's going," Raine said, as the mother-dragon soared into the low-lying clouds.

"Who cares, as long as it isn't coming our direction?"

"I care." Raine glared at her over Mica's head. "Thunder and Nolan headed that way."

Tem-aki jerked her head in Nimri's direction. "She told me this staff would protect us. Thunder had the other one. Won't that protect him, too?"

Raine visibly brightened. "I'd forgotten that. Thanks for reminding me."

Surprise rippled through Tem-aki. "You really believe this skinny piece of wood can protect us from a madrox!" More likely it would burst into flames.

"If Nimri said it will protect us, it will."

Did the woman brainwash everyone? Tem-aki's jaws clenched so hard her molars hurt. "Right, you think she is so honest." Tem-aki felt like spitting. "She told me I'd broken my leg and the next thing she told me was to run down here." Tem-aki pulled up her robes. "Does that look broken to you? Could I have gotten up and run on it, if it had been?"

"She is an excellent healer," Raine said. Tem-aki stared at her. How blind could anyone be? "Don't you realize that she told you the truth?"

"About what?"

"Everything." Raine made a helpless gesture. "I've never known her to lie."

"Everyone lies."

"On our worlds, yes, but not here." Raine put her hand on top of hers, so they both held the staff. "I know that you haven't had much time to get to know her, but Nimri is a woman of honor and she would not knowingly lie."

"Boy, does she have you brainwashed."

Raine shook her head. "Given time, you will get to know her, as I have."

Unbelievable! "So you think that in the few short weeks that you have known her that you can tell when she is lying. Are you willing to bet your life on that?"

"What do you mean?"

"If she is telling the truth and this stick can protect us from the madrox. Mind you, I don't buy that, but since it seems to be the only option, I'll hang onto it... But if it is the only protection, and her energy signature is the thin air that attracts the beast, then explain to me why she gave the stick to me and went the other direction."

"Did she tell you why?"

"She just told me to take it to you and Mica."

"Well, there you have the answer to your question."

"Excuse me?"

"Nimri is a mother, who is willing to lay her life on the line to protect her child." Raine gave her a level look. "If Mica was yours, would you do any less?"

Tem-aki opened her mouth to retort, but no sound came out.

"That's what I thought," Raine said. "You're one of those people who can dish out venom, but don't know how to deal with the truth. Well, get this, if Nimri said your leg was broken, it was broken. If she said this so-called-stick would protect us, it will protect us. Right now, she's up on that hill probably trying to fix whatever is broken and I hope for her sake that she doesn't need to use her myst-energy to do it, because I don't know how she can protect herself, while she's protecting everyone else."

~o~

"If you believe that you can, it becomes possible," Nimri muttered as she fiddled with the confusing black box.

"Need some help with that?"

She jerked upright, surprised that someone had managed to sneak up on her. Even Kazza rarely managed to do that.

"Yes," she thrust the box at Tem-aki. "This fell off the rock and now it isn't working. Is it broken?"

"Probably just needs recalibrating." Tem-aki knelt down next to her and punched a few knobs. Suddenly, white symbols glowed. "That should do it, but I don't know if it helps, now that the madrox is gone."

"It will return."

"How can you be sure?"

"Do you know many species that abandon their young?"

"Yes." Nimri raised a brow. "Many reptiles do and amphibians, as well," Tem-aki said. "I'm sure they aren't amphibians."

"Reptiles?" Nimri asked.

Tem-aki shrugged. "Madrox look a lot like they could be some sort of reptile."

Nimri frowned. "Judging by its response when the other

three approached its hatchling, I strongly doubt that it is gone for good. If you'd like to test that theory, feel free to go touch the baby." Putting her hand to shade her eyes, she scanned the sky.

"No thanks."

"Wise choice, particularly when I suspect that it's returning, now." She pointed into the distance. "You'd better get back to the boat."

"I'd rather take my chances here."

Nimri gave her a long look, as she wondered what had changed, then she shrugged and realized that it didn't matter. "As you wish."

They sat side by side on the rocky ground and watched the dragon approach. "Do you think Thunder and Nolan are okay?"

"Yes."

Tem-aki looked at her in surprise. "You didn't even pause to think about your answer."

"Thunder has Cameron's staff and knows how to use it." She turned to study Tem-aki. "Do you care if they're all right?"

"Of course."

"Why?" This time, Tem-aki didn't seem to have an answer. Nimri grimaced, "Not so easy knowing why, is it?"

Tem-aki shook her head. "Do you always understand why you do what you do?"

"I try to do what it correct, which is why I'm trying to find a way to do as Cameron asks and still protect both human and dragon lives."

"Have you always been so focused on helping others?"

"It's what I was raised to do."

Tem-aki laughed, but when she didn't join her, she got a strange look on her face. "You're serious."

Nimri nodded. "My ancestors have been our tribe's healers

and keepers of the peace since we came to this world."

"Cameron said his people arrived on this world 1,066 years ago."

"Then, they must be some of the ones my tribe calls the lost." Nimri ran her hand over the smooth top of the skull. "This Summoning Skull has been taken care of by members of my family since then, but until you and GEA-4 managed to activate the one here and tell us where you were, I had no clue how they worked. In truth, I was surprised to learn that they could create a cone of protection."

"Summoning Skull? I like the name."

Nimri grinned, "That's the official one, but Bryta always called it the Skull of Doom." Nimri looked Tem-aki in the eye. "I never understood why, but now that I've learned that Cameron's tribe had one, I suspect that sometime in history, people lost the knowledge of what the skulls' purpose was or perhaps they assumed the lost tribes had met a horrible fate."

"Sounds reasonable," Tem-aki said, but her attention was now on the dragon, which had begun flying in looping circles around the two hatchlings. She gripped the lumpy black box, as if it was a lifeline, and Nimri wondered if she was even breathing. "I don't think it plans to land, so I can trap it."

Nimri watched the beast circle wide, dipping low over the flimsy boat, where Raine clung to the staff and Mica. As the dragon's wings beat the air, the calm water in the harbor seemed to boil. Even if the staff could protect them from the dragon, Nimri wasn't certain it would protect them from drowning, if the boat collapsed.

Something had to be done, and the only thing she could think of doing was use herself as bait. Nimri took a deep breath, to calm her racing heart. "Get ready. I'll get it to land."

"How will you-"

"-do that?" Tem-aki finished lamely, as Nimri's body briefly glowed, then slumped, apparently lifeless, to the ground.

Overhead, the madrox bellowed.

Tem-aki lightly pressed her fingers against Nimri's neck. Despite appearances, her life-force seemed steady.

Again, the madrox shrieked. As she turned her attention to the sky, it nearly got its wings tangled, by turning too quickly. "What the heck?" she said aloud. Tem-aki stared, at the madrox's suddenly adversarial behavior. Squinting against the sunlight, she thought she saw an unnatural glimmer of light zigzagging through the air.

Could what she thought she was seeing actually be happening?

She blinked several times, then tried to refocus, but now thought she saw two unexplainable glimmers. Tem-aki looked from the sky to the crumpled form next to her.

If her eyes were telling her the truth, Nimri could do some amazing things. And she'd said she would get the creature to land and to be ready. Tem-aki made a couple small adjustments, then waited for the promised opportunity.

~o~

As Nimri ducked into a fat white cloud, she spotted Kazza's myst-energy. She'd wondered where he'd gone and was glad to have his help.

Once inside the cloud's cool humidity, she changed direction and soared upward, then, as the dragon's heat passed below, she shot down, onto the back of its neck. She quickly knelt on its scaly hide. Was it her imagination, or was this dragon much cooler than the other one had been? Pushing the thought aside, she worked her fingers beneath the closest scale and yanked.

The creature cried out.

She pulled harder.

The dragon twisted and turned, but Nimri held on, all the time pulling at the scale in order to distract it from Mica and buy herself time to figure out a plan to get it to land. Suddenly, the dragon dove earth-ward. She tried to leap free, but a wing slapped her, then, before she knew what happened, they entered a dark, cold area.

By the time Nimri kicked free of the tangled wings, she realized the dragon had gone head-first into the harbor. She could only imagine the waves its dive had made. Fighting her way to the surface, she frantically looked for the boat, but it was nowhere to be seen.

With a scream, she returned to her body.

Tem-aki was staring, mouth open, at the harbor.

Nimri sat upright, still looking for Raine and Mica. "Where is the boat?"

Tem-aki literally jumped. "How did you do that?"

Nimri grabbed her upper arm. "The boat. What happened to it?"

Tem-aki's eyes widened in horror, as she looked where it should be tied. "I don't know. I was watching the madrox, ready to set the shield, then suddenly, it dove straight into the middle of the harbor and water splashed everywhere." She turned huge eyes to her. "How did you do that?"

Without pausing to answer her, Nimri scrambled to her feet and ran downhill to where the boat should be.

Mica had to be alive, he just had to be!

"Watch out," Tem-aki screamed, "There's something going on in the water."

Nimri noticed that it seemed to be boiling in the middle, and that made her run faster. Arriving at the shore, all she saw of the boat was shredded rope tied to a boulder.

Mica had to be down there, somewhere.

And she would find him.

Nimri dove in.

~o~

Tem-aki watched helplessly, as Nimri went head-first into the water, where they had last seen the boat and in the middle of the harbor, a familiar golden nose emerged.

Then the head, followed by the shoulders.

The water boiled with beating wings, but the creature seemed unable to fly.

Hadn't someone said that water supposedly killed madrox?

It didn't look very dead to Tem-aki. In fact, the scarlet eyes looked furious.

Shivering, she wondered if she should try to trap the dragon in the water, but just as quickly, she decided that would be a bad choice, since she didn't know if the shield-thing worked in the water.

Fortunately, the madrox splashed its way to the far shore, pulled itself out of the water and began to drag itself toward the hatchlings.

Tem-aki turned back to where she had last seen Nimri. There was nothing but furiously lapping water.

Chapter 33

Tem-aki wished she could do something besides sit and wait for the beast to get into position, so she could reactivate the containment, but she couldn't swim, and didn't know where anyone else was, so all she could do was wait and hope the shield would hold, if the thing ever got into a good position. Slow as it was moving, that would take a while.

Eyes watering, she did the only things she could do: think, wait and wonder.

If the shield failed, again, would she die, here on this desolate rock?

She wiped a tear from her cheek.

Was Nimri actually a horrible person or had she treated her that way because she wanted to punish someone for her brother's choice to stay here?

She wiped away more tears.

If Nimri hadn't healed her, would everyone have been lost?

The tears fell so thick and fast that she no longer bothered to hide them. After all, who was left to see? There wasn't even a bird in the sky.

She had always assumed that being a Stardust Warrior was exciting. In reality, had Larwin's previous life been as boring as this tedious waiting for Shaka-uma to drag herself across a quarter mile of rock?

By the time the madrox managed to struggle to its hatchlings, the second one was halfway out of its ovum and Tem-aki had no more tears left. Her eyes burned as she watched the beast painfully coil itself around the two young ones, then very carefully, she activated the tricorder.

When the shield shimmered over the madrox, she sighed in relief. At least the creatures couldn't harm anyone else.

"You know as prisons go, that's a beautiful one."

Tem-aki whirled around to see a half-sodden Raine sitting on a rock behind her. "How long have you been there?"

"Hard to say, but I guess I've seen at least half of the dragon's efforts to coil around the hatchlings." She scratched her ear. "I've watched them for years and never realized what devoted mothers they were."

Nimri had been so devoted to Mica that she'd drowned herself. Pressure and pain clutched Tem-aki's heart, but she managed to ask, "How did you survive?"

She picked up the staff that had been lying at her side. "Somehow this thing saved me. It's amazingly buoyant."

Buoyant? Wasn't it the one she'd found at the bottom of the ocean?

"I'm surprised the others haven't returned, now that the shield is in place."

Who did she think was alive to return? Wasn't it just the two of them? She cleared her throat. "Who do you expect?"

Raine gave her a surprised look. "Mica and Kazza for starters." Then, she got a worried look. "What happened to Nimri?"

"I think she drowned."

"Why?"

Tem-aki couldn't answer.

"When?" Raine demanded.

To Tem-aki's surprise, she began to cry, again. "After she saw that the boat wasn't there, she went head-first into the water." She sniffed. "I think she was trying to save you and Mica."

"But Kazza grabbed him before the dragon hit the water and I swim better than I walk."

Of course, Raine and anyone growing up on a water world would know how to swim. Why hadn't she considered that? "Kazza grabbed Mica?" Tem-aki looked around the barren slope. "Where are they?"

"I have no idea. In fact, things went so fast that I'm not clear about where Kazza came from. I just know that he seemed to be moving very fast and seemed to come from nowhere, grab Mica, then they were gone. In fact, I know this sounds crazy, but I had the impression he was flying and I know cats can't fly." Raine massaged her temples. "Then, before I could blink, the dragon hit the water and everything went upside down. Next thing I knew, the boat was gone and I was under water, being pushed along in a riptide."

Tem-aki didn't know what a riptide was, but it didn't sound good.

"By the time I managed to get my head above water, I was halfway out the channel. I was miles offshore by the time I managed to get out of the current, so it took a while to swim back."

"And all that way, you managed to hold onto the staff."

Raine gave a rueful laugh. "I'd tied it to my arm because it was too slick to hold onto. I think it saved me, not vice-versa."

"Amazing," Tem-aki said, and meant it, since she was certain she would not have survived.

Raine nodded. After several minutes when the only sound was the soft lap of water against the shore, Raine asked, "Have you decided what you are going to do?"

"About what?" Tem-aki swallowed as she wondered what Raine expected of her.

"With your life. You have a lot of options."

"If you say so. I was trained as a geologist."

"Don't limit yourself. I was trained as a dragon herder, but I've learned that I'm really good at weaving wool."

Whatever that was.

"Seriously," Raine continued, "have you at least decided if you'll return with us or will you stay here?" She got an odd smile on her face. "I'm sure Cameron would prefer you to stay, but we all know that your goal has always been to find Larwin."

"And instead, he found me." Tem-aki rubbed her aching eyes. "You really think Cameron would like me to stay?"

Raine laughed and nodded.

"Why?"

"I've seen the way you two look at each other when the other one isn't looking."

A sliver of warmth began to bloom in Tem-aki's heart. "I'll talk to him."

"You do that." Raine raised her hand to shield her eyes from the sun. "Ah, it's about time."

Tem-aki looked to see what held her attention. Kazza, Nimri and Mica were making their way through the strange geometric rocks, which scattered the shore. Seeing the proof of Nimri's philosophy, 'If you believe, it becomes possible' was like witnessing a miracle.

~o~

Days later, when everything for the shield was in place and after everyone, except Dirk and Varlet, had returned to his home, the sun was inching downward. As soon as it dropped below the horizon, it would be time to begin the Solstice Celebration – an event, which had been hastily organized to replace the Solstice Celebration and

Pilgrimage.

Cameron had spent years imagining how he would feel if he ever had the honor of officiating at the order's major event. But, now that it was time, and dragons had even returned, all he wanted to do was convince Tem-aki to stay with him. Unfortunately, the best way to do that seemed to be taking her and her brother's family to his home, so as the sun began to sink, Cameron ushered Larwin, Thunder, Raine, Nimri, Mica, Kazza and Tem-aki down the steep stairs to the main pier, where it seemed like half the town had gathered. It seemed like everyone wanted to look at, speak to and touch the strangers before they departed, so the walk took a lot longer than he expected. By the time they all climbed aboard The Sirocco, the sun was halfway hidden by the horizon.

His fingers tightened around Tem-aki's hand, holding her with him, on deck, as the others went below to ready themselves for their part of the coming festivities. Turning to the shore, he faced the townspeople, who stood shoulder to shoulder along the quay, their expression mirrored many emotions; many seemed confused by the rumors that dragons had returned and proven to be deadly, instead of purely beneficial. The announcement that this year, instead of a pilgrimage, they would be celebrating the return of the dragons, here in town, had meant that nearly everyone had turned out for the celebration, instead of those who were devote followers.

Seeing that he was looking their way, one farmer, who had been forced to move outside the new protective barrier, shook his fist and shouted an insult. Since the energy shield could not be seen and the dragons had not ventured near, Cameron understood why the man was angry, and he hoped the plan would work, so that everyone not only could hear that the dragons had returned, but see them and understand the danger.

Benji and Tristan removed the boarding plank and loosened the mooring ropes, then they raised the sail and stood by to trim it, when the off-shore breeze arrived.

As the sun vanished, Cameron raised his arm. Slowly the crowd became silent. "I know that you have all heard rumors of why this year's Solstice Ceremony and Pilgrimage were cancelled."

A surge of sound rumbled across the water.

"Shaka-uma has risen." A shout drowned him out, so he patiently waited for silence. "As have three of her hatchlings."

"Lies!"

Cameron held up his hand for silence. "You will see with your own eyes." Again the noise swelled.

Tem-aki leaned close, "I see why you wanted to speak to them from here. Much safer."

"That plus they all can see and hear me better."

"At least they could if they ever shut up and listened."

"They will. Right now, they are reacting to a change. Most humans don't do well with that."

"Yet, life is always changing."

"But usually not this quickly." As the crowd quieted, Cameron told them about the shield and explained that it was for their protection. Many of the farmers used the opportunity to publicly protest, but he knew that the offshore breeze would come soon and he didn't have time to waste. Then, he told everyone that Nolan would officiate over the festivities, while he left on an important voyage."

"Because he doesn't want to face his lies!" a rough voice shouted.

Cameron made the pre-arranged signal to Annosha, who was in her tethered dragon balloon. In turn, Annosha signaled Malin and Emmet, who were on the dragon-side of the shield, waiting to release the lanterns.

Tem-aki stared skyward, hoping that the bizarre plan would work. Worried that it wouldn't.

For the longest time, nothing seemed to happen, then there was a flurry of movement and a harsh voice shouted, "Aw, lookie there, he figures we be stupid enough to mistake a balloon for a live dragon." Raucous laughter floated over the water.

Tem-aki's fingers tightened around his. "How can they be so horrible?"

"They are human."

"Are you sure you want to return here, after we take Larwin and everyone home?"

"I belong here."

"We belong."

Cameron gave her a tender smile, as the expected offshore breeze began to fill the sail. The Sirocco began moving toward the harbor exit, which would take her through the channel and into the ocean.

The first airborne lantern hit the dragon-shield and instantly disintegrated in a starburst, while at the same time, it briefly looked as if a huge rainbow-like dome curved over Fire Island's interior. A shout from the shore acknowledged the existence of the shield, then under the protective arc, a bolt of azure lightening rippled. And people went wild with the proof that the shield was there to protect them from Skaka-uma.

It had begun.

His fingers instinctively tightened around Tem-aki's hand.

"Tell me, again, that they will be okay," she said.

"I can't, but I don't think they would do this if they weren't sure," he said, his attention never straying from Shaka-uma and her three hatchings as they flew in a strange flight-dance with two barely discernible humans and two myst cats, which was eerily similar to what Tem-aki claimed she'd seen in the skull. "It was their idea to lure the dragons here for the Ceremony, so that all could see." Cameron continued, "I would never have asked them to risk their lives, just so the doubters could believe. Larwin thought it was important for everyone to understand the new restrictions and why only those who had no apparent myst-energy could work on the other side of the shield."

As more and more lanterns hit the dragon-shield, the mammoth iridescent dome became more visible. "This demonstration certainly shows them the massive energy. and how dangerous it is," Tem-aki said. "Larwin has always been good at strategy." She turned her attention to shore, where some were staring at the sight in silent awe, while others screamed and jumped. Then Tem-aki looked at him, the light of floating lanterns and dome reflecting in her eyes. "You have been planning this celebration since I met you. It is the pinnacle of your career."

"And far more spectacular than I ever have imagined possible." He looked at the lanterns, which still were thick as stars around the four dragons.

"Why leave, now? People finally believe you."

"I am only head draco because Nolan didn't want to accept the post for fear that our sect would fail. Besides, he actually likes officiating at this sort of thing and dealing with groups."

"Bu-"

He put his finger over her lips. "My position will be here when I return, as will be the responsibility to protect everyone." While he'd spent years believing that officiating at the Solstice Ceremony would be the highlight of his life, now that it was here, he realized that convincing Tem-aki to spend the rest of her life as his partner was much more important.

Tem-aki tugged his hand guiding him away from where Kazza and Saphera sprawled on the bow, to join Larwin, Nimri, Mica, Raine and Thunder who were all safe and watching the festivities on Sirocco's stern.

How could he ask her to choose between a life with him and one with her family?

"Why do you think I must make a choice?" Tem-aki asked.

Cameron swallowed, as he realized he had spoken aloud. "If I were to ask you to stay with me, you'd lose your family."

Tem-aki looked from him to the shimmering shield, which looked like a dark wind-bow in the moonlight. "How can you believe that, after all we've been through?" Tem-aki took his face in her hands "I think Nimri is right about anything being possible, if we just believe." She tightened her grip on his hands. "I believe that if I choose to stay with you, you are added to my family and I will gain, not lose."

Cameron wrapped her in him arms and kissed her, as he looked forward to an amazing future.

The End

Other books by Jeanne Foguth

Kazza's Chatterre Trilogy (Sci-Fantasy)

Star Bridge
Nimri, an herbal healer and Chatterer's new Keeper of the Peace, must safeguard her tribe from their bitter rivals. To do this, she must find her 'magic core'.
Many light years away, Colonel Larwin Atano, an elite Guerreterre Shadow Warrior, fights to save his intergalactic star-fighter. Despite all efforts, he crashes.
Larwin perceives Chatterre's resources as a means to gain power and prestige and views the planet's inhabitants as a minor inconvenience.
Nimri believes Larwin is a supernatural Guardian, who will protect her tribe from their rivals.
Who will survive the coming conflict?

Thunder Moon
Thunder Cartwright dreams that madrox will invade Chatterre and destroy his world unless the Star Bridge is closed.

Raine, a Kalamaran Dragon Shepard, must catch a rogue mooncalf and return it to the herd or face possible death.
Who will win and who will die?

Fire Island
Tem-aki Atano fell through a rift when the Star Bridge was destroyed and now must find a way to survive on an island which worships Fire Dragons.
Cameron must figure out a way to keep the dragons, which are hatching near an extinct volcano at his island's core, dormant, so that they do not destroy things, yet keep the faith alive.
But the beasts are hatching... will they destroy the island and everyone living on it?

Xander's Sea Purrtector Files - Fantasy

Latitudes & Cattitudes
~ a short & free prequel to The Sea Purrtector Files ~
Xander de Hunter is a rising star on Catamondo's kick-boxing circuit and dreams of becoming a Purrtector. After a match in Seattle, he is asked to help find Cha-Cha, a white Norwegian beauty, who is missing.
With Merlin's assistance, they follow Cha-Cha's trail into the Puget Sound where Xander must face his biggest fear – water.

The Red Claw
Dame Esmeralda, the Purrsident's littermate, has been catnapped. Xander de Hunter, Catamondo's Sea Purrtector hurries to Jamaica to help rescue her, even though Jamaica is one of Dogdom's strongholds.
Could this be a trap?

Purr-a-noia
Catamondo and Dogdom's peace treaty is in jeopardy. In Haiti, witchcraft and voodoo seem to be involved in a plot to hex the Purrsident.
Will Xander be able to restore the peace?

The Vi-Purrs - coming in 2016
The Daily Mews reports continued violence in the Dominican Republic Purrtectorate.

Xander discovers that the Moreau situation is still affecting the ability of Catamondo to purrtect cats. Worse, the office of the Purrtectorate seems to be involved.

Will Xander be able to save the integrity of the Purrtectorate and restore peace?

Contemporary Suspense/Romance

Deadly Rumors
Kelsey MacLennan and Devlin Doran both want to make the world better.
Doran believes the rumors about the MacLennans dealing drugs, so his goal is to bring them down.
Kelsey MacLennan's campaign turns deadly and rumors abound, because the incumbent will be killed if he does not win. Devlin Doran's younger sister died of an overdose, so his goal is to prosecute pushers. Rumors abound that the MacLennans are high in the local drug network and he is targeting Kelsey MacLennan.
Will they be able to separate fact from fiction or will the rumors be deadly to them?

Fatal Attractions

Ariel and Tempest Danner have escaped Tempest's homicidal father for the sixth time in five years. Armed with new identities and disguises, they are determined that Fairbanks, Alaska will be a sanctuary where they can live in peace.

Stone O'Banyon, their new landlord, has been divorced for three years. All his energy is focused on his job and Dolly, who would never hurt him.

The last thing Ariel needs or wants is the attraction she feels for another tall, dark man, who seems hard as the granite he is named for.

Things seem calm, then Ariel and Tempest catch sight of the man they had hoped they would never encounter and things turn fatal...again.

Passion's Fire

Prior to the blaze that killed her husband, Jacqueline Cardew believed her husband wrote the "fiery messages' she received. Now she finds a new note inside her locked house. Jacqueline suspects her faceless stalker murdered Adam and she is next. She flees north, where she joins Link Gavallan's group on a two week long Alaskan wilderness canoe trip. As they float down the desolate river, she receives another message...

Instead of finding a sanctuary, has she made it easier for the unknown person to trap her?

Connect with Jeanne Foguth

Here are her social media coordinates:

Visit her website:
http://www.jeannefoguth.com

Subscribe to her blog for pet tips and humor:
https://foguth.wordpress.com

Follow her on Twitter:
http://twitter.com/jeannefoguth

Friend her on Facebook:
 https://www.facebook.com/jeannefoguth

www.ingramcontent.com/pod-product-compliance
Lightning Source LLC
Chambersburg PA
CBHW062114170626
46813CB00002B/445